A TALE OF TWO CITIES

Published by Priory Books,
© Peter Haddock Publishing,
United Kingdom, YO16 6BT.

A TALE OF TWO CITIES

BOOK 1

RECALLED TO LIFE

CHAPTER 1

The Period

It was the best of times, it was the worst of times, it was the age of wisdom, it was the age of foolishness, it was the epoch of belief, it was the epoch of incredulity. It was the season of Light, it was the season of Darkness, it was the spring of hope, it was the winter of despair, we had everything before us, we had nothing before us, we were all going direct to Heaven, we were all going direct the other way.

There were a king with a large jaw and a queen with a plain face, on the throne of England; there were a king with a large jaw and a queen with a fair face, on the throne of France. In both countries it was clearer than crystal to the lords of the State that things in general were settled forever.

It was the year of Our Lord 1775. Messages in the earthly order of events had lately come to the English Crown and People, from a congress of British subjects in America, which, strange to relate, have proved most important to the human race.

France, less favoured on the whole as to matters spiritual than her sister of the shield and trident, rolled with exceeding smoothness down hill, making paper money and spending it. Under the guidance of her Christian pastors, she entertained herself. In the woods of France and Norway, there were trees growing, which were already marked by the Woodman, Fate, to be cut down and sawn into boards, to make a certain movable framework with a sack and a knife in it, terrible in history. It is also probable that in the rough outhouses of farmers near Paris, there were basic carts, spattered with mud, snuffed about by pigs, and roosted in by poultry, which were already set apart by the Farmer, Death, to be his tumbrils of the Revolution.

In England, there was scarcely an amount of order and protection to justify much national boasting. Every night in the capital there were daring burglaries and highway robberies. Prisoners in London gaols fought battles with their turnkeys, and the majesty of the law fired blunderbusses in among them, loaded with rounds of shot and ball. Thieves snipped off diamond crosses from the necks of noble lords at Court drawing rooms. Musketeers went into St Giles's, to search for contraband goods, and the mob fired on the musketeers. The musketeers then fired on the mob, and nobody thought any of these occurrences much out of the common way. In the midst of them, the hangman, ever busy and ever worse than useless, was in constant requisition.

All these things, and a thousand like them, came to pass in and close upon the dear old year 1775. Environed by them, while the Woodman and the Farmer worked unheeded, those two of the large jaws, and those other two of the plain and the fair faces, carried their divine rights with a high hand. Thus did the year 1775 conduct their Greatnesses, and myriads of small creatures – the creatures of this chronicle among the rest – along the roads that lay before them.

CHAPTER 2

The Mail

It was the Dover road that lay, on a Friday night late in November, before the first of the persons with whom this history has business. He walked up Shooter's Hill in the mire by the side of the mail carriage, as did the rest of the passengers. This was because the hill, harness, mud and the mail, were all so heavy, that the horses had stopped three times already.

With drooping heads, the horses mashed their way through the thick mud, floundering and stumbling, as if they were falling to pieces at the larger joints.

There was a steaming mist in all the hollows, and it had roamed up the hill, like an evil spirit, seeking rest and finding none. It was dense enough to shut out everything from the light of the coach-lamps but a few yards of road.

Two other passengers were plodding up the hill by the side of the mail. All three were wrapped to the cheekbones and over the ears, and wore jack-boots. Not one could have said, from anything he saw, what either of the other two was like. In those days, travellers were very shy of being confidential on a short notice, for anybody on the road might be a robber or in league with robbers. The guard stood on his own particular perch behind the mail, keeping an eye and a hand on the arm-chest before him, where a loaded blunderbuss lay at the top of six or eight loaded horse-pistols.

The Dover mail was in its usual genial position that the guard suspected the passengers, the passengers suspected one another and the guard. The coachman was sure of nothing but the horses; that they were not fit for the journey.

"Wo-ho!" said the coachman. "So, then! One more pull and you're at the top and be damned to you, for I have had trouble enough to get you to it! Joe!"

"Halloa!" the guard replied.

"What o'clock do you make it, Joe?"

"Ten minutes, good, past eleven."

"My blood!" ejaculated the vexed coachman, "and not atop of Shooter's yet! Tst! Yah! Get on with you!"

The horses made a decided scramble for it. The last burst carried the mail to the summit of the hill. The horses stopped to breathe again, and the guard got down to skid the wheel for the descent, and open the coach-door to let the passengers in.

"Joe!" cried the coachman in a warning voice, looking from his box.

"What do you say, Tom?"

They both listened.

"I say a horse at a canter coming up, Joe."

"I say a horse at a gallop, Tom," said the guard, letting go of the door, and mounting nimbly to his place. "Gentlemen! In the king's name, all of you!"

He then cocked his blunderbuss, and stood on the offensive.

The passenger of this history was on the coach-step, getting in; the two other passengers were close behind him, and about to follow. They all looked from the coachman to the guard, and from the guard to the coachman, and listened.

5

The stillness following the cessation of the rumbling and labouring of the coach, added to the stillness of the night, making it very quiet indeed.

The sound of a galloping horse came fast and furiously up the hill.

"So-ho!" the guard sang out, as loud as he could roar. "Yo there! Stand or I shall fire!"

The pace was suddenly checked, and, with much splashing and floundering, a man's voice called from the mist, "Is that the Dover mail?"

"Never you mind what it is!" the guard retorted. "What are you?"

"*Is* that the Dover mail?"

"Why do you want to know?"

"I want a passenger, if it is."

"What passenger?"

"Mr Jarvis Lorry."

Our booked passenger showed in a moment that it was his name. The guard, the coachman, and the two other passengers eyed him distrustfully.

"Keep where you are," the guard called to the voice in the mist, "because, if I should make a mistake, it could never be set right in your lifetime. Gentleman of the name of Lorry answer straight."

"What is the matter?" asked the passenger, then, with mildly quavering speech. "Who wants me? Is it Jerry?"

"Yes, Mr Lorry."

"What is the matter?"

"A despatch sent after you from over yonder. T. and Co."

"I know this messenger, guard," said Mr Lorry, getting down into the road. "He may come close; there's nothing wrong."

"I hope there ain't," said the guard. "Hallo you!"

"Well! And hallo you!" said Jerry, more hoarsely than before.

"Come on at a footpace! D'ye mind me? And if you've got holsters to that saddle o' yourn, don't let me see your hand go nigh 'em. For I'm a devil at a quick mistake, and when I make one, it takes the form of Lead. So now let's look at you."

The figures of a horse and rider came slowly through the swirling mist, and came to the side of the mail, where the passenger stood. The rider stooped, and, casting up his eyes at the guard, handed the passenger a small folded paper. The rider's horse was blown, and both horse and rider were covered with mud.

"Guard!" said the passenger, in a tone of quiet confidence. "I belong

6

to Tellson's Bank in London. I am going to Paris on business. I may read this?"

"If so be as you're quick, sir."

He opened it in the light of the coach-lamp on that side, and read – first to himself and then aloud: "'Wait at Dover for Mam'selle.' It's not a long note, you see, guard. Jerry, say that my answer was, *recalled to life*."

Jerry started in his saddle. "That's a Blazing strange answer, too," said he, at his hoarsest.

"Take that message back, and they will know that I received this. Make the best of your way. Good night."

With those words the passenger opened the coach-door and got in – not at all assisted by his fellow-passengers, who had secreted their watches and purses in their boots, and were now pretending to be asleep.

The coach lumbered on again, with heavier wreaths of mist closing round it as it began the descent. The guard soon replaced his blunderbuss in his arm-chest.

Jerry, left alone in the mist and darkness, dismounted meanwhile, not only to ease his spent horse, but to wipe the mud from his face, and shake the wet out of his hat-brim. After standing with the bridle over his arm, until the wheels of the mail were no longer within hearing and the night was quite still again, he turned to walk down the hill.

"After that there gallop from Temple Bar, old lady, I won't trust your fore-legs till I get you on the level," said this hoarse messenger, glancing at his mare. "'Recalled to life.' That's a Blazing strange message. You'd be in a Blazing bad way, if recalling to life was to come into fashion, Jerry!"

CHAPTER 3

The Night Shadows

The messenger rode back at an easy trot, stopping pretty often at ale-houses by the way to drink, but tending to keep his own counsel, and to keep his hat cocked over his eyes. He had eyes that assorted very well with that decoration, being of a surface black. They had a sinister expression, under an old cocked-hat like a three-cornered spittoon, and

7

over a great muffler for the chin and throat, which descended nearly to the wearer's knees. When he stopped for drink, he moved this muffler with his left hand, only while he poured his liquor in with his right; as soon as that was done, he muffled again.

"No, Jerry, no!" said the messenger, harping on one theme as he rode. "It wouldn't do for you, it wouldn't suit *your* line of business! Recalled – ! Bust me if I don't think he'd been a drinking!"

He trotted back with the message he was to deliver to the night watchman in his box at the door of Tellson's Bank, by Temple Bar, who was to deliver it to greater authorities within.

What time, the mail-coach lumbered, and bumped upon its tedious way, with its three fellow inscrutables inside. The bank passenger, his arm drawn through the leathern strap to keep him from pounding against the next passenger, nodded in his place.

He was on his way to dig some one out of a grave.

In the shadows of the night he saw faces – faces of a man of five-and-forty by years, and they differed principally in the passions they expressed. Pride, contempt, defiance, stubbornness, submission, lamentation, succeeded one another; so did varieties of sunken cheek, cadaverous colour, emaciated hands and figures. But the face was in the main one face, and every head was prematurely white. A hundred times the dozing passenger inquired:

"Buried how long?"

The answer was always the same: "Almost eighteen years."

"I hope you care to live?"

"I can't say."

Dig, dig, dig, until an impatient movement from one of the two passengers would admonish him to pull up the window. He would draw his arm securely through the leathern strap, and speculate upon the two slumbering forms, until his mind lost its hold of them, and they again slid away into the Banking house and the grave.

"Buried how long?"

"Almost eighteen years."

"You had abandoned all hope of being dug out?"

"Long ago."

The words were still in his hearing as just spoken – distinctly in his hearing as ever spoken words had been in his life – when the weary passenger started to the consciousness of daylight, and found that the shadows of the night were gone.

He lowered the window, and looked out at the rising sun. Though the earth was cold and wet, the sky was clear, and the sun rose bright, placid, and beautiful.

"Eighteen years!" said the passenger, looking at the sun. "Gracious Creator of day! To be buried alive for eighteen years!"

CHAPTER 4

The Preparation

When the mail got successfully to Dover, in the course of the forenoon, the head drawer at the Royal George Hotel opened the coach-door as his custom was. The passenger, Mr Lorry, stepped down.

"There will be a packet to Calais, tomorrow, drawer?"

"Yes, sir, if the weather holds and the wind sets tolerable fair. The tide will serve pretty nicely at about two in the afternoon, sir. Bed, sir?"

"I shall not go to bed till night; but I want a bedroom, and a barber."

"And then breakfast, sir? Yes, sir. That way, sir, if you please. Show Concord! Gentleman's valise and hot water to Concord. Fetch barber to Concord. Stir about there, now, for Concord!"

The Concord bedchamber was always assigned to a passenger by the mail, and passengers by the mail being always heavily wrapped from head to foot, the room had the odd interest for the Royal George. This being that but one kind of man was seen to go into it, whereas all kinds of men came out of it. Consequently, several maids and the landlady were loitering at various points of the road between the Concord and the coffee-room. A gentleman of sixty, formally dressed in a brown suit of clothes, pretty well worn, but very well kept, with large square cuffs and large flaps to the pockets, passed along on his way to his breakfast.

The coffee-room had no other occupant, that forenoon, than the gentleman in brown. His breakfast-table was drawn before the fire. Very orderly and methodical he looked, with a hand on each knee. He wore an odd little sleek, crisp, flaxen wig, setting very close to his head. A face habitually suppressed and quiet, was still lighted up under the quaint wig by a pair of moist bright eyes. He had a healthy colour in his cheeks, and his face, though lined, bore few traces of anxiety.

Mr Lorry dropped off to sleep. The arrival of his breakfast roused him, and he said to the drawer, as he moved his chair to it:

"I wish accommodation prepared for a young lady who may come here at any time today. She may ask for Mr Jarvis Lorry, or a gentleman from Tellson's Bank."

When Mr Lorry had finished his breakfast, he went out for a stroll on the beach. The beach was a desert of heaps of sea and stones tumbling wildly about, and the sea did what it liked, and what it liked was destruction. It thundered at the town, and thundered at the cliffs, and brought the coast down, madly.

The day declined into the afternoon, and when it was dark, and he sat before the coffee-room fire, awaiting his dinner as he had awaited his breakfast, his mind was busily digging in the live red coals.

Mr Lorry had been idle a long time, and had just poured out his last glassful of wine, when a rattling of wheels rumbled into the inn-yard.

He set down his glass untouched. "This is Mam'selle!" said he.

In a very few minutes the waiter came in to announce that Miss Manette had arrived from London, and would be happy to see the gentleman from Tellson's.

"So soon?"

Miss Manette had taken some refreshment on the road, and required none then, and was extremely anxious to see the gentleman from Tellson's immediately, if it suited his pleasure and convenience.

The gentleman from Tellson's had nothing left for it but to empty his glass, settle his odd little flaxen wig at the ears, and follow the waiter to Miss Manette's apartment. It was a large, dark room, furnished in a funereal manner with black horsehair, and loaded with heavy dark tables. He saw standing to receive him by the table before the fire, a young lady of not more than seventeen, in a riding-cloak, and still holding her straw travelling hat by its ribbon in her hand. His eyes rested on a short, slight, pretty figure, a quantity of golden hair, and a pair of blue eyes that met his own with an inquiring look. Thoughts of a sudden vivid likeness passed before him, of a child whom he had held in his arms on the passage across that very Channel, one cold time, when the hail drifted heavily and the sea ran high. The likeness passed away and he made his formal bow to Miss Manette.

"Pray take a seat, sir." In a very clear and pleasant young voice, a little foreign in its accent, but a very little indeed.

"I kiss your hand, miss," said Mr Lorry, with the manners of an earlier date, as he made his formal bow again, and took his seat.

"I received a letter from the Bank, sir, yesterday, informing me that some intelligence – or discovery – "

"Either word will do, miss."

" – respecting the small property of my poor father, whom I never saw – so long dead – "

Mr Lorry moved in his chair.

" – rendered it necessary that I should go to Paris, there to communicate with a gentleman of the Bank, so good as to be despatched to Paris for the purpose."

"Myself."

"As I was prepared to hear, sir."

She curtseyed to him, to convey to him that she felt how much older and wiser he was than she. He made her another bow.

"I replied to the Bank, sir, that as it was considered necessary that I should go to France, I should esteem it highly if I might be permitted to place myself under that worthy gentleman's protection. The gentleman had left London, but I think a messenger was sent after him to beg the favour of his waiting for me here."

"I was happy," said Mr Lorry, "to be entrusted with the charge. I shall be more happy to execute it."

"Sir, I thank you indeed. I was told by the Bank, that the gentleman would explain to me the details of the business, and that I must prepare myself to find them of a surprising nature. I have done my best to prepare myself, and I naturally have a strong and eager interest to know what they are."

"Naturally," said Mr Lorry. "Yes – I – "

After a pause, he added, again settling the crisp, flaxen wig at the ears, "It is very difficult to begin."

He did not begin, but, in his indecision, met her glance. The young forehead lifted itself into a singular expression and she raised her hand, as if with an involuntary action she caught at, or stayed some passing shadow.

11

"Are you quite a stranger to me, sir?"

"Am I not?" Mr Lorry opened his hands, and extended them outwards with an argumentative smile.

Between the eyebrows and just over the little feminine nose, the expression deepened itself as she took her seat thoughtfully in a chair. He watched her as she mused, and the moment she raised her eyes again, went on: "In your adopted country, I presume, I cannot do better than address you as a young English lady, Miss Manette?"

"If you please, sir."

"Miss Manette, I am a man of business. I have a business charge to acquit myself of. In your reception of it, don't heed me any more than if I was a speaking machine – truly, I am not much else. I will, with your leave, relate to you, miss, the story of one of our customers."

"Story!"

He seemed wilfully to mistake the word she had repeated, when he added, in a hurry, "Yes, customers; in the banking business we usually call our connection our customers. He was a French gentleman; a scientific gentleman; a man of great acquirements – a Doctor."

"Not of Beauvais?"

"Why, yes, of Beauvais. Like Monsieur Manette, your father, the gentleman was of Beauvais. Like Monsieur Manette, your father, the gentleman was of repute in Paris. I had the honour of knowing him there. Our relations were business relations, but confidential. I was at that time in our French House, and had been – oh! twenty years."

"At that time – I may ask, at what time, sir?"

"I speak, miss, of twenty years ago. He married – an English lady – and I was one of the trustees. His affairs were entirely in Tellson's hands. To go on – "

"But this is my father's story, sir; and I begin to think" – the curiously roughened forehead was very intent upon him – "that when I was left an orphan through my mother's surviving my father only two years, it was you who brought me to England. I am almost sure it was you."

Mr Lorry took the hesitating little hand that confidingly advanced to take his, and he put it with some ceremony to his lips. He then lead the young lady back to her chair. He stood looking down into her face while she sat looking up into his.

"Miss Manette, it *was* I. I have never seen you since. No; you have

12

been the ward of Tellson's House since, and I have been busy with the other business of Tellson's House since. Feelings! I have no time for them, no chance of them."

Mr Lorry flattened his flaxen wig upon his head with both hands, and resumed his former attitude.

"So far, miss (as you have remarked), this is the story of your regretted father. Now comes the difference. If your father had not died when he did – don't be frightened! How you start!"

She did, indeed, start. And she caught his wrist with both her hands.

"Pray," said Mr Lorry, in a soothing tone, bringing his left hand from the back of the chair to lay it on the supplicatory fingers that clasped him in so violent a tremble: "pray control your agitation – a matter of business. As I was saying – "

Her look so discomposed him that he stopped, wandered, and began anew: "As I was saying; if Monsieur Manette had not died, but had suddenly and silently disappeared or been spirited away. If he had an enemy in some compatriot who could exercise a privilege that made even the boldest people afraid to speak of in a whisper, for instance, filling blank forms for the consignment of any one to the oblivion of a prison for any length of time. If his wife had implored the king, the queen, the court, the clergy, for any tidings of him, and all quite in vain – then the history of your father would have been the history of this unfortunate gentleman, the Doctor of Beauvais."

"I entreat you to tell me more, sir."

"I will. I am going to. You can bear it?"

"I can bear anything but the uncertainty you leave me in at this moment."

"You speak collectedly, and you – *are* collected. That's good! A matter of business. Regard it as business that must be done. Now if this doctor's wife, though a lady of great courage and spirit, had suffered so intensely from this cause before her little child was born – "

"The little child was a daughter, sir?"

"A daughter. A – a – matter of business – don't be distressed. Miss, if the poor lady had suffered so intensely before her little child was born, that she decided to spare the poor child the agony she had known, by rearing her in the belief that her father was dead – No, don't kneel! In Heaven's name why should you kneel to me?"

13

"For the truth. O dear, good, compassionate sir, for the truth!"

"A – a matter of business. You confuse me, and how can I transact business if I am confused? Let us be clear-headed. If you could kindly mention now, for instance, what nine times ninepence are, or how many shillings in twenty guineas, it would be so encouraging. I should be so much more at my ease about your state of mind."

Without directly answering to this appeal, she sat so still when he had very gently raised her, and the hands that had not ceased to clasp his wrists were so much more steady than they had been, that she communicated some reassurance to Mr Jarvis Lorry.

"That's right, that's right. Courage! Business! You have business before you – useful business. Miss Manette, your mother took this course with you. And when she died – I believe broken-hearted – having never given up on her search for your father, she left you, at two years old, to grow to be blooming, beautiful, and happy. She left you without the dark cloud of living in uncertainty as to whether your father soon wore his heart out in prison, or wasted there through many lingering years."

As he said the words he looked down, with an admiring pity, on the flowing golden hair as if he pictured to himself that it might have been already tinged with grey.

"You know that your parents had no great possession, and that what they had was secured to your mother and to you. There has been no new discovery, of money, or of any other property; but – "

He felt his wrist held closer, and he stopped. The expression in the forehead, which had so particularly attracted his notice, and which was now immovable, had deepened into one of pain and horror.

"But he has been found. He is alive. Greatly changed, it is too probable; almost a wreck, it is possible; though we will hope the best. Still, alive. Your father has been taken to the house of an old servant in Paris, and we are going there: I, to identify him if I can: you, to restore him to life, love, duty, rest, comfort."

A shiver ran through her body, and from it through his. She said, in a low, distinct, awe-stricken voice, as if she were saying it in a dream, "I am going to see his Ghost! It will be his Ghost – not him!"

Mr Lorry quietly chafed the hands that held his arm. "There, there, there! See now, see now! The best and the worst are known to you, now. You are well on your way to the poor wronged gentleman, and, with a fair sea voyage, and a fair land journey, you will be soon at his dear side."

She repeated in the same tone, sunk to a whisper, "I have been free, I have been happy, yet his Ghost has never haunted me!"

"Only one thing more," said Mr Lorry, laying stress upon it as a wholesome means of enforcing her attention: "he has been found under another name; his own, long forgotten or long concealed. It would be worse than useless to seek to know whether he has been for years overlooked, or always designedly held prisoner. It would be worse than useless now to make any inquiries, because it would be dangerous. Better not to mention the subject, and to remove him – for a while at all events – out of France. Even I, safe as an Englishman, and even Tellson's, important as they are to French credit, avoid all naming of the matter. I carry about me, not a scrap of writing openly referring to it. This is a secret service altogether. My credentials, entries, and memoranda, are all comprehended in the one line, 'Recalled to Life'; which may mean anything. But what is the matter! She doesn't notice a word! Miss Manette!"

Perfectly still and silent, and not even fallen back in her chair, she sat under his hand, utterly insensible; with her eyes open and fixed upon him, and with that last expression looking as if it were carved or branded into her forehead. He called out loudly for assistance without moving.

A wild-looking woman entered, whom even in his agitation, Mr Lorry observed to have red hair, and to be dressed in some extraordinary tight-fitting fashion. She came running into the room in advance of the inn servants and soon settled the question of his detachment from the poor young lady, by laying a brawny hand upon his chest, and sending him flying back against the nearest wall.

"Why, look at you all!" bawled this figure, addressing the inn servants. "Why don't you go and fetch things, instead of standing there staring at me? I'll let you know, if you don't bring smelling-salts, cold water, and vinegar, quick, I will."

There was an immediate dispersal for these restoratives, and she softly laid the patient on a sofa, and tended her with great skill and gentleness.

"And you in brown!" she said, indignantly turning to Mr Lorry. "Couldn't you tell her what you had to tell her, without frightening her to death? Look at her, with her pretty pale face and her cold hands. Do you call *that* being a Banker?"

Mr Lorry was so exceedingly disconcerted by a question so hard to answer, that he could only look on.

"I hope she will do well now," he said.

"No thanks to you, if she does. My darling pretty!"

"I hope," said Mr Lorry, after another pause of feeble sympathy and humility, "that you accompany Miss Manette to France?"

"A likely thing, too!" replied the strong woman. "If it was ever intended that I should go across salt water, do you suppose Providence would have cast my lot in an island?"

This being another question hard to answer, Mr Jarvis Lorry withdrew to consider it.

CHAPTER 5

The Wine Shop

A cask of wine had been dropped, in the street. The cask had tumbled out of a cart, the hoops had burst, and it lay shattered on the stones just outside the door of the wine shop.

All the people within reach had run to the spot to drink the wine. The rough, irregular stones of the street, had dammed it into little pools; these were surrounded, each by its own jostling group. Some men kneeled down, made scoops of their two hands joined, and sipped, or tried to help women, who bent over their shoulders, to sip, before the wine had all run out between their fingers. Others dipped in the puddles with little mugs of mutilated earthenware, or even with handkerchiefs from women's heads. Others, directed by those up at high windows, darted here and there, to cut off little streams of wine. Others devoted themselves to the sodden and lee-dyed pieces of the cask, licking, and even champing the moister wine-rotted fragments with eager relish.

A shrill sound of laughter and of amused voices – men, women, and children – resounded in the street while this wine game lasted. There was little roughness in the sport, and much playfulness. When the wine was gone, and the places where it had been most abundant were raked into a gridiron-pattern by fingers, these demonstrations ceased, as suddenly as they had broken out. The man who had left his saw sticking in the firewood he was cutting, set it in motion again. The woman who had left on a door-step the little pot of hot ashes, at which she had been trying to soften the pain in her own starved fingers and toes, or in those of her child, returned to it. Men with bare arms, matted locks, and cadaverous faces, who had emerged into the winter light from cellars, moved away, to descend again.

The wine was red wine, and had stained the ground of the narrow street in the suburb of Saint Antoine, in Paris. It had stained many hands, too, and many faces. The forehead of the woman who nursed her baby, was stained with the stain of the old rag she wound about her head again. One joker scrawled upon a wall with his finger dipped in muddy wine-lees – *blood*.

The time was to come, when that wine too would be spilled on the street-stones, and when the stain of it would be red upon many there.

And now that the cloud settled on Saint Antoine, which a momentary gleam had driven from his sacred countenance, the darkness of it was heavy – cold, dirt, sickness, ignorance, and want. Samples of a people that had undergone a terrible grinding and regrinding in the mill shivered at every corner, passed in and out at every doorway, looked from every window, fluttered in every vestige of a garment that the wind shook. The mill which had worked them down, was the mill that grinds young people old; the children had ancient faces and grave voices; and upon them, and upon the grown faces, and ploughed into every furrow of age and coming up afresh, was the sign, Hunger. It was prevalent everywhere. Hunger was pushed from the tall houses, in the wretched clothing that hung upon poles and lines. Hunger was patched into them with straw and rag and wood and paper. Hunger was repeated in every fragment of the small modicum of firewood that the man sawed off. Hunger was the inscription on the baker's shelves, written in every small loaf of his scanty stock of bad bread; at the sausage-shop, in every dead-dog preparation that was offered for sale. Hunger rattled its dry bones among the roasting chestnuts in the turned cylinder; Hunger was shred into atoms in every farthing porringer of husky chips of potato, fried with some reluctant drops of oil.

The trade signs were, all, grim illustrations of Want. The butcher and the porkman painted up only the leanest scrags of meat; the baker, the coarsest of meagre loaves. Nothing was represented in a flourishing condition, save tools and weapons; the cutler's knives and axes were sharp and bright, the smith's hammers were heavy, and the gunmaker's stock was murderous. The kennel ran down the middle of the street – when it ran at all: which was only after heavy rains, and then it ran, by many eccentric fits, into the houses.

Every wind that blew over France shook the rags of the scarecrows in vain, for those birds, fine of song and feather, took no warning.

The wine shop was a corner shop, better than most others in its appearance and degree, and the master of the wine shop had stood outside it, in a yellow waistcoat and green breeches, looking on at the struggle for the lost wine. "It's not my affair," said he, with a final shrug of the shoulders. "The people from the market did it. Let them bring another."

This wine shop keeper was a bull-necked, martial-looking man of thirty, and he should have been of a hot temperament, for, although it was a bitter day, he wore no coat, but carried one slung over his shoulder. His shirt-sleeves were rolled up, too, and his brown arms were bare to the elbows. Neither did he wear anything more on his head than his own crisply-curling short dark hair. He was a dark man altogether, with good eyes and a good bold breadth between them. Good-humoured looking on the whole, but implacable-looking, too; evidently a man of a strong resolution and a set purpose; a man not desirable to be met, rushing down a narrow pass with a gulf on either side, for nothing would turn the man.

Madame Defarge, his wife, sat in the shop behind the counter as he came in. Madame Defarge was a stout woman of about his own age, with a watchful eye that seldom seemed to look at anything, a large hand heavily ringed, a steady face, strong features, and great composure of manner. There was a character about Madame Defarge, from which one might have predicated that she did not often make mistakes. Madame Defarge being sensitive to cold, was wrapped in fur, and had a quantity of bright shawl twined about her head, though not to the concealment of her large earrings. Her knitting was before her, but she had laid it down to pick her teeth with a toothpick. Thus engaged, with her right elbow supported by her left hand, Madame Defarge said nothing when her lord came in, but coughed just one grain of cough. This, together with the slight lifting of her darkly defined eyebrows, suggested to her husband that he would do well to look round the shop for any new customer who had dropped in while he stepped over the way.

The wine shop keeper accordingly rolled his eyes about, until they rested upon an elderly gentleman and a young lady, who were seated in a corner. As he passed behind the counter, he took notice that the elderly gentleman said in a look to the young lady, "This is our man."

"What the devil do *you* do in that galley there?" said Monsieur Defarge to himself. "I don't know you." But, he feigned not to notice the two strangers, and fell into discourse with the triumvirate of customers who were drinking at the counter.

"How goes it, Jacques?" said one of these three to Monsieur Defarge. "Is all the spilt wine swallowed?"

"Every drop, Jacques," answered Monsieur Defarge.

When this interchange of Christian name was effected, Madame Defarge, picking her teeth with her toothpick, coughed another grain of cough, and raised her eyebrows by the breadth of another line.

"It is not often," said the second of the three, addressing Monsieur Defarge, "that many of these miserable beasts know the taste of wine, or of anything but black bread and death. Is it not so, Jacques?"

"It is so, Jacques," Monsieur Defarge returned.

At this second interchange of the Christian name, Madame Defarge, still using her toothpick with profound composure, coughed another grain of cough, and raised her eyebrows by the breadth of another line.

The last of the three now said his say, as he put down his empty drinking vessel and smacked his lips.

"Ah! So much the worse! A bitter taste it is that such poor cattle always have in their mouths, and hard lives they live, Jacques. Am I right, Jacques?"

"You are right, Jacques," was the response of Monsieur Defarge.

This third interchange of the Christian name was completed at the moment when Madame Defarge put her toothpick by, kept her eyebrows up, and slightly rustled in her seat.

"Hold then! True!" muttered her husband. "Gentlemen – my wife!"

The three customers pulled off their hats to Madame Defarge, with three flourishes. She acknowledged their homage by bending her head, and giving them a quick look. Then she glanced in a casual manner round the wine shop, took up her knitting with great apparent calmness and repose of spirit, and became absorbed in it.

"Gentlemen," said her husband, who had kept his bright eye observantly upon her, "good day."

The eyes of Monsieur Defarge were studying his wife at her knitting when the elderly gentleman advanced from his corner, and begged the favour of a word.

"Willingly, sir," said Monsieur Defarge, and quietly stepped with him to the door.

Their conference was very short, but very decided. Almost at the first word, Monsieur Defarge started and became deeply attentive. It had not lasted a minute, when he nodded and went out. The gentleman then beckoned to the young lady, and they, too, went out. Madame Defarge knitted with nimble fingers and steady eyebrows, and saw nothing.

Mr Jarvis Lorry and Miss Manette, emerging from the wine shop thus, joined Monsieur Defarge in the doorway. It opened from a stinking little black courtyard, and was the general public entrance to a great pile of houses, inhabited by a great number of people. In the gloomy tile-paved entry to the gloomy tile-paved staircase, Monsieur Defarge bent down on one knee to the child of his old master, and put her hand to his lips. It was a gentle action, but not at all gently done; a very remarkable transformation had come over him in a few seconds. He had no good-humour in his face, nor any openness of aspect left, but had become a secret, angry, dangerous man.

"It is very high; it is a little difficult. Better to begin slowly." Thus, Monsieur Defarge, in a stern voice, to Mr Lorry, as they began ascending the stairs.

"Is he alone?" the latter whispered.

"Alone! God help him, who should be with him!" said the other, in the same low voice.

"Is he always alone, then?"

"Yes."

"Of his own desire?"

"Of his own necessity. As he was, when I first saw him after they found me and demanded to know if I would take him, and, at my peril be discreet – as he was then, so he is now."

"He is greatly changed?"

"Changed!"

The keeper of the wine shop stopped to strike the wall with his hand, and mutter a tremendous curse. No direct answer could have been half so forceful. Mr Lorry's spirits grew heavier and heavier, as he and his two companions ascended higher and higher.

Such a staircase was vile indeed to unaccustomed and unhardened senses. Every little habitation within the great foul nest of one high building left its own heap of refuse on its own landing, besides flinging other refuse from its own windows. Through such an atmosphere, by a steep dark shaft of dirt and poison, the way lay. Mr Jarvis Lorry twice stopped to rest. Each of these stoppages was made at a doleful grating. Through the rusted bars, tastes, rather than glimpses, were caught of the jumbled neighbourhood; and nothing within range, nearer or lower than the summits of the two great towers of Notre-Dame, had any promise on it of healthy life or wholesome aspirations.

At last, the top of the staircase was gained, and they stopped for the third time. There was yet another steeper and narrower staircase, before the garret story was reached. The keeper of the wine shop always went a little in advance. It was as though he dreaded to be asked any question by the young lady. He turned himself about here, and took out a key.

"The door is locked then, my friend?" said Mr Lorry, surprised.

"Ay. Yes," was the grim reply of Monsieur Defarge.

"You think it necessary to keep the unfortunate gentleman so retired?"

"I think it necessary to turn the key." Monsieur Defarge whispered it closer in his ear, and frowned heavily.

"Why?"

"Why! Because he has lived so long, locked up, that he would be frightened – rave – tear himself to pieces – die – come to I know not what harm – if his door was left open."

"Is it possible?" exclaimed Mr Lorry.

"Is it possible?" repeated Defarge, bitterly. "Yes. And a beautiful world we live in, when it *is* possible, and when many other such things are possible, and not only possible, but done – done, see you! Long live the Devil. Let us go on."

This dialogue had been held in so very low a whisper, that not a word of it had reached the young lady's ears. But, by this time she trembled under such strong emotion, and her face expressed such deep anxiety, and, above all, such dread and terror, that Mr Lorry felt it incumbent on him to speak a word or two of reassurance.

"Courage, dear miss! Courage! Business! The worst will be over in a moment; it is but entering the room and the worst is over. Then, all the good you bring to him begins. Let our good friend here assist you on that side. That's well, friend Defarge. Come, now. Business, business!"

They went up slowly and softly. The staircase was short, and they were soon at the top. There appeared to be no other door on that floor. Defarge struck twice or thrice upon the door – evidently with no other object than to make a noise there. With the same intention, he drew the key across it, three or four times, before he put it clumsily into the lock, and turned it as heavily as he could.

The door slowly opened inward under his hand, and he looked into the room and said something. A faint voice answered something. Little more than a single syllable could have been spoken on either side.

He looked back over his shoulder, and beckoned them to enter. Mr Lorry got his arm securely round the daughter's waist, and held her.

"A – a – a – business, business!" he urged, with a moisture that was not of business shining on his cheek. "Come in, come in!"

"I am afraid of it," she answered, shuddering.

"Of it? What?"

"I mean of him. Of my father."

Rendered in a manner desperate, by her state and by the beckoning of their conductor, he drew over his neck the arm that shook upon his shoulder, lifted her a little, and hurried her into the room.

Defarge drew out the key, closed the door, locked it on the inside, took out the key again, and held it in his hand. All this he did, methodically, and as loudly as he could. Finally, he walked across the room with a measured tread to where the window was. He stopped there, and turned round.

The garret was dim and dark; the window was unglazed, and closing up the middle in two pieces, like any other door of French construction. To exclude the cold, one half of this door was fast closed, and the other was opened but a very little way. Such a scanty portion of light was admitted through these means, that it was difficult, on first coming in, to see anything; and long habit alone could have slowly formed in any one, the ability to do any work requiring nicety in such obscurity. Yet, work of that kind was being done in the garret; for, with his back towards the door, and his face towards the window where the keeper of the wine shop stood looking at him, a white-haired man sat on a low bench, stooping forward and very busy, making shoes.

CHAPTER 6

The Shoemaker

"Good day!" said Monsieur Defarge, looking down at the white head that bent low over the shoemaking.

It was raised for a moment, and a very faint voice responded to the salutation, as if it were at a distance:

"Good day!"

"You are still hard at work, I see?"

After a long silence, the head was lifted for another moment, and the voice replied, "Yes – I am working." This time, a pair of haggard eyes had looked at the questioner, before the face had dropped again.

The faintness of the voice was pitiable and dreadful. It was not the faintness of physical weakness, though confinement and hard fare no doubt had their part in it. It was the faintness of solitude and disuse. It was like the last feeble echo of a sound made long ago. So entirely had it lost the life and resonance of the human voice, that it affected the senses like a once beautiful colour faded away into a poor weak stain.

Some minutes of silent work had passed, and the haggard eyes had looked up again, not with any interest or curiosity, but with a dull mechanical perception, beforehand, that the spot where the only visitor they were aware of had stood, was not yet empty.

"I want," said Defarge, who had not removed his gaze from the shoemaker, "to let in a little more light here. You can bear a little more?"

The shoemaker stopped his work; looked with a vacant air of listening, at the floor on one side of him; then similarly, at the floor on the other side of him; then, upward at the speaker.

"What did you say?"

"You can bear a little more light?"

"I must bear it, if you let it in."

The opened half-door was opened a little further. A broad ray of light fell into the garret, and showed the workman with an unfinished shoe upon his lap, pausing in his labour. His few common tools and various scraps of leather were at his feet and on his bench. He had a white beard, raggedly cut, but not very long, a hollow face, and exceedingly bright eyes. The hollowness and thinness of his face would have caused them to

23

look large, under his yet dark eyebrows and his confused white hair, though they had been really otherwise; but, they were naturally large, and looked unnaturally so. His yellow rags of shirt lay open at the throat, and showed his body to be withered and worn. He, and his old canvas frock, and his loose stockings, and all his poor tatters of clothes, had, in a long seclusion from direct light and air, faded down to such a dull uniformity of parchment-yellow, that it would have been hard to say which was which.

He had put up a hand between his eyes and the light, and the very bones of it seemed transparent. So he sat, with a steadfastly vacant gaze, pausing in his work. He never looked at the figure before him, without first looking down on this side of himself, then on that, as if he had lost the habit of associating place with sound; he never spoke, without first wandering in this manner, and forgetting to speak.

"Are you going to finish that pair of shoes today?" asked Defarge, motioning to Mr Lorry to come forward.

"What did you say?"

"Do you mean to finish that pair of shoes today?"

"I can't say that I mean to. I suppose so. I don't know."

But, the question reminded him of his work, and he bent over it again.

Mr Lorry came silently forward, leaving the daughter by the door. When he had stood, for a minute or two, by the side of Defarge, the shoemaker looked up. He showed no surprise at seeing another figure, but the unsteady fingers of one of his hands strayed to his lips as he looked at it (his lips and his nails were of the same pale lead-colour). Then the hand dropped to his work, and he once more bent over the shoe. The look and the action had occupied but an instant.

"You have a visitor, you see," said Monsieur Defarge.

"What did you say?"

"Here is a visitor."

The shoemaker looked up as before, but without removing a hand from his work.

"Come!" said Defarge. "Here is monsieur, who knows a well-made shoe when he sees one. Show him that shoe you are working at. Take it, monsieur."

Mr Lorry took it in his hand.

"Tell monsieur what kind of shoe it is, and the maker's name."

There was a longer pause, before the shoemaker replied:

"I forget what it was you asked me. What did you say?"

"I said, couldn't you describe the kind of shoe, for monsieur's information?"

"It is a lady's shoe. It is a young lady's walking-shoe. It is in the present mode. I never saw the mode. I have had a pattern in my hand." He glanced at the shoe with some little passing touch of pride.

"And the maker's name?" said Defarge.

Now that he had no work to hold, he laid the knuckles of the right hand in the hollow of the left, and then the knuckles of the left hand in the hollow of the right. He then passed a hand across his bearded chin, and so on in regular changes, without a moment's intermission. The task of recalling him from the vagrancy into which he always sank when he had spoken, was like recalling some very weak person from a swoon, or endeavouring, in the hope of some disclosure, to stay the spirit of a fast-dying man.

"Did you ask me for my name?"

"Assuredly I did."

"One Hundred and Five, North Tower."

"Is that all?"

"One Hundred and Five, North Tower."

With a weary sound that was not a sigh, nor a groan, he bent to work again, until the silence was again broken.

"You are not a shoemaker by trade?" said Mr Lorry, looking steadfastly at him.

His haggard eyes turned to Defarge as if he would have transferred the question to him: but as no help came from that quarter, they turned back on the questioner when they had sought the ground.

"I am not a shoemaker by trade? No, I was not a shoemaker by trade. I – I learnt it here. I taught myself. I asked leave to – "

He lapsed away, even for minutes, ringing those measured changes on his hands the whole time. His eyes came slowly back, at last, to the face from which they had wandered; when they rested on it, he started, and resumed, in the manner of a sleeper that moment awake, reverting to a subject of last night.

"I asked leave to teach myself, and I got it with much difficulty after a long while, and I have made shoes ever since."

25

As he held out his hand for the shoe that had been taken from him, Mr Lorry said, still looking steadfastly in his face:

"Monsieur Manette, do you remember nothing of me?"

The shoe dropped to the ground, and he sat looking fixedly at the questioner.

"Monsieur Manette." Mr Lorry laid his hand upon Defarge's arm; "do you remember nothing of this man? Look at him. Look at me. Is there no old banker, no old business, no old servant, no old time, rising in your mind, Monsieur Manette?"

As the captive of many years sat looking fixedly, by turns, at Mr Lorry and at Defarge, some long obliterated marks of an actively intent intelligence in the middle of the forehead, gradually forced themselves through the black mist that had fallen on him. They were overclouded again, they were fainter, they were gone; but they had been there. And so exactly was the expression repeated on the fair young face of her who had crept along the wall to a point where she could see him, and where she now stood looking at him. Her hands were now extending towards him, trembling with eagerness to lay the spectral face upon her warm young breast, and love it back to life and hope. So exactly was the expression repeated (though in stronger characters) on her fair young face, that it looked as though it had passed like a moving light, from him to her.

He looked at the two, less and less attentively, and his eyes sought the ground and looked about him in the old way. Finally, with a deep long sigh, he took the shoe up, and resumed his work.

"Have you recognised him, monsieur?" asked Defarge in a whisper.

"Yes; for a moment. At first I thought it quite hopeless, but I have unquestionably seen, for a moment, the face that I once knew so well. Hush! Let us draw further back. Hush!"

She had moved from the wall of the garret, very near to the bench on which he sat. He was totally unaware of the figure that could have touched him as he worked.

Not a word was spoken, not a sound was made. She stood, like a spirit, beside him, and he bent over his work.

It happened, at length, that he had occasion to change the instrument in his hand, for his shoemaker's knife. He had taken it up, and was stooping to work again, when his eyes caught the skirt of her dress. He raised them, and saw her face. The two spectators started forward, but she stayed them with a motion of her hand. She had no fear of his striking with the knife, though they had.

He stared at her with a fearful look, and after a while his lips began to form some words, though no sound proceeded from them. By degrees, he was heard to say: "What is this?"

With the tears streaming down her face, she put her two hands to her lips, and kissed them to him; then clasped them on her breast, as if she laid his ruined head there.

"You are not the gaoler's daughter?"

She sighed. "No."

"Who are you?"

Not yet trusting the tones of her voice, she sat down on the bench beside him. He recoiled, but she laid her hand upon his arm. A strange thrill struck him when she did so, and visibly passed over his frame; he laid the knife down softly, as he sat staring at her.

Her golden hair, which she wore in long curls, had been hurriedly pushed aside, and fell down over her neck. Advancing his hand by little and little, he took it up and looked at it. In the midst of the action he went astray, and, with another deep sigh, fell to work at his shoemaking.

But not for long. Releasing his arm, she laid her hand upon his shoulder. After looking doubtfully at it, two or three times, as if to be sure that it was really there, he laid down his work, put his hand to his neck, and took off a blackened string with a scrap of folded rag attached to it. He opened this, carefully, on his knee, and it contained a very little quantity of hair: not more than one or two long golden hairs, which he had, in some old day, wound off upon his finger.

He took her hair into his hand again, and looked closely at it. "It is the same. How can it be! When was it! How was it!"

As the concentrated expression returned to his forehead, he seemed to become conscious that it was in hers too. He turned her full to the light, and looked at her.

"She had laid her head upon my shoulder, that night when I was summoned out – she had a fear of my going, though I had none – and when I was brought to the North Tower they found these upon my sleeve. 'You will leave me them? They can never help me to escape in the body, though they may in the spirit.' Those were the words I said. I remember them very well."

He formed this speech slowly.

"How was this? *Was it you?*"

Once more, the two spectators started, as he turned upon her with a frightful suddenness. But she sat perfectly still in his grasp, and only said, in a low voice, "I entreat you, good gentlemen, do not come near us, do not speak, do not move!"

"Hark!" he exclaimed. "Whose voice was that?"

His hands released her as he uttered this cry, and went up to his white hair, which they tore in a frenzy. It died out, as everything but his shoemaking did die out of him, and he refolded his little packet and tried to secure it in his breast; but he still looked at her, and gloomily shook his head.

"No, no, no; you are too young, too blooming. It can't be. See what the prisoner is. These are not the hands she knew, this is not the face she knew, this is not a voice she ever heard. No, no. She was – and He was – before the slow years of the North Tower – ages ago. What is your name, my gentle angel?"

Hailing his softened tone and manner, his daughter fell upon her knees before him, with her appealing hands upon his breast.

"O, sir, at another time you shall know my name, and who my mother was, and who my father, and how I never knew their hard, hard history. But I cannot tell you here and now. All that I may tell you is, that I pray to you to bless me. Kiss me! O my dear!"

His cold white head mingled with her radiant hair, which warmed and lighted it as though it were the light of Freedom shining on him.

"If you hear in my voice – I don't know that it is so, but I hope it is – any resemblance to a voice that once was sweet music in your ears, weep for it! If you touch, in touching my hair, anything that recalls a beloved head that lay on your breast when you were young and free, weep for it! If, when I hint to you of a Home that is before us, where I will be true to you with all my duty and with all my faithful service, I bring back the remembrance of a Home long desolate, weep for it, weep for it!"

She held him closer round the neck, and rocked him on her breast like a child.

"Dearest dear, your agony is over, and I have come here to take you from it, and we go to England to be at peace and at rest. Our native France was so wicked to you – weep for it! When I tell you my name, and that

28

of my father who is living and of my mother who is dead – you will learn that I must kneel to my honoured father, and beg his pardon for never having striven all day or lain awake and wept all night. The love of my poor mother hid his torture from me. Weep for her, then, and for me! Good gentlemen, thank God! I feel his sacred tears upon my face, and his sobs strike against my heart. O, see! Thank God for us, thank God!"

He had sunk in her arms, and his face dropped on her breast: a sight so touching, yet so terrible in the tremendous wrong and suffering which had gone before it, that the two beholders covered their faces.

When the quiet of the garret had been long undisturbed, they came forward to raise the father and daughter from the ground. He had gradually dropped to the floor, and lay there in a stupor, worn out. She had nestled down with him, that his head might lie upon her arm; and her hair drooping over him curtained him from the light.

"If, without disturbing him," she said, raising her hand to Mr Lorry as he stooped over them, after repeated blowings of his nose, "all could be arranged for our leaving Paris at once, so that, from the very door, he could be taken away – "

"But, consider. Is he fit for the journey?" asked Mr Lorry.

"More fit for that, I think, than to remain in this city, so dreadful to him."

"It is true," said Defarge, who was kneeling to look on and hear. "More than that; Monsieur Manette is, for all reasons, best out of France. Say, shall I hire a carriage and post-horses?"

"That's business," said Mr Lorry, resuming on the shortest notice his methodical manners; "and if business is to be done, I had better do it."

"Then be so kind," urged Miss Manette, "as to leave us here. You see how composed he has become, and you cannot be afraid to leave him with me now. Why should you be? I will take care of him until you return, and then we will remove him straight."

Both Mr Lorry and Defarge were in favour of one of them remaining. But, as there were not only carriage and horses to be seen to, but travelling papers; and as time pressed, for the day was drawing to an end, it came at last to their hastily dividing the business that was necessary to be done, and hurrying away to do it.

Then, as the darkness closed in, the daughter laid her head down on the hard ground close at the father's side, and watched him. The darkness deepened and deepened, and they both lay quiet, until a light gleamed through the chinks in the wall.

Mr Lorry and Monsieur Defarge had made all ready for the journey, and had brought with them, besides travelling cloaks and wrappers, bread and meat, wine, and hot coffee. Monsieur Defarge put this provender, and the lamp he carried, on the shoemaker's bench (there was nothing else in the garret but a pallet bed), and he and Mr Lorry roused the captive, and assisted him to his feet.

Whether he knew what had happened, whether he recollected what they had said to him, whether he knew that he was free, were questions that no sagacity could have solved. They tried speaking to him; but he was so confused, that they took fright at his bewilderment, and agreed for the time to tamper with him no more. He had a wild, lost manner of occasionally clasping his head in his hands, that had not been seen in him before; yet, he had some pleasure in the mere sound of his daughter's voice, and invariably turned to it when she spoke.

In the submissive way of one long accustomed to obey under coercion, he ate and drank what they gave him to eat and drink, and put on the cloak and other wrappings, that they gave him to wear. He readily responded to his daughter's drawing her arm through his, and took – and kept – her hand in both his own.

They began to descend; Monsieur Defarge going first with the lamp, Mr Lorry closing the little procession. They had not traversed many steps of the long main staircase when he stopped, and stared at the roof and round at the walls. They heard him mutter, "One Hundred and Five, North Tower;" and when he looked about him, it evidently was for the strong fortress-walls that had long encompassed him. On their reaching the courtyard he instinctively altered his tread, as being in expectation of a drawbridge; and when there was no drawbridge, and he saw the carriage waiting in the open street, he dropped his daughter's hand and clasped his head again.

Only one soul was to be seen, and that was Madame Defarge – who leaned against the door-post, knitting, and saw nothing.

The prisoner had got into a coach, and his daughter had followed him, when Mr Lorry's feet were arrested on the step by his asking, miserably, for his shoemaking tools and the unfinished shoes. Madame Defarge immediately called to her husband that she would get them, and went, knitting, out of the lamplight, through the courtyard. She quickly brought them down and handed them in, and immediately afterwards leaned against the door-post, knitting, and saw nothing.

Defarge got upon the box, and gave the word "To the Barrier!" The postilion cracked his whip, and they clattered away under the feeble over-swinging lamps.

Under the over-swinging lamps – swinging ever brighter in the better streets, and ever dimmer in the worse – and by lighted shops, gay crowds, illuminated coffee-houses, and theatre-doors, to one of the city gates. Soldiers with lanterns, at the guard-house there. "Your papers, travellers!"

"See here then, Monsieur the Officer," said Defarge, getting down, and taking him gravely apart, "these are the papers of monsieur inside, with the white head. They were consigned to me, with him, at the –." He dropped his voice, there was a flutter among the military lanterns, and one of them being handed into the coach by an arm in uniform, the eyes connected with the arm looked at monsieur with the white head. "It is well. Forward!" from the uniform. "Adieu!" from Defarge. And so, under a short grove of feebler and feebler over-swinging lamps, out under the great grove of stars.

Beneath that arch of unmoved and eternal lights the shadows of the night were broad and black. All through the cold and restless interval, until dawn, they once more whispered in the ears of Mr Jarvis Lorry – sitting opposite the buried man who had been dug out, and wondering what subtle powers were for ever lost to him, and what were capable of restoration – the old inquiry:

"I hope you care to be recalled to life?"

And the old answer:

"I can't say."

BOOK 2

THE GOLDEN THREAD

CHAPTER 1

Five Years Later

Tellson's Bank by Temple Bar was an old-fashioned place, even in the year 1780. It was very small, very dark, very ugly. It was an old-fashioned place, moreover, in the moral attribute that the partners in the House were proud of its smallness, proud of its darkness, proud of its ugliness.

Any one of these partners would have disinherited his son on the question of rebuilding Tellson's. In this respect the House was much on a par with the Country; which did very often disinherit its sons for suggesting improvements in laws and customs that had long been highly objectionable, but were only the more respectable.

Cramped in all kinds of dun cupboards and hutches at Tellson's, the oldest of men carried on the business gravely. When they took a young man into Tellson's London house, they hid him somewhere till he was old. They kept him in a dark place, like a cheese. Then only was he permitted to be seen, spectacularly poring over large books, and casting his breeches and gaiters into the general weight of the establishment.

Outside Tellson's – never by any means in it, unless called in – was an odd-job man, an occasional porter and messenger. He was never absent during business hours, unless upon an errand, and then he was represented by his son: a grisly urchin of twelve, who was his express image. People understood that Tellson's, in a stately way, tolerated the odd-job man. The house had always tolerated some person in that capacity, and time and tide had drifted this person to the post. His name was Jerry Cruncher.

The scene was Mr Cruncher's private lodging in Hanging-sword Alley, Whitefriars: the time, half-past seven on a windy March morning, Anno Domini 1780. (Mr Cruncher himself always spoke of the year of our Lord as Anna Dominoes: apparently under the impression that the Christian era dated from the invention of a popular game, by a lady who had bestowed her name upon it.)

Mr Cruncher's apartments were not in a savoury neighbourhood, and were but two in number, even if a closet with a single pane of glass in it might be counted as one. But they were very decently kept. Early as it was, on the windy March morning, the room in which he lay a-bed was already scrubbed throughout; and between the cups and saucers arranged for breakfast, and the lumbering deal table, a very clean white cloth was spread.

Mr Cruncher reposed under a patchwork counterpane, like a Harlequin at home. At first, he slept heavily, but, by degrees, began to roll and surge in bed, until he rose above the surface, with his spiky hair looking as if it must tear the sheets to ribbons. He threw a boot at the woman in the room (his wife). It was a very muddy boot, and may introduce the odd circumstance connected with Mr Cruncher's domestic economy, that, whereas he often came home after banking hours with clean boots, he often got up next morning to find the same boots covered with clay.

"What," said Mr Cruncher, "what are you up to, Aggerawayter?"

"I was only saying my prayers."

"Saying your prayers! What do you mean by praying agin me?"

"I was not praying against you; I was praying for you."

"You weren't. And if you were, I won't be took the liberty with. Here! Your mother's a nice woman, young Jerry, going a praying agin your father's prosperity. You've got a religious mother, you have, my boy, and praying that the bread-and-butter may be snatched out of the mouth of her only child."

Master Cruncher (who was in his shirt) took this very ill, and, turning to his mother, strongly deprecated any praying away of his personal board.

"And what do you suppose," said Mr Cruncher, "that the worth of *your* prayers may be?"

"They only come from the heart, Jerry. They are worth no more than that."

"Worth no more than that," repeated Mr Cruncher. "They ain't worth much, then. Whether or no, I won't be prayed agin, I can't afford it. I'm not a going to be made unlucky by *your* sneaking. Young Jerry, dress yourself, my boy, and while I clean my boots keep a eye upon your mother now and then, and if you see any signs of more praying, give me a call. For, I tell you," here he addressed his wife once more, "I won't be gone agin, in this manner."

Growling, Mr Cruncher betook himself to his boot-cleaning and his general preparation for business. In the meantime, his son, whose head was garnished with tenderer spikes, and whose young eyes stood close by one another, as his father's did, kept the required watch upon his mother.

Mr Cruncher's temper was not at all improved when he came to his breakfast. He resented Mrs Cruncher's saying grace.

"Now, Aggerawayter! What are you up to? At it agin?"

His wife explained that she had merely "asked a blessing."

"Don't do it!" said Mr Cruncher, looking about, as if he rather expected to see the loaf disappear under the efficacy of his wife's petitions. "I ain't a going to be blest out of house and home. I won't have my wittles blest off my table. Keep still!"

Jerry Cruncher worried his breakfast rather than ate it. Towards nine o'clock he smoothed his ruffled aspect, and, presenting as respectable and business-like an exterior as he could overlay his natural self with, issued forth to the occupation of the day.

His stock consisted of a wooden stool. Young Jerry carried this, walking at his father's side, every morning to beneath the banking-house window that was nearest Temple Bar. There, with the addition of the first handful of straw that could be gleaned from any passing vehicle to keep the cold and wet from the odd-job man's feet, it formed the encampment for the day. On this post of his, Mr Cruncher was as well known to Fleet Street and the Temple, as the Bar itself.

Encamped at a quarter before nine, in good time to touch his three-cornered hat to the oldest of men as they passed in to Tellson's, Jerry took up his station on this windy March morning. Young Jerry stood by him. Father and son, extremely like each other, looking silently on at the morning traffic in Fleet Street, with their two heads as near to one another as the two eyes of each were, bore a considerable resemblance to a pair of monkeys.

The head of one of the regular indoor messengers attached to Tellson's establishment was put through the door, and the word was given:

"Porter wanted!"

"Hooray, father! Here's an early job to begin with!"

Having thus given his parent God speed, young Jerry seated himself on the stool, and cogitated.

"Al-ways rusty! His fingers is al-ways rusty!" muttered young Jerry. "Where does my father get all that iron rust from? He don't get no iron rust here!"

CHAPTER 2

A Sight

"You know the Old Bailey, well, no doubt?" said one of the oldest of clerks to Jerry the messenger.

"Ye-es, sir," returned Jerry, in something of a dogged manner. "I *do* know the Bailey."

"Just so. And you know Mr Lorry."

"I know Mr Lorry, sir, much better than I know the Bailey. Much better," said Jerry, not unlike a reluctant witness at the establishment in question, "than I, as a honest tradesman, wish to know the Bailey."

"Very well. Find the door where the witnesses go in, and show the door-keeper this note for Mr Lorry. He will then let you in."

"Into the court, sir?"

"Into the court."

"Am I to wait in the court, sir?" he asked.

"I am going to tell you. The door-keeper will pass the note to Mr Lorry. You must make a gesture to attract Mr Lorry's attention, to show him where you stand. Then you remain there until he wants you."

"Is that all, sir?"

"That's all. He wishes to have a messenger at hand. This will tell him you are there."

As the ancient clerk deliberately folded and superscribed the note, Mr Cruncher, after surveying him in silence, remarked:

"I suppose they'll be trying Forgeries this morning?"

"Treason!"

"That's quartering," said Jerry. "Barbarous!"

"It is the law," remarked the ancient clerk, turning his surprised spectacles upon him. "It is the law."

"It's hard in the law to spile a man, I think. It's hard enough to kill him, but it's wery hard to spile him, sir."

"Not at all," retained the ancient clerk. "Speak well of the law. Take care of your chest and voice, my good friend, and leave the law to take care of itself. I give you that advice."

"It's the damp, sir, what settles on my chest and voice," said Jerry. "I leave you to judge what a damp way of earning a living mine is."

"Well, well," said the old clerk; "we all have our various ways of gaining a livelihood. Some of us have damp ways, and some of us have dry ways. Here is the letter. Go along."

Jerry took the letter, and went his way.

They hanged at Tyburn, in those days, so the street outside Newgate had not obtained one infamous notoriety that has since attached to it. But, the gaol was a vile place, in which most kinds of debauchery and villainy were practised, and where dire diseases were bred, that came into court with the prisoners, and sometimes rushed straight from the dock at my Lord Chief Justice himself, and pulled him off the bench. It had more than once happened, that the Judge in the black cap pronounced his own doom as certainly as the prisoner's, and even died before him.

Making his way through the tainted crowd, with the skill of a man accustomed to make his way quietly, the messenger found out the door he sought, and handed in his letter through a trap in it. For, people then paid to see the play at the Old Bailey, just as they paid to see the play in Bedlam – only the former entertainment was much the dearer. Therefore, all the Old Bailey doors were well guarded – except, indeed, the social doors by which the criminals got there, and those were always left wide open.

After some delay and demur, the door grudgingly turned on its hinges a very little way, and allowed Mr Jerry Cruncher to squeeze himself into court.

"What's on?" he asked, in a whisper, of the man he found himself next to.

"Nothing yet."

"What's coming on?"

"The Treason case."

"The quartering one, eh?"

36

"Ah!" returned the man, with relish. "He'll be drawn on a hurdle to be half hanged, and then he'll be taken down and sliced before his own face, and then his inside will be taken out and burnt while he looks on, and then his head will be chopped off, and he'll be cut into quarters. That's the sentence."

"If he's found Guilty, you mean to say?" Jerry added, by way of proviso.

"Oh! they'll find him guilty," said the other.

Mr Cruncher's attention was here diverted to the door-keeper, whom he saw making his way to Mr Lorry, with the note in his hand. Mr Lorry sat at a table, among the gentlemen in wigs, not far from a wigged gentleman, the prisoner's counsel. He had a great bundle of papers before him: and nearly opposite another wigged gentleman with his hands in his pockets, whose whole attention, when Mr Cruncher looked at him then or afterwards, seemed to be concentrated on the ceiling of the court. After some gruff coughing and rubbing of his chin and signing with his hand, Jerry attracted the notice of Mr Lorry, who had stood up to look for him, and who quietly nodded and sat down again.

"What's *he* got to do with the case?" asked the man he had spoken with.

"Blest if I know," said Jerry.

"What have *you* got to do with it, then, if a person may inquire?"

"Blest if I know that either," said Jerry.

The entrance of the Judge, and a consequent great stir and settling down in the court, stopped the dialogue. Presently, the dock became the central point of interest. Two gaolers, who had been standing there, went out, and the prisoner was brought in, and put to the bar.

Everybody present, except the one wigged gentleman who looked at the ceiling, stared at him. Eager faces strained round pillars and corners, to get a sight of him. Spectators in back rows stood up, not to miss a hair of him; people on the floor of the court, laid their hands on the shoulders of the people before them, to help themselves, at anybody's cost, to a view of him. Conspicuous among these, like an animated bit of the spiked wall of Newgate, Jerry stood.

The object of all this staring and blaring, was a young man of about five-and-twenty, well-grown and well-looking, with a sunburnt cheek and a dark eye. His condition was that of a young gentleman. He was plainly dressed in black, or very dark grey, and his hair, which was long and dark, was gathered in a ribbon at the back of his neck; more to be out of his way than for ornament. As an emotion of the mind will express itself through any covering of the body, so the paleness that his situation engendered came through the brown upon his cheek, showing the soul to be stronger than the sun. He was otherwise quite self-possessed, bowed to the Judge, and stood quiet.

The sort of interest with which this man was stared and breathed at, was not a sort that elevated humanity. Had he stood in peril of a less horrible sentence, by just so much would he have lost in his fascination. The form that was to be doomed to be so shamefully mangled, was the sight; the immortal creature that was to be so butchered and torn asunder, yielded the sensation.

Whatever gloss the various spectators put upon the interest, according to their several arts and powers of self-deceit, the interest was, at the root of it, Ogreish.

Silence in the court! Charles Darnay had yesterday pleaded Not Guilty to an indictment denouncing him (with infinite jingle and jangle) for that he was a false traitor to our serene, illustrious, excellent, and so forth, prince, our Lord the King. By reason of his having, on divers occasions, and by divers means and ways, assisted Lewis, the French King, in his wars against our said serene, illustrious, excellent, and so forth. By coming and going between the dominions of our said serene, illustrious, excellent, and so forth, and those of the said French Lewis. By wickedly, falsely, traitorously, and otherwise, revealing to the said French Lewis the forces our said serene, illustrious, excellent, and so forth, had ready to send to Canada and North America. This much, Jerry made out with huge satisfaction. He arrived circuitously at the understanding that the aforesaid, and over and over again aforesaid, Charles Darnay, stood there before him upon his trial; that the jury were swearing in; and that Mr Attorney-General was making ready to speak.

The accused, who was (and who knew he was) being mentally hanged, beheaded, and quartered, by everybody there, neither flinched from the situation, nor assumed any theatrical air in it. He was quiet and attentive; watched the opening proceedings with a grave interest; and stood with his hands resting on the slab of wood before him, so composedly, that they had not displaced a leaf of the herbs with which it was strewn. The court was all bestrewn with herbs and sprinkled with vinegar, as a precaution against gaol air and gaol fever.

Over the prisoner's head there was a mirror, to throw the light down upon him. Crowds of the wicked and the wretched had been reflected in it, and had passed from its surface and this earth's together. A change in his position making him conscious of a bar of light across his face, he looked up; and when he saw the glass his face flushed, and his right hand pushed the herbs away.

It happened, that the action turned his face to that side of the court on his left. About on a level with his eyes, there sat, in that corner of the Judge's bench, two persons upon whom his look immediately rested; so immediately, and so much to the changing of his aspect, that all the eyes that were tamed upon him, turned to them.

The spectators saw in the two figures, a young lady of little more than twenty, and a gentleman who was evidently her father. The man was of a very remarkable appearance in respect of the absolute whiteness of his hair, and a certain indescribable intensity of face. When this expression was upon him, he looked as if he were old; but when it was stirred and broken up – as it was now, in a moment, on his speaking to his daughter – he became a handsome man, not past the prime of life.

His daughter had one of her hands drawn through his arm, as she sat by him, and the other pressed upon it. She had drawn close to him, in her dread of the scene, and in her pity for the prisoner. Her forehead had been strikingly expressive of an engrossing terror and compassion that saw nothing but the peril of the accused. This had been so very noticeable, so very powerfully and naturally shown, that starers who had had no pity for him were touched by her; and the whisper went about, "Who are they?"

Jerry, the messenger, stretched his neck to hear who they were. The crowd about him had pressed and passed the inquiry on to the nearest attendant, and from him it had been more slowly pressed and passed back; at last it got to Jerry:

"Witnesses against the prisoner's side."

The Judge, whose eyes had gone in the general direction, recalled them, leaned back in his seat, and looked steadily at the man whose life was in his hand, as Mr Attorney-General rose to spin the rope, grind the axe, and hammer the nails into the scaffold.

CHAPTER 3

A Disappointment

Mr Attorney-General had to inform the jury, that the prisoner before them, though young in years, was old in the treasonable practices which claimed the forfeit of his life. This correspondence with the public enemy was not a correspondence of today, or of yesterday, or even of last year, or of the year before. It was certain the prisoner had, for longer than that, been in the habit of passing and repassing between France and England, on secret business of which he could give no honest account. If it were in the nature of traitorous ways to thrive (which happily it never was), the real wickedness and guilt of his business might have remained undiscovered. That Providence, however, had put it into the heart of a person who was beyond fear and beyond reproach, to ferret out the nature of the prisoner's schemes, and, struck with horror, to disclose them to his Majesty's Chief Secretary of State and most honourable Privy Council. This patriot would be produced before them. His position and attitude were, on the whole, sublime. He had been the prisoner's friend, but, at once in an auspicious and an evil hour detecting his infamy, had resolved to immolate the traitor he could no longer cherish in his bosom, on the sacred altar of his country. If statues were decreed in Britain, as in ancient Greece and Rome, to public benefactors, this shining citizen would assuredly have had one. As they were not so decreed, he probably would not have one. Virtue, as had been observed by the poets (in many passages which he well knew the jury would have, word for word, on the tips of their tongues; whereat the jury's faces showed a guilty consciousness that they knew nothing about the passages), was in a manner contagious; more especially the bright virtue known as patriotism, or love of country. The lofty example of this immaculate and unimpeachable witness for the Crown, to refer to whom however unworthily was an honour, had communicated itself to the prisoner's servant, and had engendered in him a holy determination to examine his master's table-drawers and pockets, and secrete his papers. He (Mr Attorney-General) was prepared to hear some disparagement attempted of this admirable servant; but that, in a general way, he preferred him to his (Mr Attorney-General's) brothers and sisters, and honoured him more

40

than his (Mr Attorney-General's) father and mother. He called with confidence on the jury to come and do likewise. The evidence of these two witnesses, coupled with the documents of their discovering that would be produced, would show the prisoner to have been furnished with lists of his Majesty's forces, and of their disposition and preparation, both by sea and land. It would leave no doubt that he had habitually conveyed such information to a hostile power. These lists could not be proved to be in the prisoner's handwriting; but it was all the better for the prosecution, as showing the prisoner to be artful in his precautions. The proof would go back five years, and would show the prisoner already engaged in these pernicious missions, within a few weeks before the date of the very first action fought between the British troops and the Americans. For these reasons, the jury, being a loyal jury (as he knew they were), and being a responsible jury (as *they* knew they were), must positively find the prisoner Guilty, and make an end of him, whether they liked it or not. Mr Attorney-General concluded by demanding of them the head of the prisoner, in the name of everything he could think of with a round turn in it, and on the faith of his solemn asseveration that he already considered the prisoner as good as dead and gone.

When the Attorney-General ceased, a buzz arose in the court as if a cloud of great blue-flies were swarming about the prisoner, in anticipation of what he was soon to become. When toned down again, the unimpeachable patriot appeared in the witness box.

Mr Solicitor-General then, following his leader's lead, examined the patriot: John Barsad, gentleman, by name. The story of his pure soul was exactly what Mr Attorney-General had described it to be – perhaps, if it had a fault, a little too exactly. Having released his noble bosom of its burden, he would have modestly withdrawn himself, but the wigged gentleman with the papers before him, sitting not far from Mr Lorry, begged to ask him a few questions. The wigged gentleman sitting opposite, still looked at the ceiling of the court.

Had he ever been a spy himself? No, he scorned the base insinuation. What did he live upon? His property. Where was his property? He didn't precisely remember where it was. What was it? Nobody's business. Had he inherited it? Yes, he had. From whom? A distant relation. Very distant? Rather. Ever been in prison? Certainly not. Never in a debtors' prison? Didn't see what that had to do with it. Never in a debtors' prison? – Come, once again. Never? Yes. How many times? Two or three times. Not five or six? Perhaps. Of what profession? Gentleman. Ever been kicked downstairs? Decidedly not; once received a kick on the top of a staircase, and fell downstairs of his own accord. Kicked on that occasion for cheating at dice? Something to that effect was said by the intoxicated liar who committed the assault, but it was not true. Swear it was not true? Positively. Ever live by cheating at play? Never. Ever live by play? Not more than other gentlemen do. Ever borrow money off the prisoner? Yes. Ever pay him? No. Was not this intimacy with the prisoner, in reality a very slight one, forced upon the prisoner in coaches, inns, and packets? No. Sure he saw the prisoner with these lists? Certain. Knew no more about the lists? No. Had not procured them himself, for instance? No. Expect to get anything by this evidence? No. Not in regular government pay and employment, to lay traps? Oh dear no. Or to do anything? Oh dear no. Swear that? Over and over again. No motives but motives of sheer patriotism? None whatever.

The virtuous servant, Roger Cly, swore his way through the case at a great rate. He had taken service with the prisoner, in good faith and simplicity, four years ago. He had asked the prisoner, aboard the Calais packet, if he wanted a handy fellow, and the prisoner had engaged him. He began to have suspicions of the prisoner, and to keep an eye upon him, soon afterwards. In arranging his clothes, while travelling, he had seen similar lists to these in the prisoner's pockets, over and over again. He had taken these lists from the drawer of the prisoner's desk. He had not put them there first. He had seen the prisoner show these identical lists to French gentlemen at Calais, and similar lists to French gentlemen, both at Calais and Boulogne. He loved his country, and couldn't bear it, and had given information. He had never been suspected of stealing a silver tea-pot; he had been maligned respecting a mustard-pot, but it turned out to be only a plated one. He had known the last witness seven or eight years; that was merely a coincidence. He didn't call it a particularly curious coincidence. Neither did he call it a curious coincidence that true patriotism was *his* only motive too. He was a true Briton, and hoped there were many like him.

The blue-flies buzzed again, and Mr Attorney-General called Mr Jarvis Lorry.

"Mr Jarvis Lorry, are you a clerk in Tellson's bank?"

"I am."

"On a certain Friday night in November 1775, did business occasion you to travel between London and Dover by the mail?"

"It did."

"Were there any other passengers in the mail?"

"Two."

"Did they alight on the road in the course of the night?"

"They did."

"Mr Lorry, look upon the prisoner. Was he one of those two passengers?"

"I cannot undertake to say that he was."

"Does he resemble either of these two passengers?"

"Both were so wrapped up, and the night was so dark, and we were all so reserved, that I cannot undertake to say even that."

"You will not swear, Mr Lorry, that he was not one of them?"

"No."

"So at least you say he may have been one of them?"

"Yes. Except that I remember them both to have been – like myself – wary of highwaymen, and the prisoner has not a shy air."

"Did you ever see a counterfeit of timidity, Mr Lorry?"

"I certainly have seen that."

"Mr Lorry, look once more upon the prisoner. Have you seen him, to your certain knowledge, before?"

"I have."

"When?"

"I was returning from France a few days afterwards, and, at Calais, the prisoner came on board the packet-ship in which I returned, and made the voyage with me."

"At what hour did he come on board?"

"At a little after midnight."

"Was he the only passenger who came on board at that untimely hour?"

"He happened to be the only one."

"Never mind about 'happening,' Mr Lorry. He was the only passenger who came on board in the dead of the night?"

"He was."

"Were you travelling alone, Mr Lorry, or with any companion?"

"With two companions. A gentleman and lady. They are here."

"Had you any conversation with the prisoner?"

"Hardly any. The weather was stormy, and the passage long and rough, and I lay on a sofa, almost from shore to shore."

"Miss Manette!"

The young lady, to whom all eyes had been turned before, and were now turned again, stood up where she had sat. Her father rose with her, and kept her hand drawn through his arm.

"Miss Manette, look upon the prisoner."

To be confronted with such pity, and such earnest youth and beauty, was far more trying to the accused than to be confronted with the crowd. Standing, as it were, with her on the edge of his grave – not all the staring curiosity that looked on, could, for the moment, nerve him to remain quite still. His right hand parcelled out the herbs before him into imaginary beds of flowers; and his efforts to steady his breathing shook the lips from which the colour rushed to his heart. The buzz of the great flies was loud again.

"Miss Manette, have you seen the prisoner before?"

"Yes, sir."

"Where?"

"On board of the packet-ship just now referred to, sir, and on the same occasion."

"You are the young lady just now referred to?"

"O! Most unhappily, I am!"

The plaintive tone of her compassion merged into the less musical voice of the Judge, as he said something fiercely: "Answer the questions put to you, and make no remark upon them."

"Miss Manette, had you any conversation with the prisoner on that passage across the Channel?"

"Yes, sir."

"Recall it."

In the midst of a profound stillness, she faintly began: "When the gentleman came on board – "

"Do you mean the prisoner?" inquired the Judge, knitting his brows.

"Yes, my Lord."

"Then say the prisoner."

"When the prisoner came on board, he noticed that my father," turning her eyes lovingly to him as he stood beside her, "was in a very weak state

44

of health. My father was so reduced that I was afraid to take him out of the air, and I had made a bed for him on the deck near the cabin steps, and I sat on the deck at his side to take care of him. There were no other passengers. The prisoner was so good as to beg permission to advise me how I could shelter my father from the weather, better than I had done. He did it for me. He expressed great gentleness and kindness for my father's state, and I am sure he felt it. That was the manner of our beginning to speak together."

"Let me interrupt you for a moment. Had he come on board alone?"

"No."

"How many were with him?"

"Two French gentlemen."

"Had any papers been handed about among them, similar to these lists?"

"Some papers had been handed about among them, but I don't know what papers."

"Like these in shape and size?"

"Possibly, but indeed I don't know. They spoke very low, and I did not hear what they said, and saw only that they looked at papers."

"Now, to the prisoner's conversation, Miss Manette."

"The prisoner was as open in his confidence with me – which arose out of my helpless situation – as he was kind, and good, and useful to my father. I hope," bursting into tears, "I may not repay him by doing him harm today."

Buzzing from the blue-flies.

"Miss Manette, if the prisoner does not perfectly understand that you give the evidence which it is your duty to give – which you must give – and which you cannot escape from giving – with great unwillingness, he is the only person present in that condition. Please to go on."

"He told me that he was travelling on business of a delicate and difficult nature, which might get people into trouble, and that he was therefore travelling under an assumed name. He said that this business had, within a few days, taken him to France, and might, at intervals, take him backwards and forwards between France and England for a long time to come."

"Did he say anything about America, Miss Manette? Be particular."

"He tried to explain to me how that quarrel had arisen, and he said that, so far as he could judge, it was a wrong and foolish one on England's part. He added, in a jesting way, that perhaps George Washington might gain almost as great a name in history as George the Third. But there was no harm in his way of saying this: it was said laughingly."

The Judge looked up from his notes to glare at that tremendous heresy about George Washington.

Mr Attorney-General now signified to my Lord, that he deemed it necessary, as a matter of precaution and form, to call the young lady's father, Doctor Manette. Who was called accordingly.

"Doctor Manette, look upon the prisoner. Have you ever seen him before?"

"Once. When he called at my lodgings in London. Some three or three years and a half ago."

"Can you identify him as your fellow-passenger on board the packet, or speak to his conversation with your daughter?"

"Sir, I can do neither."

"Is there any particular and special reason for your being unable to do either?"

He answered, in a low voice, "There is."

"Has it been your misfortune to undergo a long imprisonment, without trial, or even accusation, in your native country, Doctor Manette?"

He answered, in a tone that went to every heart, "A long imprisonment."

"Were you newly released on the occasion in question?"

"They tell me so."

"Have you no remembrance of the occasion?"

"None. My mind is a blank, from some time – I cannot even say what time – when I employed myself, in my captivity, in making shoes, to the time when I found myself living in London with my dear daughter here. She had become familiar to me, when a gracious God restored my faculties; but I am quite unable even to say how she had become familiar. I have no remembrance of the process."

Mr Attorney-General sat down, and the father and daughter sat down together.

A witness was called to identify Charles Darnay as having been at the precise time required, in the coffee-room of an hotel in a garrison-and-dockyard town just off the mail route, those five years before, waiting for another person. The prisoner's counsel was cross-examining this witness with no result, except that he had never seen the prisoner on any other occasion. The wigged gentleman who was still looking at the ceiling of the court, suddenly wrote a word or two on a little piece of paper, screwed it up, and tossed it to him. Opening this piece of paper in the next pause, the counsel looked with great attention and curiosity at the prisoner.

"You say again you are quite sure that it was the prisoner?"

The witness was quite sure.

"Did you ever see anybody very like the prisoner?"

Not so like (the witness said) as that he could be mistaken.

"Look well upon that gentleman, my learned friend there," pointing to him who had tossed the paper over, "and then look well upon the prisoner. Are they very like each other?"

Allowing for my learned friend's appearance being careless and slovenly if not debauched, they were sufficiently like each other to surprise, not only the witness, but everybody present, when they were thus brought into comparison. My Lord being prayed to bid my learned friend lay aside his wig, and giving no very gracious consent, the likeness became much more remarkable. My Lord inquired of Mr Stryver (the prisoner's counsel), whether they were next to try Mr Carton (name of my learned friend) for treason?

But, Mr Stryver replied to my Lord, no. But he would ask the witness to tell him whether what happened once, might happen twice. The upshot of which, was, to smash this witness like a crockery vessel, and shiver his part of the case to useless lumber.

Mr Cruncher had by this time taken quite a lunch of rust off his fingers in his following of the evidence. He had now to attend while Mr Stryver fitted the prisoner's case on the jury, like a compact suit of clothes. By showing them how the patriot, Barsad, was a hired spy and traitor, an unblushing trafficker in blood, and one of the greatest scoundrels upon earth since accursed Judas – which he certainly did look rather like. How the virtuous servant, Cly, was his friend and partner. How the watchful eyes of those forgers and false swearers had rested on the prisoner as a victim, because some family affairs in France, he being of French extraction, did require his making those passages across the Channel. Though what those affairs were, a consideration for others who were near and dear to him, forbade him, even for his life, to disclose. How the

47

evidence that had been warped and wrested from the young lady, whose anguish in giving it they had witnessed, came to nothing. It was merely the little innocent gallantries and politenesses likely to pass between any young gentleman and young lady so thrown together – with the exception of that reference to George Washington, which was altogether too extravagant and impossible to be regarded in any other light than as a monstrous joke. But, there my Lord interposed (with as grave a face as if it had not been true), saying that he could not sit upon that Bench and suffer those allusions.

Mr Stryver then called his few witnesses, and Mr Cruncher had next to attend while Mr Attorney-General turned the whole suit of clothes Mr Stryver had fitted on the jury, inside out. How Barsad and Cly were even a hundred times better than he had thought them, and the prisoner a hundred times worse. Lastly, came my Lord himself, turning the suit of clothes, now inside out, now outside in, but on the whole decidedly trimming and shaping them into grave-clothes for the prisoner.

And now, the jury turned to consider, and the great flies swarmed again.

Mr Carton, who had so long sat looking at the ceiling of the court, changed neither his place nor his attitude, even in this excitement. While his learned friend, Mr Stryver, massing his papers before him, whispered with those who sat near, and from time to time glanced anxiously at the jury. While even my Lord himself arose from his seat, and slowly paced up and down his platform, this one man sat leaning back, with his torn gown half off him, his untidy wig put on anyhow, his hands in his pockets, and his eyes on the ceiling as they had been all day. Something in his demeanour not only gave him a disreputable look, but so diminished the strong resemblance he undoubtedly bore to the prisoner, that many of the lookers-on said to one another they would hardly have thought the two were so alike.

Yet, this Mr Carton took in more of the details of the scene than he appeared to take in; for now, when Miss Manette's head dropped upon her father's breast, he was the first to see it, and to say audibly: "Officer! Look to that young lady. Help the gentleman to take her out. Don't you see she will fall!"

There was much commiseration for her as she was removed, and much sympathy with her father. It had evidently been a great distress to him, to have the days of his imprisonment recalled. As he passed out, the jury, who had turned back and paused a moment, spoke, through their foreman.

They were not agreed, and wished to retire. My Lord (perhaps with George Washington on his mind) showed some surprise that they were not agreed, but signified his pleasure that they should retire under watch and ward, and retired himself. The trial had lasted all day, and the lamps in the court were now being lighted. It began to be rumoured that the jury would be out a long while. The spectators dropped off to get refreshment, and the prisoner withdrew to the back of the dock, and sat down.

Mr Lorry, who had gone out when the young lady and her father went out, now reappeared, and beckoned to Jerry.

"Jerry, if you wish to eat, you can. But, keep in the way. You will be sure to hear when the jury come in. Don't be a moment behind them, for I want you to take the verdict back to the bank. You are the quickest messenger I know, and will get to Temple Bar long before I can."

Mr Carton came up at the moment, and touched Mr Lorry on the arm. "How is the young lady?"

"She is greatly distressed; but her father is comforting her, and she feels the better for being out of court."

"I'll tell the prisoner so. It won't do for a respectable bank gentleman like you, to be seen speaking to him publicly."

Mr Lorry reddened as if he were conscious of having debated the point in his mind, and Mr Carton made his way to the outside of the bar. The way out of court lay in that direction, and Jerry followed him, all eyes, ears, and spikes.

"Mr Darnay!"

The prisoner came forward directly.

"You will naturally be anxious to hear that Miss Manette will do very well. You have seen the worst of her agitation."

"I am deeply sorry to have been the cause of it. Could you tell her so for me?"

"Yes, I could. I will, if you ask it."

Mr Carton's manner was so careless as to be almost insolent. He stood, half turned from the prisoner, lounging with his elbow against the bar.

"I do ask it. Accept my cordial thanks."

"What," said Carton, still only half turned towards him, "do you expect, Mr Darnay?"

49

"The worst."

"It's the wisest thing to expect, and the likeliest. But I think their withdrawing is in your favour."

Loitering on the way out of court not being allowed, Jerry heard no more: but left them – so like each other in feature, so unlike each other in manner – standing side by side, both reflected in the glass above them.

An hour and a half limped heavily away in the thief-and-rascal crowded passages below, even though assisted off with mutton pies and ale. The hoarse messenger, uncomfortably seated on a form after taking that refection, had dropped into a doze, when a loud murmur and a rapid tide of people setting up the stairs that led to the court, carried him along with them.

"Jerry! Jerry!" Mr Lorry was already calling at the door when he got there.

"Here, sir! It's a fight to get back again. Here I am, sir!"

Mr Lorry handed him a paper through the throng. "Quick! Have you got it?"

"Yes, sir."

Hastily written on the paper was the word "*Acquitted*."

"If you had sent the message, 'Recalled to Life,' again," muttered Jerry, as he turned, "I should have known what you meant, this time."

He had no opportunity of saying, or so much as thinking, anything else, until he was clear of the Old Bailey. The crowd came pouring out with a vehemence that nearly took him off his legs, and a loud buzz swept into the street as if the baffled blue-flies were dispersing in search of other carrion.

CHAPTER 4

Congratulatory

From the dimly lighted passages of the court, the last sediment of the human stew that had been boiling there all day, was straining off, when Doctor Manette, Lucie Manette, his daughter, Mr Lorry, the solicitor for the defence, and its counsel, Mr Stryver, stood gathered round Mr Charles

Darnay. They were congratulating him on his escape from death.

It would have been difficult by a far brighter light, to recognise in Doctor Manette, the shoemaker of the garret in Paris. Yet, no one could have looked at him twice, without looking again. There was always a gloom over him, as incomprehensible to those unacquainted with his story as if they had seen the shadow of the actual Bastille thrown upon him by a summer sun, when the substance was three hundred miles away.

Only his daughter had the power of charming this black brooding from his mind. She was the golden thread that united him to a Past beyond his misery, and to a Present beyond his misery: and the sound of her voice, the light of her face, the touch of her hand, had a strong beneficial influence with him almost always. Not absolutely always, for she could recall some occasions on which her power had failed; but they were few and slight, and she believed them over.

Mr Darnay had kissed her hand fervently and gratefully, and had turned to Mr Stryver, whom he warmly thanked. Mr Stryver, a man of little more than thirty, but looking twenty years older than he was. Stout, loud, red, bluff, and free from any drawback of delicacy, he had a pushing way of shouldering himself (morally and physically) into companies and conversations.

He still had his wig and gown on, and he said, squaring himself at his late client to that degree that he squeezed the innocent Mr Lorry clean out of the group: "I am glad to have brought you off with honour, Mr Darnay. It was an infamous prosecution, grossly infamous; but not the less likely to succeed on that account."

"You have laid me under an obligation to you for life – in two senses," said his late client, taking his hand.

"I have done my best for you, Mr Darnay; and my best is as good as another man's, I believe."

It clearly being incumbent on some one to say, "Much better," Mr Lorry said it; perhaps not quite disinterestedly, but with the interested object of squeezing himself back again.

"You think so?" said Mr Stryver. "Well! You have been present all day, and you ought to know. You are a man of business, too."

"And as such," quoth Mr Lorry, whom the counsel learned in the law had now shouldered back into the group, just as he had previously shouldered him out of it – "as such I will appeal to Doctor Manette, to break up this conference and order us all to our homes. Miss Lucie looks ill, Mr Darnay has had a terrible day, we are worn out."

Dr Manette's face had become frozen, as it were, in a very curious look at Darnay: an intent look, deepening into a frown of dislike and distrust, not even unmixed with fear. With this strange expression on him his thoughts had wandered away.

"My father," said Lucie, softly laying her hand on his.

He slowly shook the shadow off, and turned to her.

"Shall we go home, my father?"

With a long breath, he answered "Yes."

The friends of the acquitted prisoner had dispersed, under the impression – which he himself had originated – that he would not be released that night. The lights were nearly all extinguished in the passages, the iron gates were being closed with a jar and a rattle, and the dismal place was deserted until tomorrow morning. Walking between her father and Mr Darnay, Lucie Manette passed into the open air. A hackney-coach was called, and the father and daughter departed in it.

Mr Stryver had left them in the passages, to shoulder his way back to the robing-room. Another person, who had not joined the group, or interchanged a word with any one of them, but who had been leaning against the wall where its shadow was darkest, had silently strolled out after the rest, and had looked on until the coach drove away. He now stepped up to where Mr Lorry and Mr Darnay stood upon the pavement.

"So, Mr Lorry! Men of business may speak to Mr Darnay now?"

Nobody had made any acknowledgment of Mr Carton's part in the day's proceedings; nobody had known of it. He was unrobed, and was none the better for it in appearance.

"If you knew what a conflict goes on in the business mind, when the business mind is divided between good-natured impulse and business appearances, you would be amused, Mr Darnay."

Mr Lorry reddened, and said, warmly, "You have mentioned that before, sir. We men of business, who serve a House, are not our own masters. We have to think of the House more than ourselves."

"I know, I know," rejoined Mr Carton, carelessly. "Don't be nettled, Mr Lorry. You are as good as another, I have no doubt: better, I dare say."

"And indeed, sir," pursued Mr Lorry, not minding him, "I really don't know what you have to do with the matter. If you'll excuse me, as very much your elder, for saying so, I really don't know that it is your business."

"Business! Bless you, *I* have no business," said Mr Carton.

"It is a pity you have not, sir."

"I think so, too."

"If you had," pursued Mr Lorry, "perhaps you would attend to it."

"Lord love you, no! I shouldn't," said Mr Carton.

"Well, sir!" cried Mr Lorry, thoroughly heated by his indifference, "business is a very good thing, and a very respectable thing. Mr Darnay, good night, God bless you, sir! I hope you have been this day preserved for a prosperous and happy life. Chair there!"

Perhaps a little angry with himself, as well as with the barrister, Mr Lorry bustled into the chair, and was carried off to Tellson's.

Carton, who smelt of port wine, and did not appear to be quite sober, laughed then, and turned to Darnay:

"This is a strange chance that throws you and me together. This must be a strange night to you, standing alone here with your counterpart on these street stones?"

"I hardly seem yet," returned Charles Darnay, "to belong to this world again."

"I don't wonder at it; it's not so long since you were pretty far advanced on your way to another. You speak faintly."

"I begin to think I *am* faint."

"Then why the devil don't you dine? I dined, myself, while those numskulls were deliberating which world you should belong to. Let me show you the nearest tavern to dine well at."

Drawing his arm through his own, he took him down Ludgate Hill to Fleet Street, and so, up a covered way, into a tavern. Here, they were shown into a little room, where Charles Darnay was soon recruiting his strength with a good plain dinner and good wine. Carton sat opposite to him at the same table, with his separate bottle of port before him, and his fully half-insolent manner upon him.

"Do you feel, yet, that you belong to this terrestrial scheme again, Mr Darnay?"

"I am frightfully confused regarding time and place; but I am so far mended as to feel that."

"It must be an immense satisfaction!"

He said it bitterly, and filled up his glass again: which was a large one.

"As to me, the greatest desire I have, is to forget that I belong to it. It has no good in it for me – except wine like this – nor I for it. So we are not much alike in that particular. Indeed, I begin to think we are not much alike in any particular, you and I."

Confused by the emotion of the day, Charles Darnay was at a loss how to answer; finally, answered not at all.

"Now your dinner is done," Carton presently said, "why don't you call a health, Mr Darnay; why don't you give your toast?"

"What health? What toast?"

"Why, it's on the tip of your tongue. It ought to be, it must be, I'll swear it's there."

"Miss Manette, then!"

"Miss Manette, then!"

Looking his companion full in the face while he drank the toast, Carton flung his glass over his shoulder against the wall, where it shivered to pieces; then, rang the bell, and ordered in another.

"That's a fair young lady to hand to a coach in the dark, Mr Darnay!" he said, filling his new goblet.

A slight frown and a laconic, "Yes," were the answer.

"That's a fair young lady to be pitied by and wept for by! How does it feel? Is it worth being tried for one's life, to be the object of such sympathy and compassion, Mr Darnay?"

Again Darnay answered not a word.

"She was mightily pleased to have your message, when I gave it her. Not that she showed she was pleased, but I suppose she was."

The allusion served as a timely reminder to Darnay that this disagreeable companion had, of his own free will, assisted him in the strait of the day. He turned the dialogue to that point, and thanked him for it.

"I neither want any thanks, nor merit any," was the careless rejoinder. "It was nothing to do, in the first place; and I don't know why I did it, in the second. Mr Darnay, let me ask you a question."

"Willingly, and a small return for your good offices."

"Do you think I particularly like you?"

"Really, Mr Carton," returned the other, oddly disconcerted, "I have not asked myself the question."

"But ask yourself the question now."

"You have acted as if you do; but I don't think you do."

"I don't think I do," said Carton. "I begin to have a very good opinion of your understanding."

"Nevertheless," pursued Darnay, rising to ring the bell, "there is nothing in that, I hope, to prevent my calling the reckoning, and our parting without ill-blood on either side."

Carton rejoining, "Nothing in life!" Darnay rang. "Do you call the whole reckoning?" said Carton. On his answering in the affirmative, "Then bring me another pint of this same wine, drawer, and come and wake me at ten."

The bill being paid, Charles Darnay rose and wished him good night. Without returning the wish, Carton rose too, with something of a threat of defiance in his manner, and said, "A last word, Mr Darnay: you think I am drunk?"

"I think you have been drinking, Mr Carton."

"Think? You know I have been drinking."

"Since I must say so, I know it."

"Then you shall likewise know why. I am a disappointed drudge, sir. I care for no man on earth, and no man on earth cares for me."

"Much to be regretted. You might have used your talents better."

"May be so, Mr Darnay; may be not. Don't let your sober face elate you, however; you don't know what it may come to. Good night!"

When he was left alone, this strange being took up a candle, went to a glass that hung against the wall, and surveyed himself minutely in it.

"Do you particularly like the man?" he muttered, at his own image; "why should you particularly like a man who resembles you? There is nothing in you to like; you know that. Ah, confound you! What a change you have made in yourself! A good reason for taking to a man, that he shows you what you have fallen away from, and what you might have been! Change places with him, and would you have been looked at by those blue eyes as he was, and commiserated by that agitated face as he was? Come on, and have it out in plain words! You hate the fellow."

He resorted to his pint of wine for consolation, drank it all in a few minutes, and fell asleep on his arms, with his hair straggling over the table, and a long winding-sheet in the candle dripping down upon him.

CHAPTER 5

Hundreds of People

The quiet lodgings of Doctor Manette were in a quiet street-corner not far from Soho Square. One fine Sunday when the waves of four months had rolled over the trial for treason, and carried it far out to sea, Mr Jarvis Lorry walked along the sunny streets from Clerkenwell where he lived, on his way to dine with the Doctor. Mr Lorry had become the Doctor's friend, and the quiet street-corner was the sunny part of his life.

A quainter corner than the corner where the Doctor lived, was not to be found in London. There was no way through it, and the front windows of the Doctor's lodgings commanded a pleasant little vista of street that had a congenial air of retirement on it. There were few buildings then, north of the Oxford Road, and forest-trees flourished, and wild flowers grew, and the hawthorn blossomed, in the now vanished fields. As a consequence, country airs circulated in Soho; and there was many a good south wall, not far off, on which the peaches ripened in their season.

The summer light struck into the corner brilliantly earlier in the day; but, when the streets grew hot, the corner was in shadow. It was a cool spot, staid but cheerful, a wonderful place for echoes, and a very harbour from the raging streets.

There ought to have been a tranquil bark in such an anchorage, and there was. The Doctor occupied two floors of a large stiff house, where several callings purported to be pursued by day, but whereof little was audible any day, and which was shunned by all of them at night. Occasionally, a stray workman putting his coat on, traversed the hall, or a stranger peered about there, or a distant clink was heard across the courtyard.

Doctor Manette received such patients here as his old reputation, and its revival in the floating whispers of his story, brought him. His scientific knowledge, and his vigilance and skill in conducting ingenious experiments, brought him otherwise into moderate request, and he earned as much as he wanted.

These things were within Mr Jarvis Lorry's knowledge, thoughts, and notice, when he rang the door bell of the tranquil house in the corner, on the fine Sunday afternoon.

"Doctor Manette at home?"

Expected home.

"Miss Lucie at home?"

Expected home.

"Miss Pross at home?"

Possibly at home, but of a certainty impossible for handmaid to anticipate intentions of Miss Pross, as to admission or denial of the fact.

"As I am at home myself," said Mr Lorry. "I'll go upstairs."

Although the Doctor's daughter had known nothing of the country of her birth, she appeared to have innately derived from it that ability to make much of little means. Simple as the furniture was, it was set off by so many little adornments of no value but for their taste and fancy, that its effect was delightful.

There were three rooms on a floor, and, the doors by which they communicated were open that the air might pass freely through them all. The first was the best room, and in it were Lucie's birds, and flowers, and books, and desk, and work-table, and box of water-colours. The second was the Doctor's consulting-room, used also as the dining-room; and the third, was the Doctor's bedroom. There, in a corner, stood the disused shoemaker's bench and tray of tools, much as it had stood on the fifth floor of the dismal house by the wine shop, in the suburb of Saint Antoine in Paris.

"I wonder," said Mr Lorry, pausing in his looking about, "that he keeps that reminder of his sufferings about him!"

"And why wonder at that?" was the abrupt inquiry that made him start.

It proceeded from Miss Pross, the wild red woman, strong of hand, whose acquaintance he had first made at the Royal George Hotel at Dover, and had since improved.

"I should have thought – " Mr Lorry began.

"Pooh! You'd have thought!" said Miss Pross; and Mr Lorry left off.

"I am very much put out about my Ladybird."

"May I ask the cause?"

"I don't want dozens of people who are not at all worthy of Ladybird, to come here looking after her," said Miss Pross. "It really is trebly hard to have crowds and multitudes of people turning up after Dr Manette (I can forgive him), to take Ladybird's affections away from me."

Mr Lorry knew Miss Pross to be very jealous, but he also knew her to

57

be, under the show of eccentricity, one of those unselfish creatures – found only among women – who will, for pure love and admiration, bind themselves to youth when they have lost it. She was bound to beauty that she never had, to accomplishments that she was never fortunate enough to gain, to bright hopes that never shone upon her own sombre life. He stationed Miss Pross much nearer to the lower Angels than many ladies immeasurably better got up both by Nature and Art, who had balances at Tellson's.

"There never was, nor will be, but one man worthy of Ladybird," said Miss Pross; "and that was my brother Solomon, if he hadn't made a mistake in life."

Here again Mr Lorry's inquiries into Miss Pross's personal history had established the fact that her brother Solomon was a heartless scoundrel who had stripped her of everything she possessed, as a stake to speculate with, and had abandoned her in her poverty for evermore, with no touch of compunction. Miss Pross's fidelity of belief in Solomon (deducting a mere trifle for this slight mistake) was quite a serious matter with Mr Lorry, and had its weight in his good opinion of her.

"As we happen to be alone for the moment," he said, when they had got back to the drawing room. "Let me ask you – does the Doctor, in talking with Lucie, refer to the shoemaking time, yet?"

"Never."

"And yet keeps that bench and those tools beside him?"

"Ah!" returned Miss Pross, shaking her head. "But I don't say he don't refer to it within himself."

"Do you believe that he thinks of it much?"

"I do," said Miss Pross.

"Do you imagine – " Mr Lorry had begun, when Miss Pross took him up short with:

"Never imagine anything. Have no imagination at all."

"I stand corrected; do you suppose – you go so far as to suppose, sometimes?"

"Now and then," said Miss Pross.

"Do you suppose," Mr Lorry went on, with a laughing twinkle in his bright eye, as it looked kindly at her, "that Doctor Manette has any theory of his own? Preserved through all those years, relative to the cause of his being so oppressed; perhaps, even to the name of his oppressor?"

"I don't suppose anything about it but what Ladybird tells me."

"And that is –?"

"That she thinks he has."

"Now don't be angry at my asking all these questions. Is it not remarkable that Doctor Manette, unquestionably innocent of any crime as we are all well assured he is, should never touch upon that question? I will not say with me, though he had business relations with me many years ago, and we are now intimate; I will say with the fair daughter to whom he is so devotedly attached, and who is so devotedly attached to him? Believe me, Miss Pross, I don't approach the topic with you, out of curiosity, but out of zealous interest."

"Well! To the best of my understanding, and bad's the best, you'll tell me," said Miss Pross, softened by the tone of the apology, "he is afraid of the whole subject."

"Afraid?"

"It's plain enough, I should think, why he may be. It's a dreadful remembrance. Not knowing how he lost himself, or how he recovered himself, he may never feel certain of not losing himself again. That alone wouldn't make the subject pleasant, I should think."

It was a profounder remark than Mr Lorry had looked for. "True," said he, "and fearful to reflect upon. Yet, a doubt lurks in my mind, Miss Pross, whether it is good for Doctor Manette to have that suppression always shut up within him. Indeed, it is this doubt and the uneasiness it sometimes causes me that has led me to our present confidence."

"Can't be helped," said Miss Pross, shaking her head. "Touch that string, and he instantly changes for the worse. Better leave it alone. Sometimes, he gets up in the dead of the night, and will be heard, by us overhead there, walking up and down, in his room. Ladybird has learnt to know then that his mind is walking up and down in his old prison. She hurries to him, and they go on together, walking up and down, until he is composed. But he never says a word of the true reason of his restlessness, to her, and she finds it best not to hint at it to him. In silence they go walking up and down together, till her love and company have brought him to himself."

The corner has been mentioned as a wonderful corner for echoes; it had begun to echo so resoundingly to the tread of coming feet, that it seemed as though the very mention of that weary pacing to and fro had set it going.

"Here they are!" said Miss Pross, rising to break up the conference; "and now we shall have hundreds of people pretty soon!"

It was such a curious corner in its acoustical properties, such a peculiar Ear of a place, that as Mr Lorry stood at the open window, looking for the father and daughter whose steps he heard, he fancied they would never approach. Not only would the echoes die away, as though the steps had gone; but, echoes of other steps that never came would be heard in their stead, and would die away for good when they seemed close at hand. However, father and daughter did at last appear, and Miss Pross was ready at the street door to receive them.

Miss Pross was a pleasant sight, albeit wild, and red, and grim, taking off her darling's bonnet when she came up-stairs, and touching it up with the ends of her handkerchief. Her darling was a pleasant sight too, embracing her and thanking her, and protesting against her taking so much trouble for her – which last she only dared to do playfully, or Miss Pross, sorely hurt, would have retired to her own chamber and cried. The Doctor was a pleasant sight too, looking on at them, and telling Miss Pross how she spoilt Lucie, in accents and with eyes that had as much spoiling in them as Miss Pross had, and would have had more if it were possible. Mr Lorry was a pleasant sight too, beaming at all this in his little wig, and thanking his bachelor stars for having lighted him in his declining years to a Home. But, no Hundreds of people came to see the sights, and Mr Lorry looked in vain for the fulfilment of Miss Pross's prediction.

Dinner-time, and still no Hundreds of people. Miss Pross took charge of the lower regions, and always acquitted herself marvellously. Her dinners, of a very modest quality, were so well cooked and so well served, and so neat in their contrivances, half English and half French, that nothing could be better.

On Sundays, Miss Pross dined at the Doctor's table, but on other days persisted in taking her meals at unknown periods, either in the lower regions, or in her own room on the second floor. On this occasion, Miss Pross, responding to Ladybird's pleasant face and pleasant efforts to please her, unbent exceedingly; so the dinner was very pleasant, too.

It was an oppressive day, and, after dinner, Lucie proposed that the wine should be carried out under the plane-tree, and they should sit there in the air. As everything turned upon her, and revolved about her, they went out under the plane-tree, and she carried the wine down for the special benefit of Mr Lorry. She had installed herself, some time before, as Mr Lorry's cup-bearer; and while they sat under the plane-tree, talking, she kept his glass replenished. The plane-tree whispered to them in its own way above their heads.

Still, the Hundreds of people did not present themselves. Mr Darnay presented himself while they were sitting under the plane-tree, but he was only One.

Doctor Manette received him kindly, and so did Lucie. But, Miss Pross suddenly became afflicted with a twitching in the head and body, and retired into the house. She was not unfrequently the victim of this disorder, and she called it, in familiar conversation, "a fit of the jerks."

The Doctor was in his best condition, and looked specially young. The resemblance between him and Lucie was very strong at such times, and as they sat side by side, she leaning on his shoulder, and he resting his arm on the back of her chair, it was very agreeable to trace the likeness.

He had been talking all day, on many subjects, and with unusual vivacity. "Pray, Doctor Manette," said Mr Darnay, as they sat under the plane-tree – and he said it in the natural pursuit of the topic in hand, which happened to be the old buildings of London – "have you seen much of the Tower?"

"Lucie and I have been there; but only casually. We have seen enough of it, to know that it teems with interest; little more."

"I have been there, as you remember," said Darnay, with a smile, though reddening a little angrily, "in another character, and not in a character that gives facilities for seeing much of it. They told me a curious thing when I was there."

"What was that?" Lucie asked.

"In making some alterations, the workmen came upon an old dungeon, which had been, for many years, built up and forgotten. Every stone of its inner wall was covered by inscriptions which had been carved by prisoners – dates, names, complaints, and prayers. Upon a corner stone in an angle of the wall, one prisoner, who seemed to have gone to execution, had cut as his last work, three letters. They were done with some very poor instrument, and hurriedly, with an unsteady hand. At first, they were read as D. I. C.; but, on being more carefully examined, the last letter was found to be G. There was no record or legend of any prisoner with those

61

initials. At length, it was suggested that the letters were not initials, but the complete word, Dig. The floor was examined very carefully under the inscription, and, in the earth beneath a stone, or some fragment of paving, were found the ashes of a paper, mingled with the ashes of a small leathern case or bag. What the unknown prisoner had written will never be read, but he had written something, and hidden it away to keep it from the gaoler."

"My father," exclaimed Lucie, "you are ill!"

He had suddenly started up, with his hand to his head. His manner and his look quite terrified them all.

"No, my dear, not ill. There are large drops of rain falling, and they made me start. We had better go in."

He recovered himself almost instantly. Rain was really falling in large drops, and he showed the back of his hand with rain-drops on it. But, he said not a single word in reference to the discovery that had been told of. As they went into the house, the business eye of Mr Lorry detected, or fancied it detected, on his face, as it turned towards Charles Darnay, the same singular look that had been upon it when it turned towards him in the passages of the Court House.

He recovered himself so quickly, however, that Mr Lorry had doubts of his business eye.

Tea-time, and Miss Pross making tea, with another fit of the jerks upon her, and still no Hundreds of people. Mr Carton had lounged in, but he made only Two.

The night was so very sultry, that although they sat with doors and windows open, they were overpowered by heat. When the tea table was done with, they all moved to one of the windows, and looked out into the heavy twilight. Lucie sat by her father; Darnay sat beside her; Carton leaned against a window. The curtains were long and white, and some of the thunder-gusts that whirled into the corner, caught them up to the ceiling, and waved them like spectral wings.

"The rain-drops are still falling, large, heavy, and few," said Doctor Manette. "It comes slowly."

"It comes surely," said Carton.

They spoke low, as people watching and waiting mostly do; as people in a dark room, watching and waiting for Lightning, always do.

There was a great hurry in the streets of people speeding away to get shelter before the storm broke; the wonderful corner for echoes resounded with the echoes of footsteps coming and going, yet not a footstep was there.

"A multitude of people, and yet a solitude!" said Darnay, when they had listened for a while.

"Is it not impressive, Mr Darnay?" asked Lucie. "Sometimes, I have sat here of an evening, until I have fancied – but even the shade of a foolish fancy makes me shudder tonight, when all is so black and solemn – "

"Let us shudder too. We may know what it is."

"It will seem nothing to you. I have sometimes sat alone here of an evening, listening, until I have made the echoes out to be the echoes of all the footsteps that are coming by-and-by into our lives."

"There is a great crowd coming one day into our lives, if that be so," Sydney Carton struck in, in his moody way.

The footsteps were incessant, and the hurry of them became more and more rapid. The corner echoed with the tread of feet; some, as it seemed, under the windows; some, as it seemed, in the room; some coming, some going; all in the distant streets, and not one within sight.

"Are all these footsteps destined to come to all of us, Miss Manette, or are we to divide them among us?"

"I don't know, Mr Darnay; I told you it was a foolish fancy, but you asked for it. When I have yielded myself to it, I have been alone, and then I have imagined them the footsteps of the people who are to come into my life, and my father's."

"I take them into mine!" said Carton. "I ask no questions and make no stipulations. There is a great crowd bearing down upon us, Miss Manette, and I see them – by the Lightning." He added the last words, after there had been a vivid flash that had shown him lounging in the window.

"And I hear them!" he added again, after a peal of thunder. "Here they come, fast, fierce, and furious!"

It was the rush and roar of rain that he typified, and it stopped him, for no voice could be heard in it. A memorable storm of thunder and lightning broke with that sweep of water, and there was not a moment's interval in crash, and fire, and rain, until after the moon rose at midnight.

The great bell of Saint Paul's was striking one in the cleared air, when Mr Lorry, escorted by Jerry, bearing a lantern, set forth on his return-passage to Clerkenwell. There were solitary patches of road on the way between Soho and Clerkenwell, and Mr Lorry, mindful of foot-pads, always retained Jerry for this service.

"What a night! Almost a night, Jerry, to bring the dead out of their graves."

"I never see the night myself, master – nor yet I don't expect to – what would do that," answered Jerry.

"Good night, Mr Carton," said the man of business. "Good night, Mr Darnay. Shall we ever see such a night again, together!"

Perhaps. Perhaps, see the great crowd of people with its rush and roar, bearing down upon them, too.

CHAPTER 6

Monseigneur in Town

Monseigneur, one of the great lords in power at the Court, held his fortnightly reception in his grand hotel in Paris. Monseigneur was in his inner room, his sanctuary of sanctuaries, the Holiest of Holiests. Monseigneur was about to take his chocolate. Monseigneur could swallow a great many things with ease, and was by some few sullen minds supposed to be rather rapidly swallowing France; but, his morning's chocolate could not so much as get into the throat of Monseigneur, without the aid of four strong men besides the Cook.

Yes. It took four men, all four ablaze with gorgeous decoration, and the Chief of them unable to exist with fewer than two gold watches in his pocket. One lackey carried the chocolate-pot into the sacred presence; a second, milled and frothed the chocolate with the little instrument he bore for that function; a third, presented the favoured napkin; a fourth (he of the two gold watches), poured the chocolate out. It was impossible for Monseigneur to dispense with one of these attendants on the chocolate and hold his high place under the admiring Heavens. Deep would have been the blot upon his escutcheon if his chocolate had been ignobly waited on by only three men; he must have died of two.

Monseigneur had one truly noble idea of general public business, which was, to let everything go on in its own way; of particular public business, Monseigneur had the other truly noble idea that it must all go his way – tend to his own power and pocket. Of his pleasures, general and particular, Monseigneur had the other truly noble idea, that the world was made for them. The text of his order (altered from the original by only a pronoun, which is not much) ran: "The earth and the fulness thereof are mine, saith Monseigneur."

Yet, Monseigneur had slowly found that vulgar embarrassments crept into his affairs, both private and public; and he had allied himself perforce with a Farmer-General. As to finances public, because Monseigneur could not make anything at all of them, and must consequently let them out to somebody who could; as to finances private, because Farmer-Generals were rich, and Monseigneur, after generations of great luxury and expense, was growing poor. Hence Monseigneur had taken his sister from a convent, while there was yet time to ward off the impending veil, and had bestowed her as a prize upon a very rich Farmer-General, poor in family. Which Farmer-General, carrying an appropriate cane with a golden apple on the top of it, was now among the company in the outer rooms, much prostrated before by mankind.

A sumptuous man was the Farmer-General. Thirty horses stood in his stables, twenty-four male domestics sat in his halls, six body-women waited on his wife. As one who pretended to do nothing but plunder and forage where he could, the Farmer-General was at least the greatest reality among the personages who attended at the hotel of Monseigneur that day.

For, the rooms, though a beautiful scene to look at, were, in truth, not a sound business. Military officers destitute of military knowledge, naval officers with no idea of a ship, ci.. officers without a notion of affairs, brazen ecclesiastics, of the worst world worldly, with sensual eyes, loose tongues, and looser lives; all totally unfit for their several callings. All lying horribly in pretending to belong to them, but all nearly or remotely of the order of Monseigneur, and therefore foisted on all public employments from which anything was to be got. People not immediately connected with Monseigneur or the State, yet equally unconnected with anything that was real, were no less abundant. Doctors who made great fortunes out of dainty remedies for imaginary disorders that never existed, smiled upon their courtly patients in the ante-chambers of Monseigneur. Unbelieving Philosophers who were remodelling the world with words, and making card-towers of Babel to scale the skies with, talked with Unbelieving Chemists who had an eye on the transmutation of metals, at this wonderful gathering accumulated by Monseigneur. Spies among the assembled devotees of Monseigneur – forming a goodly half of the polite company – would have found it hard to discover among the angels of that sphere one solitary wife, who, in her manners and appearance, owned to being a Mother. Indeed, except for the mere act of bringing a troublesome creature into this world – which does not go far towards the realisation of the name of mother – there was no such thing known to the fashion. Peasant women kept the unfashionable babies close, and brought them up, and charming grandmammas of sixty dressed and supped as at twenty.

In the outermost room were half a dozen exceptional people who had had, for a few years, some vague misgiving in them that things in general were going rather wrong.

But, the comfort was, that all the company at the grand hotel of Monseigneur were perfectly dressed. If the Day of Judgment had only been ascertained to be a dress day, everybody there would have been eternally correct. The exquisite gentlemen of the finest breeding wore little pendant trinkets that chinked as they languidly moved. These golden fetters rang like precious little bells; and what with that ringing, and with the rustle of silk and brocade and fine linen, there was a flutter in the air that fanned Saint Antoine and his devouring hunger far away.

Dress was the one unfailing talisman and charm used for keeping all things in their places. Everybody was dressed for a Fancy Ball that was never to leave off. From the Palace of the Tuileries, through Monseigneur and the whole Court, through the Chambers, the Tribunals of Justice, and all society (except the scarecrows), the Fancy Ball descended to the Common Executioner. He, in pursuance of the charm, was required to officiate "frizzled, powdered, in a gold-laced coat, pumps, and white silk stockings". And who among the company at Monseigneur's reception in that 1780th year of our Lord, could possibly doubt, that a system rooted in a frizzled hangman, powdered, gold-laced, pumped, and white-silk stockinged, would see the very stars out!

Monseigneur having eased his four men of their burdens and taken his chocolate, caused the doors of the Holiest of Holiests to be thrown open, and issued forth. Then, what submission, what cringing and fawning, what servility, what abject humiliation!

Bestowing a word of promise here and a smile there, a whisper on one happy slave and a wave of the hand on another, Monseigneur affably passed through his rooms to the remote region of the Circumference of Truth. There, Monseigneur turned, and came back again, and so in due course of time got himself shut up in his sanctuary by the chocolate sprites, and was seen no more.

The show being over, the flutter in the air became quite a little storm, and the precious little bells went ringing downstairs. There was soon but one person left of all the crowd, and he, with his hat under his arm and his snuff-box in his hand, slowly passed among the mirrors on his way out.

"I devote you," said this person, stopping at the last door on his way, and turning in the direction of the sanctuary, "to the Devil!"

With that, he shook the snuff from his fingers as if he had shaken the dust from his feet, and quietly walked downstairs.

He was a man of about sixty, handsomely dressed, haughty in manner, and with a face like a fine mask. A face of a transparent paleness; every feature in it clearly defined.

Its owner went downstairs into the courtyard, got into his carriage, and drove away. Not many people had talked with him at the reception; he had stood in a little space apart, and Monseigneur might have been warmer in his manner. It appeared, under the circumstances, rather agreeable to him to see the common people dispersed before his horses, and often barely escaping from being run down. His man drove as if he were charging an enemy, and the furious recklessness of the man brought no check from the master. The complaint had sometimes made itself audible, even in that deaf city and dumb age, that, in the narrow streets without footways, the fierce patrician custom of hard driving endangered and maimed the mere vulgar in a barbarous manner. But, few cared enough for that to think of it a second time, and, in this matter, as in all others, the common wretches were left to get out of their difficulties as they could.

With a wild rattle and clatter, and an inhuman abandonment of consideration not easy to be understood in these days, the carriage dashed through streets and swept round corners, with women screaming before it, and men clutching each other and children out of its way. At last, swooping at a street corner by a fountain, one of its wheels gave a sickening little jolt, and there was a loud cry from a number of voices, and the horses reared and plunged.

But for the latter inconvenience, the carriage probably would not have stopped. Carriages were often known to drive on, and leave their wounded behind, and why not? But the frightened valet had got down in a hurry, and there were twenty hands at the horses' bridles.

"What has gone wrong?" said Monsieur, calmly looking out.

A tall man in a nightcap had caught up a bundle from among the feet of the horses, and had laid it on the basement of the fountain, and was down in the mud and wet, howling over it like a wild animal.

"Pardon, Monsieur the Marquis!" said a ragged and submissive man. "It is a child."

"Why does he make that abominable noise? Is it his child?"

"Excuse me, Monsieur the Marquis – it is a pity – yes."

The fountain was a little removed; for the street opened into a space some ten or twelve yards square. As the tall man suddenly got up from the ground, and came running at the carriage, Monsieur the Marquis clapped his hand for an instant on his sword-hilt.

"Killed!" shrieked the man, in wild desperation, extending both arms at their length above his head, and staring at him. "Dead!"

The people closed round, and looked at Monsieur the Marquis. There was nothing revealed by the many eyes that looked at him but watchfulness and eagerness; there was no visible menacing or anger. Neither did the people say anything; after the first cry, they had been silent, and they remained so. The voice of the submissive man who had spoken, was flat and tame in its extreme submission. Monsieur the Marquis ran his eyes over them all, as if they had been mere rats come out of their holes.

He took out his purse.

"It is extraordinary to me," said he, "that you people cannot take care of yourselves and your children. One or the other of you is forever in the way. How do I know what injury you have done my horses. See! Give him that."

He threw out a gold coin for the valet to pick up, and all the heads craned forward that all the eyes might look down at it as it fell. The tall man called out again with a most unearthly cry, "Dead!"

He was stopped by the quick arrival of another man, for whom the rest made way. On seeing him, the miserable creature fell upon his shoulder, sobbing and crying, and pointing to the fountain, where some women were stooping over the motionless bundle, and moving gently about it. They were as silent, however, as the men.

"I know all, I know all," said the last comer. "Be a brave man, my Gaspard! It is better for the poor little plaything to die so, than to live. It has died in a moment without pain. Could it have lived an hour as happily?"

"You are a philosopher, you there," said the Marquis, smiling. "How do they call you?"

"They call me Defarge."

"Of what trade?"

"Monsieur the Marquis, vendor of wine."

"Pick up that, philosopher and vendor of wine," said the Marquis, throwing him another gold coin, "and spend it as you will. The horses there; are they right?"

Without deigning to look at the assemblage a second time, Monsieur the Marquis leaned back in his seat. He was on the point of being driven away with the air of a gentleman who had accidentally broken some common thing, and had paid for it, when a coin flew into his carriage, ringing on its floor.

"Hold!" said Monsieur the Marquis. "Hold the horses! Who threw that?"

He looked to the spot where Defarge the vendor of wine had stood, a moment before; but the wretched father was grovelling on his face on the pavement in that spot, and the figure that stood beside him was the figure of a dark stout woman, knitting.

"You dogs!" said the Marquis, smoothly: "I would ride over any of you very willingly, and exterminate you from the earth. If I knew which rascal threw at the carriage, and he were sufficiently near it, he should be crushed under the wheels."

Not a voice, or a hand, or even an eye was raised. Among the men, not one. But the woman who stood knitting looked up steadily, and looked the Marquis in the face. It was not for his dignity to notice it; his contemptuous eyes passed over her, and over all the other rats; and he leaned back in his seat again, and gave the word "Go on!"

He was driven on, and other carriages came whirling by in quick succession; the Minister, the State-Projector, the Farmer-General, the Doctor, the Lawyer, the Ecclesiastic, the Grand Opera, the Comedy, the whole Fancy Ball in a bright continuous flow, came whirling by. The father had long ago taken up his bundle and bidden himself away with it, when the women who had tended the bundle while it lay on the base of the fountain, sat there watching the running of the water and the rolling of the Fancy Ball. The one woman who had stood conspicuous, knitting, still knitted on with the steadfastness of Fate. The water of the fountain ran, the day ran into evening, and so much life in the city ran into death. Time and tide waited for no man, the rats were sleeping close together in their dark holes again, the Fancy Ball was lighted up at supper, all things ran their course.

CHAPTER 7

Monseigneur in the Country

A beautiful landscape, with the corn bright in it, but not abundant. Patches of poor rye where corn should have been, patches of poor peas and beans, patches of most coarse vegetable substitutes for wheat.

Monsieur the Marquis in his travelling carriage conducted by four post-horses and two postilions, fagged up a steep hill. There was a blush on the face of Monsieur the Marquis due to the setting sun.

The sunset struck so brilliantly into the travelling carriage when it gained the hill top, that its occupant was steeped in crimson. "It will die out," said Monsieur the Marquis, glancing at his hands, "directly."

The sun was so low that it dipped at the moment. What could be seen was broken country, a little village at the bottom of the hill, a broad sweep and rise beyond it, a church-tower, a windmill, a forest for the chase, and a crag with a fortress on it used as a prison. Round upon all these darkening objects as the night drew on, the Marquis looked, with the air of one who was coming near home.

The village had its one poor street, with its poor brewery, poor tannery, poor tavern, poor stable-yard for relays of post-horses, and poor fountain. It had its poor people too – many of them were sitting at their doors, shredding spare onions and the like for supper, while many were at the fountain, washing leaves, and grasses, and any such small yieldings of the

70

earth that could be eaten. What made them poor were the tax for the state, the tax for the church, the tax for the lord, tax local and tax general, to be paid here and there, according to solemn inscription.

Few children were to be seen, and no dogs. As to the men and women, their choice on earth was stated in the prospect – Life on the lowest terms that could sustain it, down in the little village under the mill; or captivity and Death in the dominant prison on the crag.

Heralded by a courier in advance, and by the cracking of his postilions' whips, Monsieur the Marquis drew up in his travelling carriage at the posting-house gate. It was hard by the fountain, and the peasants suspended their operations to look at him.

Monsieur the Marquis cast his eyes over the submissive faces that drooped before him, as he had drooped before Monseigneur of the Court – only these faces drooped merely to suffer and not to propitiate – when a grizzled mender of the roads joined the group.

"Bring that fellow here!" said the Marquis to the courier.

The fellow was brought, cap in hand, and the other fellows closed round to look and listen, in the manner of the people at the Paris fountain.

"I passed you on the road?"

"Monseigneur, it is true. I had the honour of being passed."

"What did you look at, so fixedly?"

"Monseigneur, I looked at the man."

He stooped a little, and with his tattered blue cap pointed under the carriage. All his fellows stooped to look under the carriage.

"What man, pig? And why look there?"

"Pardon, Monseigneur; he swung by a chain."

"Who?" demanded the traveller.

"Monseigneur, the man."

"May the Devil carry away these idiots! How do you call the man? You know all the men of this part of the country. Who was he?"

"Your clemency, Monseigneur! He was not of this part of the country. Of all the days of my life, I never saw him."

"Swinging by the chain? To be suffocated?"

"With your gracious permission, that was the wonder of it, Monseigneur. His head hanging over – like this!" He turned himself sideways to the carriage, and leaned back, with his face thrown up to the sky; then recovered himself.

71

"What was he like?"

"Monseigneur, he was whiter than the miller. All covered with dust, white as a spectre, tall as a spectre!"

The picture produced an immense sensation in the little crowd; but all eyes, without comparing notes with other eyes, looked at Monsieur the Marquis. Perhaps to observe whether he had any spectre on his conscience.

"Truly, you did well," said the Marquis, felicitously sensible that such vermin were not to ruffle him, "to see a thief accompanying my carriage, and not open that great mouth of yours. Bah! Put him aside, Monsieur Gabelle!"

Monsieur Gabelle was the Postmaster, and some other taxing functionary united. "Bah! Go aside!" he said.

"Lay hands on this – stranger – if he seeks to lodge in your village tonight, and be sure that his business is honest, Gabelle."

"Monseigneur, I am flattered to devote myself to your orders."

"Did he run away, fellow? Where is he –?"

The road worker was already under the carriage with some half-dozen particular friends, pointing out the chain with his blue cap. Some half-dozen others promptly hauled him out, and presented him breathless to Monsieur the Marquis.

"Did the man run away, Dolt, when we stopped for the drag?"

"Monseigneur, he precipitated himself over the hill-side, head first, as a person plunges into the river."

"See to it, Gabelle. Go on!"

The half-dozen who were peering at the chain were still among the wheels, like sheep; the wheels turned so suddenly that they were lucky to save their skins and bones; they had very little else to save, or they might not have been so fortunate.

The carriage started out of the village and up the rise beyond, its speed soon checked by the steepness of the hill. Gradually, it slowed to a foot-pace, swinging and lumbering upward among the many sweet scents of a summer night.

The carriage broke into a brisk trot, and Monseigneur was rapidly diminishing the league or two of distance that remained between him and his château.

The shadow of a large high-roofed house, and of many over-hanging trees, was soon upon Monsieur the Marquis, and the shadow was exchanged for the light of a flambeau, as his carriage stopped, and the great door of his château was opened to him.

"Monsieur Charles, whom I expect; is he arrived from England?"

"Monseigneur, not yet."

CHAPTER 8

The Gorgon's Head

It was a heavy mass of building, that château of Monsieur the Marquis, with a large stone courtyard before it, and two stone sweeps of staircase meeting in a stone terrace before the principal door. A stony business altogether, with heavy stone balustrades, and stone urns, and stone flowers, and stone faces of men, and stone heads of lions, in all directions. As if the Gorgon's head had surveyed it, when it was finished, two centuries ago.

Up the broad flight of shallow steps, Monsieur the Marquis, flambeau preceded, went from his carriage, disturbing an owl in the roof of the great pile of stable building away among the trees. All else was quiet.

The great door clanged behind him, and Monsieur the Marquis crossed a hall grim with certain old boar-spears, swords, and knives of the chase.

Avoiding the larger rooms, Monsieur the Marquis, with his flambeau-bearer going on before, went up the staircase to his own private apartment of three rooms: his bed chamber and two others. High vaulted rooms with cool uncarpeted floors, great dogs upon the hearths for the burning of wood in winter time, and all luxuries befitting the state of a marquis in a luxurious age and country.

A supper-table was laid for two, in the third of the rooms; a round room, in one of the château's four extinguisher-topped towers.

"My nephew," said the Marquis, glancing at the supper preparation; "they said he was not arrived."

Nor was he; but, he had been expected with Monseigneur.

"Ah! It is not probable he will arrive tonight; nevertheless, leave the table as it is. I shall be ready in a quarter of an hour."

In a quarter of an hour Monseigneur was ready, and sat down alone to his sumptuous and choice supper. His chair was opposite to the window, and he had taken his soup, and was raising his glass of Bordeaux to his lips, when he put it down.

"What is that?" he calmly asked, looking with attention at the shutters at the window.

"Monseigneur? That?"

"Outside the blinds. Open the blinds."

It was done.

"Well?"

"Monseigneur, it is nothing. The trees and the night are all that are here."

The servant who spoke, had thrown the blinds wide, had looked out into the vacant darkness, and stood with that blank behind him, looking round for instructions.

"Good," said the imperturbable master. "Close them again."

That was done too, and the Marquis went on with his supper. He was half way through it, when he again stopped with his glass in his hand, hearing the sound of wheels.

"Ask who is arrived."

It was the nephew of Monseigneur. He had been a short distance behind Monseigneur, early in the afternoon, but had not caught up with him. He had heard that Monseigneur was in front of him, at the posting-houses.

He was to be told (said Monseigneur) that supper awaited him, and that he was prayed to come to it. In a little while he came. He had been known in England as Charles Darnay.

Monseigneur received him in a courtly manner, but they did not shake hands.

"You left Paris yesterday, sir?" he said to Monseigneur, as he took his seat at table.

"Yesterday. And you?"

"I come direct from London."

"You have been a long time coming," said the Marquis, with a smile. "I mean, not a long time on the journey; a long time intending the journey."

"I have been detained by" – the nephew stopped a moment in his answer – "various things."

74

"Without doubt," said the polished uncle.

No other words passed between them while the servant was there. When coffee had been served and they were alone together, the nephew, looking at the uncle and meeting his eyes, opened a conversation.

"I have come back, sir, as you anticipate, pursuing the object that took me away. It carried me into great and unexpected peril; but it is a sacred object, and if it had carried me to death I hope it would have sustained me."

"Not to death," said the uncle; "it is not necessary to say, to death."

"I doubt, sir," returned the nephew, "whether, if it had carried me to the utmost brink of death, you would have cared to stop me there."

The uncle made a graceful gesture of protest, which was so clearly a slight form of good breeding that it was not reassuring.

"Indeed, sir," pursued the nephew, "for all I know, you may have expressly worked to give a more suspicious appearance to the suspicious circumstances that surrounded me."

"No, no, no," said the uncle, pleasantly.

"But, however that may be," resumed the nephew, glancing at him with deep distrust, "I know that your diplomacy would stop me by any means, and would know no scruple as to means. In effect, sir, I believe it to be both your bad fortune, and my good fortune, that has kept me out of a prison in France here."

"I do not quite understand," returned the uncle, sipping his coffee. "Dare I ask you to explain?"

"I believe that if you were not in disgrace with the Court, and for some years now, a *lettre de cachet* would have sent me to some fortress indefinitely."

"It is possible," said the uncle, with great calmness. "For the honour of the family, I could even resolve to incommode you to that extent. Pray excuse me!"

"I realise that, happily for me, the Reception of the day before yesterday was, as usual, a cold one," observed the nephew.

"I would not say happily, my friend," returned the uncle, with refined politeness; "These little instruments of correction, these gentle aids to the power and honour of families, these slight favours that might so incommode you, are only to be obtained now by interest and importunity. They are sought by so many, and they are granted (comparatively) to so few! It used not to be so, but France in all such things is changed for the worse. Our not remote ancestors held the right of life and death over the surrounding vulgar. From this room, many such dogs have been taken out to be hanged. We have lost many privileges; all very bad, very bad!"

The Marquis took a gentle little pinch of snuff, and shook his head.

"We have so asserted our station, both in the old time and in the modern time also," said the nephew, gloomily, "that I believe our name to be more detested than any name in France."

"Let us hope so," said the uncle. "Detestation of the high is the involuntary homage of the low."

"There is not," pursued the nephew, in his former tone, "a face I can look at, in all this country round about us, which looks at me with any deference on it but the dark deference of fear and slavery."

"A compliment," said the Marquis, "to the grandeur of the family, merited by the manner in which the family has sustained its grandeur. Hah!" And he took another gentle little pinch of snuff, and lightly crossed his legs.

But, when his nephew, leaning an elbow on the table, covered his eyes thoughtfully and dejectedly with his hand, the fine mask looked at him sideways with a strong concentration of keenness, closeness, and dislike.

"Repression is the only lasting philosophy. The dark deference of fear and slavery, my friend," observed the Marquis, "will keep the dogs obedient to the whip, as long as this roof," looking up to it, "shuts out the sky."

That might not be so long as the Marquis supposed. Had a picture of the château as it was to be a very few years hence been shown to him that night, he might have been at a loss to recognise it from the ghastly, fire-charred, plunder-wrecked ruins.

"Meanwhile," said the Marquis, "I will preserve the honour and repose of the family, if you will not. But you must be fatigued. Shall we terminate our conference for the night?"

"A moment more."

"An hour, if you please."

"Sir," said the nephew, "we have done wrong, and are reaping the fruits of wrong."

"*We* have done wrong?" repeated the Marquis, with an inquiring smile, and delicately pointing, first to his nephew, then to himself.

"In my father's time, we did a world of wrong, injuring every human creature who came between us and our pleasure, whatever it was. Why need I speak of my father's time, when it is equally yours? Can I separate my father's twin-brother, joint inheritor, and next successor, from himself?"

"Death has done that!" said the Marquis.

"And has left me," answered the nephew, "bound to a system that is frightful to me. I am responsible for it, but powerless in it. I try to carry out the last request of my dear mother's lips, and obey the last look of my dear mother's eyes, which implored me to have mercy and to redress. It tortures me to seek help and power in vain."

"Seeking them from me, my nephew," said the Marquis, touching him on the breast with his forefinger – they were now standing by the hearth – "you will for ever seek them in vain, be assured."

Every fine straight line in the clear whiteness of his face, was cruelly, craftily, and closely compressed, while he stood looking quietly at his nephew, with his snuff-box in his hand. He touched him on the breast, as though his finger were the fine point of a small sword, with which, in delicate finesse, he ran him through the body, and said, "My friend, I will die, perpetuating the system under which I have lived."

When he had said it, he took a culminating pinch of snuff, and put his box in his pocket.

"Better to be a rational creature," he added then, after ringing a small bell on the table, "and accept your natural destiny. But you are lost, Monsieur Charles, I see."

"This property and France are lost to me," said the nephew, sadly; "I renounce them."

"Are they both yours to renounce? France may be, but is the property? It is scarcely worth mentioning; but, is it yet?"

"I had no intention, in the words I used, to claim it yet. If it passed to me from you, tomorrow – "

"Which I have the vanity to hope is not probable."

"– or twenty years hence – "

"You do me too much honour," said the Marquis; "still, I prefer that supposition."

" – I would abandon it, and live otherwise and elsewhere. It is little to relinquish. What is it but a wilderness of misery and ruin!"

77

"Hah!" said the Marquis, glancing round the luxurious room.

"To the eye it is fair enough, here; but seen in daylight, it is a crumbling tower of waste, mismanagement, extortion, debt, mortgage, oppression, hunger, nakedness, and suffering."

"Hah!" said the Marquis again, in a well-satisfied manner.

"If it ever becomes mine, it shall be put into some hands better qualified to free it slowly (if such a thing is possible). The miserable people who cannot leave it and who have been long wrung to the last point of endurance, may, in another generation, suffer less; but it is not for me. There is a curse on it, and on all this land."

"And you?" said the uncle. "Forgive my curiosity; how do you, under your new philosophy, graciously intend to live?"

"I must do, to live, what others of my countrymen, even with nobility at their backs, may have to do some day – work."

"In England, for example?"

"Yes. The family honour, sir, is safe from me in this country. The family name can suffer from me in no other, for I bear it in no other."

The ringing of the bell had caused the adjoining bedchamber to be lighted. The Marquis looked that way, and listened for the retreating step of his valet.

"England is very attractive to you, seeing how indifferently you have prospered there," he observed then, turning his calm face to his nephew with a smile.

"I have already said, that for my prospering there, I am sensible I may be indebted to you, sir. For the rest, it is my Refuge."

"They say, those boastful English, that it is the Refuge of many. You know a compatriot who has found a Refuge there? A Doctor?"

"Yes."

"With a daughter?"

"Yes."

"Yes," said the Marquis. "You are fatigued. Good night!"

As he bent his head in his most courtly manner, there was a secrecy in his smiling face, and he conveyed an air of mystery to those words, which struck the eyes and ears of his nephew forcibly.

"Yes," repeated the Marquis. "A Doctor with a daughter. Yes. So commences the new philosophy! You are fatigued. Good night!"

The nephew looked at him, in vain, in passing on to the door.

"Good night!" said the uncle. "I look to the pleasure of seeing you again in the morning. Good repose! Light Monsieur my nephew to his chamber there! – And burn Monsieur my nephew in his bed, if you will," he added to himself, before he rang his little bell again, and summoned his valet to his own bedroom.

The valet come and gone, Monsieur the Marquis walked to and fro in his loose chamber-robe, to prepare himself gently for sleep, that hot still night. Rustling about the room, his softly slippered feet making no noise on the floor, he moved like a caged tiger.

He went from one end of his voluptuous bedroom to the other, recalling the day's journey; the slow toil up the hill, the setting sun, the descent, the prison, the little village in the hollow, the peasants at the fountain, and the mender of roads with his blue cap pointing out the chain under the carriage. That fountain suggested the Paris fountain, with the little bundle lying on the step, the women bending over it, and the tall man with his arms up, crying, "Dead!"

"I am cool now," said Monsieur the Marquis, "and may go to bed."

So, leaving only one light burning on the large hearth, he let his thin gauze curtains fall around him, and heard the night break its silence with a long sigh as he composed himself to sleep.

The stone faces on the outer walls stared blindly at the black night. For three heavy hours, the stone faces of the château, lion and human, stared blindly at the night. Dead darkness lay on all the landscape. In the village, taxers and taxed were fast asleep. Dreaming, perhaps, of banquets, as the starved usually do, and of ease and rest, as the driven slave and the yoked ox may, its lean inhabitants slept soundly, and were fed and freed.

The fountain in the village flowed unseen and unheard, and the fountain at the château dropped unseen and unheard through three dark hours. Then, the grey water of both began to be ghostly as the eyes of the stone faces of the château were opened. Lighter and lighter, until at last the sun touched the tops of the still trees, and poured its radiance over the hill. In the glow, the water of the château fountain seemed to turn to blood, and the stone faces crimsoned. On the weather-beaten sill of the great window of the bedchamber of Monsieur the Marquis, one little bird sang its sweetest song with all its might.

Now, the sun was full up, and movement began in the village. Casement windows opened, crazy doors were unbarred, and people came

79

forth shivering – chilled, as yet, by the new sweet air. Then began the rarely lightened toil of the day among the village population. Some, to the fountain; some, to the fields; men and women there, to see to the poor live stock, and lead the bony cows out, to such pasture as could be found by the roadside.

The château awoke later, as became its quality, but awoke gradually and surely. Doors and windows were thrown open, horses in their stables looked round over their shoulders at the light and freshness pouring in at doorways, leaves sparkled and rustled at iron-grated windows, dogs pulled hard at their chains, and reared impatient to be loosed.

All these trivial incidents belonged to the routine of life, and the return of morning. Surely, not so the ringing of the great bell of the château, nor the running up and down the stairs; nor the hurried figures on the terrace; nor the booting and tramping here and there and everywhere, nor the quick saddling of horses and riding away?

The grizzled mender of roads, already at work on the hilltop beyond the village, became aware of the fuss. He ran, as if for his life, down the hill, knee-high in dust, and never stopped till he got to the fountain.

All the people of the village were at the fountain, standing about in their depressed manner, and whispering low, but showing no other emotions than grim curiosity and surprise. The led cows, hastily brought in and tethered to anything that would hold them, were looking stupidly on. Some of the people of the château, and some of those of the posting-house, and all the taxing authorities, were armed more or less, and were crowded on the other side of the little street. Already, the mender of roads had penetrated into the midst of a group of fifty particular friends, and was smiting himself in the breast with his blue cap. Why was Monsieur Gabelle behind a servant on horseback, being taken away at a gallop?

It became clear there was one stone face too many, up at the château.

The Gorgon had surveyed the building again in the night, and had added the one stone face wanting; the stone face for which it had waited through about two hundred years.

It lay back on the pillow of Monsieur the Marquis. It was like a fine mask, suddenly startled, made angry, and petrified. Driven home into the heart of the stone figure attached to it, was a knife. Round its hilt was a frill of paper, on which was scrawled:

"Drive him fast to his tomb. This, from Jacques."

CHAPTER 9

Two Promises

Twelve months had come and gone, and Mr Charles Darnay was established in England as a higher teacher of the French language who was conversant with French literature. In this age, he would have been a Professor; in that age, he was a Tutor. He was well acquainted with the circumstances of his country, and those were of ever-growing interest. So, with great perseverance and untiring industry, he prospered.

In London, he had expected neither to walk on pavements of gold, nor to lie on beds of roses. He had expected labour, and he found it, and did it and made the best of it. In this, his prosperity consisted.

A portion of his time was passed at Cambridge, where he read with undergraduates. The rest of his time he passed in London.

Now, from the days when it was always summer in Eden, to these days when it is mostly winter in fallen latitudes, the world of a man has invariably gone one way – Charles Darnay's way – the way of the love of a woman.

He had loved Lucie Manette from the hour of his danger. He had never heard a sound so sweet and dear as the sound of her compassionate voice; he had never seen a face so tenderly beautiful, as hers when it was confronted with his own on the edge of the grave that had been dug for him. But, he had said nothing of the assassination at the deserted château far away, the solid stone château that had itself become the mere mist of a dream. It had been a year since and he had never yet, by so much as a single spoken word, disclosed to her the state of his heart.

He had his reasons for this. It was again a summer day when, lately back in London, he turned into the quiet corner in Soho, bent on seeking an opportunity of opening his mind to Doctor Manette. It was the close of the summer day, and he knew Lucie to be out.

He found the Doctor reading in his armchair at a window. He was now a very energetic man indeed, with great firmness of purpose and vigour of action. He studied much, slept little, sustained a great deal of fatigue with ease, and was equably cheerful. To him, now entered Charles Darnay, at sight of whom he laid aside his book and held out his hand.

"Charles Darnay! I rejoice to see you. We have been counting on your return these three or four days past. Sydney Carton was here yesterday, and made you out to be more than due."

"I am obliged to him for his interest in the matter," he answered, a little coldly as to him, though very warmly as to the Doctor. "Miss Manette – "

"Is well," said the Doctor, "and your return will delight us all. She has gone out on some household matters, but will soon be home."

"Doctor Manette, I knew she was from home. I took the opportunity of her being from home, to beg to speak to you."

There was a blank silence.

"Yes?" said the Doctor, with evident constraint.

"I have had the happiness, Doctor Manette, of being so intimate here," so Charles Darnay at length began, "for some year and a half, that I hope the topic on which I am about to touch may not – "

The Doctor put out his hand to stop him. When he had kept it so a little while, he said, drawing it back: "Is Lucie the topic?"

"She is."

"It is hard for me to speak of her at any time. It is very hard for me to hear her spoken of in that tone of yours, Charles Darnay."

"It is a tone of fervent admiration, true homage, and deep love, Doctor Manette!" he said deferentially.

There was another blank silence before her father rejoined:

"I believe it. I do you justice; I believe it."

His constraint so clearly originated in an unwillingness to approach the subject, that Charles Darnay hesitated.

"Shall I go on, sir?"

Another blank.

"Yes, go on."

"You anticipate what I would say. Dear Doctor Manette, I love your daughter dearly, disinterestedly, devotedly. If ever there were love in the world, I love her. You have loved yourself; let your old love speak for me!"

The Doctor sat with his face turned away, and his eyes bent on the ground. At the last words, he stretched out his hand again, hurriedly, and cried:

"Not that, sir! I beg you, do not recall that!"

His cry was so like a cry of actual pain that it rang in Charles Darnay's ears long after he had ceased. He motioned with his hand and Darnay remained silent.

"I ask your pardon," said the Doctor, in a subdued tone, after some moments. "I do not doubt your loving Lucie."

He turned towards him in his chair. "Have you spoken to Lucie?"

"No."

"Nor written?"

"Never."

"I realise that your self-denial is out of consideration for her father. Her father thanks you."

He offered his hand.

"I know," said Darnay, respectfully, "that between you and Miss Manette there is an affection so unusual, so touching, so belonging to the circumstances in which it has been nurtured, that it can have few parallels. I know, Doctor Manette, that, mingled with the affection and duty of a daughter who has become a woman, there is, in her heart, towards you, all the love and reliance of infancy itself. I know that, as in her childhood she had no parent, so she is now devoted to you with all the constancy of her present years and character, united to the trustfulness and attachment of the early days in which you were lost to her. I know that in loving you she sees and loves her mother at her own age, sees and loves you at my age, loves her mother broken-hearted, loves you through your dreadful trial and in your blessed restoration. I have known this, night and day, since I have known you in your home."

Her father sat silent, with his face bent down. His breathing was a little quickened; but he repressed all other signs of agitation.

"Dear Doctor Manette, always knowing this, always seeing her and you with this hallowed light about you, I have forborne, as long as it was in the nature of man to do it. But I love her. Heaven is my witness that I love her!"

"I believe it," answered her father, mournfully. "I have thought so before now. I believe it."

"But, do not believe," said Darnay, upon whose ear the mournful voice struck with a reproachful sound, "that I could at any time put any separation between her and you. If I had any such possibility, harboured in my thoughts, and hidden in my heart – if it ever had been there – if it ever could be there – I could not now touch this honoured hand."

He laid his own upon it as he spoke.

"No, dear Doctor Manette. Like you, a voluntary exile from France and like you, driven from it by its distractions, oppressions, and miseries. Like you, striving to live away from it by my own exertions, and trusting in a happier future – I look only to sharing your fortunes, sharing your life and home, and being faithful to you to the death. I would not divide with Lucie her privilege as your child, companion, and friend; but to come in aid of it, and bind her closer to you, if such a thing can be."

His touch still lingered on her father's hand. Answering the touch for a moment, but not coldly, her father rested his hands upon the arms of his chair, and looked up for the first time since the beginning of the conference. A struggle was evidently in his face; a struggle with that occasional look which had a tendency in it to dark doubt and dread.

"You speak so feelingly and so manfully, Charles Darnay, that I thank you with all my heart, and will open all my heart – or nearly so. Have you any reason to believe that Lucie loves you?"

"None. As yet, none."

"Is it the immediate object of this confidence, that you may at once ascertain that, with my knowledge?"

"Not even so. I might not have the hopefulness to do it for weeks; I might have that hopefulness tomorrow."

"Do you seek any guidance from me?"

"I ask none, sir. But I have thought it possible that you might have it in your power, if you should deem it right, to give me some."

"Do you seek any promise from me?"

"I do seek that."

"What is it?"

"I well understand that, without you, I could have no hope. I well understand that, even if Miss Manette held me at this moment in her innocent heart – do not think I have the presumption to assume so much – I could retain no place in it against her love for her father."

"If that be so, do you see what, on the other hand, is involved in it?"

"I understand equally well, that a word from her father in any suitor's favour, would outweigh herself and all the world. For which reason, Doctor Manette," said Darnay, modestly but firmly, "I would not ask that word, to save my life."

"I am sure of it. Charles Darnay, mysteries arise out of close love, as well as out of wide division; in the former case, they are subtle and delicate, and difficult to penetrate. My daughter Lucie is, in this

84

one respect, such a mystery to me; I can make no guess at the state of her heart."

"May I ask, sir, if you think she is – " As he hesitated, her father supplied the rest.

"Is sought by any other suitor?"

"It is what I meant to say."

Her father considered a little before he answered:

"You have seen Mr Carton here, yourself. I had not thought of him. I should not think it likely. You want a promise from me. Tell me what it is."

"It is, that if Miss Manette should bring to you at any time, on her own part, such a confidence as I have ventured to lay before you, you will bear testimony to what I have said, and to your belief in it. I hope you may be able to think so well of me, as to urge no influence against me. I say nothing more of my stake in this; this is what I ask. The condition on which I ask it, and which you have an undoubted right to require, I will observe immediately."

"I give the promise," said the Doctor, "without any condition. I believe your object to be, purely and truthfully, as you have stated it. I believe your intention is to perpetuate, and not to weaken, the ties between me and my daughter. If she should ever tell me that you are essential to her perfect happiness, I will give her to you. If there were – Charles Darnay, if there were – "

The young man had taken his hand gratefully; their hands were joined as the Doctor spoke:

"– any reasons, any misunderstandings, new or old, against the man she really loved – for which he is not directly responsible – they should all be obliterated for her sake. She is everything to me; more to me than suffering. More to me – Well! This is idle talk."

So strange was the way in which he faded into silence, and so strange his fixed look when he had ceased to speak, that Darnay felt his own hand turn cold in the hand that slowly released and dropped it.

"You said something to me," said Doctor Manette, breaking into a smile. "What was it you said to me?"

Charles Darnay was at a loss until he remembered having spoken of a condition. Relieved as his mind reverted to that, he answered:

"Your confidence in me ought to be returned with full confidence on my part. My present name, though but slightly changed from my mother's, is not, as you will remember, my own. I wish to tell you what that is, and why I am in England."

"Stop!" said the Doctor of Beauvais.

"I wish it, that I may the better deserve your confidence, and have no secret from you."

"Stop!"

For an instant, the Doctor even had his two hands at his ears; for another instant, even had his two hands laid on Darnay's lips.

"Tell me when I ask you, not now. If your suit should prosper, if Lucie should love you, you shall tell me on your marriage morning. Do you promise?"

"Willingly.

"Give me your hand. She will be home directly, and it is better she should not see us together tonight. Go! God bless you!"

Lucie came home an hour later, hurrying into the room alone, and was surprised to find his reading-chair empty.

"My father!" she called to him. "Father dear!"

Nothing was said in answer, but she heard a low hammering sound in his bedroom. She looked in at his door and came running back frightened, crying to herself, with her blood all chilled, "What shall I do! What shall I do!"

Her uncertainty lasted but a moment; she hurried back, and tapped at his door, and softly called to him. The noise ceased at the sound of her voice, and he presently came out to her, and they walked up and down together for a long time.

She came down from her bed, to look at him in his sleep that night. He slept heavily, and his tray of shoemaking tools, and his old unfinished work, were all as usual.

CHAPTER 10

The Fellow of No Delicacy

If Sydney Carton ever shone anywhere, he certainly never shone in the house of Doctor Manette. He had been there often, during a whole year, and had always been the same moody and morose lounger there. When he cared to talk, he talked well; but, the cloud of caring for nothing, which overshadowed him, was very rarely pierced by the light within him.

And yet he did care something for the streets around the house, and for the senseless stones that made their pavements. Many a night he vaguely and unhappily wandered there. Many a dreary daybreak revealed his solitary figure lingering there.

On a day in August, Sydney's feet still trod those stones. From being irresolute and purposeless, his feet became animated by an intention, and, in the working out of that intention, they took him to the Doctor's door.

He was shown upstairs, and found Lucie at her work, alone. She had never been quite at her ease with him, and received him with some little embarrassment as he seated himself near her table. But, looking up at his face she observed a change in it.

"I fear you are not well, Mr Carton!"

"No. But the life I lead, Miss Manette, is not conducive to health."

"Is it not – forgive me; I have begun the question on my lips – a pity to live no better life?"

"God knows it is a shame!"

"Then why not change it?"

Looking gently at him again, she was surprised and saddened to see that there were tears in his eyes, and voice, as he answered, "It is too late for that. I shall never be better than I am. I shall sink lower, and be worse."

He leaned an elbow on her table, and covered his eyes with his hand. The table trembled in the silence that followed.

She had never seen him softened, and was much distressed. He knew her to be so, without looking at her, and said, "Pray forgive me, Miss Manette. I break down before the knowledge of what I want to say to you. Will you hear me?"

"If it will do you any good, Mr Carton, if it would make you happier, it would make me very glad!"

"God bless you for your sweet compassion!"

He unshaded his face after a little while, and spoke steadily. "Don't be afraid to hear me. Don't shrink from anything I say. I am like one who died young."

"No, Mr Carton. I am sure that the best part of it might still be; I am sure that you might be much, much worthier of yourself."

"Say of you, Miss Manette, and although I know better – although in the mystery of my own wretched heart I know better – I shall never forget it!"

She was pale and trembling. He came to her relief with a fixed despair of himself which made the conversation unlike any other.

"If it had been possible, Miss Manette, that you could have returned the love of the man you see before yourself – flung away, wasted, drunken, poor creature of misuse as you know him to be – he would realise that he would bring you to misery, bring you to sorrow and repentance, blight you, disgrace you, pull you down with him. I know very well that you can have no tenderness for me – I ask for none; I am even thankful that it cannot be."

"Without it, can I not save you, Mr Carton? Can I not recall you to a better course?" she modestly said, after a little hesitation, and in earnest tears, "I know you would say this to no one else. Can I turn it to no good account for yourself, Mr Carton?"

He shook his head.

"To none. If you will hear me through a very little more, all you can ever do for me is done. I wish you to know that you have been the last dream of my soul. This home has been made such a home by you, and has stirred old shadows that I thought had died out of me. Since I knew you, I have been troubled by a remorse that I thought would never reproach me again, and have heard whispers from old voices impelling me upward, that I thought were silent for ever. I have had unformed ideas of striving afresh, beginning anew, and fighting out the abandoned fight. A dream, all a dream, that ends in nothing, and leaves the sleeper where he lay down, but I wish you to know that you inspired it."

"Will nothing of it remain? O Mr Carton, think again! Try again!"

"No, Miss Manette; all through it, I have known myself to be quite undeserving."

"Since it is my misfortune, Mr Carton, to have made you more unhappy than you were before you knew me – "

"Don't say that, Miss Manette, for you would have reclaimed me, if anything could. You will not be the cause of my becoming worse."

"Since the state of your mind that you describe, is, at all events, attributable to some influence of mine – can I use no influence to serve you? Have I no power for good, with you, at all?"

"The utmost good that I am capable of now, Miss Manette, I have come here to realise. Let me carry through the rest of my misdirected life, the remembrance that I opened my heart to you, last of all the world; and that there was something left in me at this time which you could deplore and pity."

"Which I entreated you to believe, again and again, most fervently, with all my heart, was capable of better things, Mr Carton!"

"Entreat me to believe it no more, Miss Manette. I have proved myself, and I know better. I distress you; I draw fast to an end. Will you let me believe, when I recall this day, that the last confidence of my life was reposed in your pure and innocent breast, and that it lies there alone, and will be shared by no one?"

"If that will be a consolation to you, yes."

"Not even by the dearest one ever to be known to you?"

"Mr Carton," she answered, after an agitated pause, "the secret is yours, not mine; and I promise to respect it."

"Thank you. And again, God bless you."

He put her hand to his lips, and moved towards the door.

"Be under no apprehension, Miss Manette, of my ever resuming this conversation by so much as a passing word. I will never refer to it again. In the hour of my death, I shall hold sacred the one good remembrance – and shall thank and bless you for it – that my last avowal of myself was made to you, and that my name, and faults, and miseries were gently carried in your heart. May it otherwise be light and happy!"

He was so unlike what he had ever shown himself to be, and it was so sad to think how much he had thrown away, that Lucie Manette wept mournfully for him as he stood looking back at her.

"Be comforted!" he said, "I am not worth such feeling, Miss Manette. An hour or two hence, and the low companions and low habits that I scorn but yield to, will render me less worth such tears as those, than any wretch who creeps along the streets. Be comforted! But, within myself, I shall always be, towards you, what I am now, though outwardly I shall be what you have heretofore seen me. The last supplication but one I make to you, is, that you will believe this of me."

"I will, Mr Carton."

"My last supplication of all, is this; and with it, I will relieve you of my presence. It is useless to say it, I know, but it rises out of my soul. For you, and for any dear to you, I would do anything. Try to hold me in your mind, at some quiet times, as ardent and sincere in this one thing. The time will come, the time will not be long in coming, when new ties will be formed about you – ties that will bind you yet more tenderly and strongly to the home you so adorn – the dearest ties that will ever grace and gladden you. O Miss Manette, when you see your own bright beauty springing up anew at your feet, think now and then that there is a man who would give his life, to keep a life you love beside you!"

He said, "Farewell!" said a last "God bless you!" and left her.

CHAPTER 11

The Honest Tradesman

To the eyes of Mr Jeremiah Cruncher, sitting on his stool in Fleet Street with his grisly urchin beside him, a vast number and variety of objects in movement were every day presented.

Looking down Fleet Street westward, Mr Cruncher made out that some kind of funeral was coming along, and that there was popular objection to this funeral, which engendered uproar.

"Young Jerry, get a top of that there seat, and look at the crowd," said Mr Cruncher.

His son obeyed, and the crowd approached; they were bawling and hissing round a dingy hearse and dingy mourning coach, in which mourning coach there was only one mourner, dressed in the dingy trappings that were considered essential to the dignity of the position. The position appeared by no means to please him. An increasing rabble surrounded the coach, deriding him, making grimaces at him, and incessantly groaning and calling out: "Yah! Spies! Tst! Yaha! Spies!"

Funerals had at all times a remarkable attraction for Mr Cruncher; he always pricked up his senses, and became excited, when a funeral passed Tellson's. He asked of the first man who ran against him: "What is it, brother? What's it about?"

"I don't know," said the man. "Spies! Yaha! Tst! Spies!"

A person better informed on the merits of the case, tumbled against him, and from this person he learned that the funeral was that of one Roger Cly.

"Was He a spy?" asked Mr Cruncher.

"Old Bailey spy," returned his informant.

"Why, to be sure!" exclaimed Jerry, recalling the Trial at which he had assisted. "I've seen him. Dead, is he?"

"Dead as mutton," returned the other.

The crowd then mobbed the two vehicles so closely that they came to a stop. On the crowd's opening the coach doors, the one mourner scuffled out and was in their hands for a moment. But he was alert, and in another moment he was scouring away up a bye-street, after shedding his cloak, hat, long hatband, white pocket-handkerchief, and other symbolical tears.

These, the people tore to pieces and scattered far and wide with great enjoyment, while the tradesmen hurriedly shut up their shops; for a crowd in those times stopped at nothing, and was a monster much dreaded. The coach was then filled with eight inside and a dozen out, while as many people got on the roof of the hearse to accompany it to the burial site. Among the first of these volunteers was Jerry Cruncher himself, who modestly concealed his spiky head from the observation of Tellson's, in the further corner of the mourning coach.

The officiating undertakers made some protest against these changes in the ceremonies; but, the river being alarmingly near, the protest was faint and brief. The remodelled procession started, with a chimney sweep driving the hearse, advised by the regular driver.

Thus, with beer-drinking, pipe-smoking, song-roaring, the disorderly procession went its way. Its destination was the old church of Saint Pancras, far off in the fields. It got there in course of time; insisted on pouring into the burial-ground; finally, accomplished the interment of the deceased Roger Cly in its own way, and highly to its own satisfaction.

Mr Cruncher did not assist at the closing sports, but had remained behind in the churchyard, to confer and condole with the undertakers.

Having smoked his pipe out, and ruminated a little longer, he turned himself about, that he might appear, before the hour of closing, on his station at Tellson's. He made a short call upon his medical adviser – a distinguished surgeon – on his way back.

Young Jerry relieved his father with dutiful interest, and reported No job in his absence. The bank closed, the ancient clerks came out, the usual watch was set, and Mr Cruncher and his son went home to tea.

"Are you going out tonight?" asked his decent wife, as he sat at the table.

"Yes, I am."

"May I go with you, father?" asked his son, briskly.

"No, you mayn't. I'm a-going a-fishing. I ain't a-going out, till you've been long a-bed."

The evening wore away with the Cruncher family, until Young Jerry was ordered to bed, and his mother, laid under similar injunctions, obeyed them.

Mr Cruncher did not start upon his excursion until nearly one o'clock. Towards that small and ghostly hour, he rose up from his chair, took a key out of his pocket, opened a locked cupboard, and brought forth a sack, a crowbar of convenient size, a rope and chain, and other fishing tackle of that nature. Disposing these articles about him in skilful manner, he extinguished the light, and went out.

Young Jerry was not long after his father. Under cover of the darkness he followed.

Keeping close to house fronts, walls, and doorways, he held his honoured parent in view. The honoured parent steering Northward, had not gone far, when he was joined by another disciple of Izaak Walton, and the two trudged on together.

Within half an hour from the first starting, they were out upon a lonely road. Another fisherman was picked up here.

The three went on, and Young Jerry went on, until the three stopped under a bank overhanging the road. Upon the top of the bank was a low brick wall, surmounted by an iron railing. Crouching down in a corner, peeping up the lane, the next object that Young Jerry saw, was the form of his honoured parent, pretty well defined against a watery and clouded moon, nimbly scaling an iron gate. He was soon over, and then the second fisherman got over, and then the third. They all dropped softly on the ground within the gate, then moved away on their hands and knees.

It was now Young Jerry's turn to approach the gate: which he did, holding his breath. Crouching down again in a corner there, and looking in, he made out the three fishermen creeping through a large churchyard. They did not creep far, before they stopped and stood upright. And then they began to fish.

They fished with a spade, at first. Presently the honoured parent appeared to be adjusting some instrument like a great corkscrew. Whatever tools they worked with, they worked hard, until the awful striking of the church clock so terrified Young Jerry, that he made off.

But, his long-cherished desire to know more about these matters, not only stopped him in his running away, but lured him back again. They were still fishing but, now they seemed to have got a bite. There was a screwing and complaining sound down below, and their bent figures were strained, as if by a weight. By slow degrees the weight broke away the earth upon it, and came to the surface. Young Jerry very well knew what it would be; but, when he saw it, and saw his honoured parent about to wrench it open, he was so frightened, being new to the sight, that he made off again, and never stopped until he had run a mile or more.

He ran all the way home, climbing the stairs and scrambling into his bed. Young Jerry in his closet was awakened after daybreak and before sunrise, by the presence of his father in the family room. Something had gone wrong.

The honest tradesman kicked off his clay-soiled boots, and lay down at his length on the floor. After taking a timid peep at him lying on his back, with his rusty hands under his head for a pillow, his son lay down too, and fell asleep again.

There was no fish for breakfast, and not much of anything else. Mr Cruncher was out of spirits, and out of temper. He was brushed and washed at the usual hour, and set off with his son to pursue his ostensible calling.

Young Jerry, walking with the stool under his arm at his father's side along sunny and crowded Fleet Street, was a very different Young Jerry from him of the previous night, running home through darkness and solitude. His cunning was fresh with the day, and his qualms were gone with the night.

"Father," said Young Jerry, as they walked along: taking care to keep at arm's length and to have the stool well between them: "what's a Resurrection-Man?"

Mr Cruncher came to a stop on the pavement. "How should I know?"

"I thought you knowed everything, father," said the artless boy.

"Hem! Well," returned Mr Cruncher, going on again, and lifting off his hat to give his spikes free play, "he's a tradesman."

"What's his goods, father?" asked Young Jerry.

"His goods," said Mr Cruncher, after turning it over in his mind, "is a branch of Scientific goods."

"Persons' bodies, ain't it, father?" asked the lively boy.

"I believe it is something of that sort," said Mr Cruncher.

"Oh, father, I should so like to be a Resurrection-Man when I'm quite growed up!"

Mr Cruncher was soothed, but shook his head in a dubious and moral way. "It depends upon how you dewelop your talents. Never to say no more than you can help to nobody." Young Jerry, thus encouraged, went on a few yards in advance, to plant the stool in the shadow of the Bar. Mr Cruncher added to himself: "Jerry, you honest tradesman, there's hopes wot that boy will yet be a blessing to you!"

CHAPTER 12

Knitting

There had been earlier drinking than usual in the wine shop. As early as six o'clock in the morning, sallow faces peeping through its barred windows had descried other faces within, bending over measures of wine. Monsieur Defarge sold a very thin wine at the best of times, but it would seem to have been an unusually sour wine that he sold at this time, for its influence on the mood of those who drank it was to make them gloomy.

This was the third morning on which there had been early drinking at the wine shop of Monsieur Defarge. It began on Monday, and it was now Wednesday. There was more brooding than drinking. The customers glided from seat to seat, and from corner to corner, swallowing talk instead of drink.

In spite of the unusual flow of company, the master of the wine shop was not visible. Spies looked in at the wine shop, as they looked in at every place, high and low, from the king's palace to the criminal's gaol.

It was high noontide, when two dusty men passed through the streets and under the swinging lamps. One was Monsieur Defarge: the other a mender of roads in a blue cap. The two entered the wine shop. Their arrival had lighted a kind of fire in the breast of Saint Antoine, fast spreading as they came along. Faces appeared at most doors and windows. Yet, no one had followed them, and no man spoke when they entered the wine shop, though every man there looked at them.

"Good day, gentlemen!" said Monsieur Defarge.

There was an answering chorus of "Good day!"

"It is bad weather, gentlemen," said Defarge, shaking his head.

Upon which, every man looked at his neighbour, and then cast down their eyes and sat silent. Except one man, who got up and went out.

"My wife," said Defarge aloud, addressing Madame Defarge: "I met this mender of roads, called Jacques – by chance – a day and half's journey out of Paris. He is a good child – give him a drink, my wife!"

A second man got up and went out. Madame Defarge set wine before the mender of roads called Jacques, who doffed his blue cap and drank. He ate some black bread from his pocket. A third man got up and went out.

Defarge refreshed himself with a draught of wine and waited until the countryman had made his breakfast. He looked at no one and no one now looked at him. Madame Defarge took up her knitting, and was at work.

"Have you finished, friend?" he asked.

"Yes, thank you."

"Come, then! You shall see the apartment that I said you could occupy. It will suit you to a marvel."

Out of the wine shop into the street, out of the street into a court-yard, out of the courtyard up a steep staircase, out of the staircase into a garret – once the garret where a white-haired man sat on a low bench, making shoes.

No white-haired man was there now; but the three men were there who had gone out of the wine shop singly.

Defarge closed the door carefully, and spoke in a subdued voice: "Jacques One, Jacques Two, Jacques Three! This is the witness I arranged to meet. He will tell you all. Speak, Jacques Five!"

The mender of roads, blue cap in hand, wiped his swarthy forehead with it, and said, "Where shall I commence, monsieur?"

"Commence," was Monsieur Defarge's not unreasonable reply, "at the commencement."

"I saw him then, messieurs," began the mender of roads, "a year ago this summer, underneath the carriage of the Marquis, hanging by the chain."

Jacques One struck in, and asked if he had ever seen the man before?

"Never," answered the mender of roads.

Jacques Three demanded how he afterwards recognised him then?

"By his tall figure," said the mender of roads, softly, and with his finger at his nose. "When Monsieur the Marquis demanded that evening, 'Say, what is he like?' I answered, 'Tall as a spectre.'"

"You should have said, short as a dwarf," returned Jacques Two.

"But what did I know? The deed was not then accomplished, neither did he confide in me."

"He is right, Jacques," murmured Defarge, to him who had interrupted. "Go on!"

"Good!" said the mender of roads, with an air of mystery. "The tall man is lost, and he is sought – how many months? Nine, ten, eleven?"

"No matter, the number," said Defarge. "He is well hidden, but at last he is unluckily found. Go on!"

"I am again at work upon the hill-side, at sunset. I am collecting my tools to go to my cottage down in the village below, where it is already dark, when I raise my eyes, and see coming over the hill six soldiers. In the midst of them is a tall man with his arms bound to his sides – like this!"

He then represented a man with his elbows bound fast at his hips, with cords that were knotted behind him.

"I stand aside, messieurs, by my heap of stones, to see the soldiers and their prisoner pass. When they advance quite near to me, I recognise the tall man, and he recognises me. Ah, but he would be well content to precipitate himself over the hill-side once again, as on the evening when he and I first encountered, close to the same spot!"

He described it as if he were there, and it was evident that he saw it vividly; perhaps he had not seen much in his life.

"I do not show the soldiers that I recognise the tall man; he does not show that he recognises me; we know it, with our eyes. 'Come on!' says the chief of that company, pointing to the village, 'bring him fast to his tomb!' and they bring him faster. I follow. His arms are swelled because of being bound so tight, his wooden shoes are large and clumsy, and he is lame and slow. So they drive him with their guns – like this!"

He imitated the action of a man's being impelled forward by the butt-ends of muskets.

"As they descend the hill like madmen running a race, he falls. They laugh and pick him up again. His face is bleeding and covered with dust, but he cannot touch it; thereupon they laugh again. They bring him into the village; all the village runs to look; they take him past the mill, and up to the prison; the prison gate opens in the darkness of the night, and swallows him – like this!"

He opened his mouth as wide as he could, and shut it with a sounding snap of his teeth. Observant of his unwillingness to mar the effect by opening it again, Defarge said, "Go on, Jacques."

"All the village," pursued the mender of roads, on tiptoe and in a low voice, "withdraws and whispers by the fountain. That night all the village sleeps and dreams of that unhappy one, within the locks and bars of the prison on the crag, never to come out of it, except to perish. In the morning, with my tools upon my shoulder, eating my morsel of black bread as I go, I make a circuit by the prison. There I see him, high up, behind the bars of a lofty iron cage, bloody and dusty as last night, looking through. He has no hand free, to wave to me; I dare not call to him; he regards me like a dead man."

Defarge and the three glanced darkly at one another as they listened to the countryman's story; the manner of all of them, while it was secret, was authoritative too. They had the air of a rough tribunal.

"Go on, Jacques," said Defarge.

"He remains up there in his iron cage some days. The village looks at him by stealth, for it is afraid. But it always looks up at the prison on the crag; and in the evening, when the work of the day is achieved and it assembles to gossip at the fountain, all faces are turned towards the prison. Formerly, they were turned towards the posting-house; now, they are turned towards the prison. They whisper at the fountain, that although condemned to death he will not be executed; they say that petitions have been presented to the king in Paris, showing that he was enraged and made mad by the death of his child. What do I know? It is possible. Perhaps yes, perhaps no."

"Listen then, Jacques," Number One of that name sternly interposed. "Know that a petition was presented to the King and Queen. All here, yourself excepted, saw the King take it, in his carriage in the street, sitting beside the Queen. It is Defarge whom you see here, who, at the hazard of his life, darted out before the horses, with the petition in his hand."

"And once again listen, Jacques!" said the kneeling Number Three. "The guards surrounded the petitioner, and struck him blows. You hear?"

"I hear, messieurs."

"Go on then," said Defarge.

"They also whisper at the fountain," resumed the countryman, "that he is brought down into our country to be executed on the spot, and that he will very certainly be executed. They even whisper that because he has slain Monseigneur, and because Monseigneur was the father of his tenants – serfs – what you will – he will be executed as a parricide. They speak of nothing else. At length, on Sunday night when the village is asleep, soldiers come and their guns ring on the stones of the little street. Workmen dig, workmen hammer, soldiers laugh and sing; in the morning, by the fountain, there is raised a gallows forty feet high, poisoning the water."

The mender of roads looked *through* rather than *at* the low ceiling, and pointed as if he saw the gallows somewhere in the sky.

"All work is stopped, all assemble there. At midday, the drums roll. Soldiers have marched into the prison in the night, and he is in the midst of many soldiers. He is bound and gagged. On the top of the gallows is fixed the knife, blade upwards, with its point in the air. He is hanged there forty feet high – and is left hanging, poisoning the water."

They looked at one another, as he used his blue cap to wipe his face.

"It is frightful, messieurs. How can the women and the children draw water! Who can gossip of an evening, under that shadow! That's all, messieurs. I left at sunset (as I had been warned to do), and I walked on, that night and half next day, until I met (as I was warned I should) this comrade. With him, I came on, now riding and now walking, through the rest of yesterday and through last night. And here you see me!"

After a gloomy silence, the first Jacques said, "Good! You have acted and recounted faithfully. Will you wait for us a little, outside the door?"

"Very willingly," said the mender of roads. Defarge escorted him to the top of the stairs, and, leaving him seated there, returned. The three had risen, and their heads were together when he came back.

"How say you, Jacques?" demanded Number One. "To be registered?"

"To be registered, as doomed to destruction," returned Defarge.

"Magnificent!" croaked the man with the craving.

"The château, and all the race?" inquired the first.

"The château and all the race," returned Defarge. "Extermination."

Number two repeated, "Magnificent!"

"Are you sure," asked Jacques Two, "that no embarrassment can arise from our manner of keeping the register? Without doubt it is safe, for no one beyond ourselves can decipher it; but shall we always be able to decipher it – or, I ought to say, will she?"

"Jacques," returned Defarge, drawing himself up, "if Madame my wife undertook to keep the register in her memory alone, she would not lose a word of it. Knitted, in her own stitches and her own symbols, it will always be as plain to her as the sun. Have confidence in Madame Defarge."

There was a murmur of confidence and approval, and then one asked: "Is this rustic to be sent back soon? I hope so. He is very simple; is he not a little dangerous?"

"He knows nothing," said Defarge; "I will take care of him, and set him on his road. He wishes to see the fine world – the King, the Queen, and Court; let him see them on Sunday."

"What?" exclaimed Jacques, staring. "Is it a good sign, that he wishes to see Royalty and Nobility?"

"Jacques," said Defarge; "show a cat milk, if you wish her to thirst for it. So show a dog his natural prey, if you wish him to bring it down one day."

Nothing more was said, and the mender of roads was advised to lay himself down on the pallet-bed and take some rest. He needed no persuasion, and was soon asleep.

Worse quarters than Defarge's wine shop, could easily have been found in Paris for a provincial slave of that degree. Saving for a mysterious dread of Madame by which he was constantly haunted, his life was very new and agreeable. The following Sunday Defarge accompanied the mender of roads to Versailles, to see the carriage of the King and Queen.

Madame Defarge kept them company, knitting as they waited.

"You work hard, madame," said a man near her.

"Yes," answered Madame Defarge; "I have a good deal to do."

"What do you make, madame?"

"Many things."

"For instance– "

"For instance," returned Madame Defarge, composedly, "shrouds."

The man moved away, as soon as he could, and the mender of roads fanned himself with his blue cap. If he needed a King and Queen to restore him, he was fortunate that soon the large-faced King and the fair-faced Queen came in their golden coach, attended by the shining Bull's Eye of their Court. A glittering multitude of laughing ladies and fine lords in jewels and silks and powder and splendour. At the marvellous sight, the mender of roads cried Long live the King, Long live the Queen, Long live everybody and everything! During the whole of this scene, which lasted some three hours, he had plenty of shouting and weeping and sentimental company, and throughout Defarge held him by the collar, as if to restrain him from flying at the objects of his brief devotion and tearing them to pieces.

"Bravo!" said Defarge, clapping him on the back when it was over, like a patron; "you are a good boy!"

The mender of roads was now coming to himself, and was mistrustful of having made a mistake in his late demonstrations; but no.

"You are the fellow we want," said Defarge, in his ear; "you make these fools believe that it will last for ever. Then, they are the more insolent, and it is the nearer ended."

"Hey!" cried the mender of roads, reflectively; "that's true."

"These fools know nothing. While they despise your breath, and would stop it forever and ever, in you or in a hundred like you rather than in one of their own horses or dogs, they only know what your breath tells them. Deceive them, then, a little longer."

CHAPTER 13

Still Knitting

Madame Defarge and monsieur her husband returned amicably to Saint Antoine, while a speck in a blue cap toiled through the darkness, and through the dust, and down the weary miles towards the château of Monsieur the Marquis, now in his grave.

Château and hut, stone face and dangling figure, the red stain on the stone floor, and the pure water in the village well – thousands of acres of land – a whole province of France – all France itself – lay under the night sky.

The Defarges, husband and wife, came lumbering under the starlight, in their public vehicle, to that gate of Paris whereunto their journey naturally tended. There was the usual stoppage at the barrier guardhouse. Monsieur Defarge alighted; knowing one or two of the soldiery there, and one of the police. The latter he was intimate with, and affectionately embraced.

When Saint Antoine had again enfolded the Defarges in his dusky wings, and they, having finally alighted near the Saint's boundaries, were picking their way on foot through his streets, Madame Defarge spoke to her husband: "Say then, my friend; what did Jacques of the police tell thee?"

"Very little tonight, but all he knows. There is another spy commissioned for our quarter. There may be many more, for all that he can say, but he knows of one."

"Eh well!" said Madame Defarge, raising her eyebrows with a cool business air. "It is necessary to register him. How do they call that man?"

"He is English."

"So much the better. His name?"

"John Barsad," said Defarge, making it French by pronunciation. He then spelt it with perfect correctness.

"Barsad," repeated Madame. "Good. His appearance; is it known?"

"Age, about forty years; height, about five feet nine; black hair; complexion dark; generally, rather handsome visage; eyes dark, face thin, long, and sallow; nose aquiline, but not straight, having a peculiar inclination towards the left cheek; expression, therefore, sinister."

"Eh my faith. It is a portrait!" said Madame, laughing. "He shall be registered tomorrow."

They turned into the wine shop, which was closed and Madame Defarge immediately took her post at her desk, turned out the contents of the bowl of money, and began knotting them up in her handkerchief, in a chain of separate knots, for safe keeping through the night. All this while, Defarge, with his pipe in his mouth, walked up and down, complacently admiring, but never interfering; in which condition, indeed, as to the business and his domestic affairs, he walked up and down through life.

"You are fatigued," said Madame, raising her glance as she knotted the money.

"I am a little tired," her husband acknowledged.

"You are a little depressed, too," said Madame.

"But my dear!" began Defarge.

"But my dear!" repeated Madame, nodding firmly. "You are faint of heart tonight, my dear!"

"Well, then," said Defarge, as if a thought were wrung out of his breast, "it *is* a long time."

"It is a long time," repeated his wife. "And when is it not a long time? Vengeance and retribution require a long time. It does not take a long time for an earthquake to swallow a town. Eh well! Tell me how long it takes to prepare the earthquake?"

"A long time, I suppose," said Defarge.

"But when it is ready, it takes place, and grinds to pieces everything before it. In the meantime, it is always preparing, though it is not seen or heard. That is your consolation. Keep it."

She tied a knot with flashing eyes, as if it throttled a foe.

"I tell thee," said Madame, extending her right hand, for emphasis, "that although it is a long time on the road, it is on the road and coming."

"My brave wife," returned Defarge, standing before her with his head a little bent, and his hands clasped at his back. "I do not question all this. But it has lasted a long time, and it is possible – you know well, my wife, it is possible that it may not come, during our lives."

"We shall have helped it," returned Madame, with her extended hand in strong action. "Nothing that we do, is done in vain. I believe, with all my soul, that we shall see the triumph. But even if I knew certainly not, show me the neck of an aristocrat and tyrant, and still I would – "

Then Madame, with her teeth set, tied a very terrible knot indeed.

"Hold!" cried Defarge, reddening a little as if he felt charged with cowardice; "I too, my dear, will stop at nothing."

"Yes! But it is your weakness that you sometimes need to see your victim and your opportunity, to sustain you. Sustain yourself without that. When the time comes, let loose a tiger and a devil; but wait with the tiger and the devil chained yet always ready."

Madame enforced the conclusion of this piece of advice by striking her little counter with her chain of money as if she knocked its brains out, and then gathering the heavy handkerchief under her arm in a serene manner, observed that it was time to go to bed.

Next noontide saw the admirable woman in her usual place in the wine shop, knitting away. A rose lay beside her, and she now and then glanced at the flower. There were a few customers, drinking or not drinking, standing or seated, sprinkled about. The day was very hot.

A figure entering at the door threw a shadow on Madame Defarge which she felt to be a new one. She laid down her knitting, and began to pin her rose in her head-dress, before she looked at the figure.

It was most curious. The moment Madame Defarge took up the rose, the customers ceased talking, and began gradually to drop out of the wine shop.

"Good day, madame," said the newcomer.

"Good day, monsieur."

She said it aloud, but added to herself, as she resumed her knitting: "Hah! Good day, age about forty, height about five feet nine, black hair, generally rather handsome visage, complexion dark, eyes dark, thin, long and sallow face, aquiline nose but not straight, having a peculiar inclination towards the left cheek imparting a sinister expression! Good day, one and all!"

"A little glass of old cognac, and a mouthful of cool fresh water, madame."

Madame complied with a polite air.

"Marvellous cognac this, madame!"

It was the first time it had ever been so complimented. She said that the cognac was flattered, and took up her knitting. The visitor watched her fingers for a few moments, and took the opportunity of observing the place in general.

"You knit with great skill, madame."

"I am accustomed to it."

"A pretty pattern too!"

"*You* think so?" said Madame, with a smile.

"Decidedly. May one ask what it is for?"

"Pastime," said Madame, still looking at him with a smile while her fingers moved nimbly.

"Not for use?"

"That depends. I may find a use for it one day. If I do – Well," said Madame, drawing a breath and nodding her head, "I'll use it!"

It was remarkable; but, a rose on the head-dress of Madame Defarge had a strange effect. Two men had entered separately, and had been about to order, when, catching sight of that novelty, they faltered, made a pretence of looking about, and went away. Of those who had been there when this visitor entered, there was none left. They had all left. The spy had kept his eyes open, but had been able to detect no sign. They had simply lounged away in a poverty-stricken, purposeless, accidental manner.

"John," thought Madame, checking off her work as her fingers knitted, and her eyes looked at the stranger. "Stay long enough, and I shall knit 'Barsad' before you go."

"You have a husband, madame?"

"I have."

"Children?"

"No children."

"Business seems bad?"

"Business is very bad; the people are so poor."

"Ah, the unfortunate, miserable people! So oppressed, too – as you say."

"As *you* say," Madame retorted, correcting him, and deftly knitting an extra something into his name that boded him no good.

"Pardon me; certainly it was I who said so, but you naturally think so. Of course."

"I think?" returned Madame, in a high voice. "I and my husband have enough to do to keep this wine shop open, without thinking. All we think, here, is how to live. And it gives us enough to think about, without embarrassing our heads concerning others. I think for others? No, no."

The spy, there to pick up any crumbs he could find or make, did not allow his baffled state to express itself in his sinister face. He stood with an air of gossiping gallantry, leaning his elbow on Madame Defarge's little counter, and occasionally sipping his cognac.

"A bad business this, madame, of Gaspard's execution. Ah! the poor Gaspard!" With a sigh of great compassion.

"My faith!" returned Madame, coolly and lightly, "if people use knives for such purposes, they have to pay for it. He knew beforehand what the price of his luxury was; he has paid the price."

"I believe," said the spy, dropping his soft voice to a tone that invited confidence, "there is much compassion and anger in this neighbourhood, touching the poor fellow? Between ourselves."

"Is there?" asked Madame, vacantly.

"Is there not?"

" – Here is my husband!" said Madame Defarge.

As the keeper of the wine shop entered at the door, the spy saluted him by touching his hat, and saying, with an engaging smile, "Good day, Jacques!" Defarge stopped short, and stared at him.

"Good day, Jacques!" the spy repeated with not quite so much confidence.

"You deceive yourself, monsieur," returned the keeper of the wine shop. "You mistake me for another. I am Ernest Defarge."

"It is all the same," said the spy, airily, but discomfited too. "Good day!"

"Good day!" answered Defarge, drily.

"I was saying to Madame that they tell me there is – and no wonder – much sympathy and anger in Saint Antoine, touching the unhappy fate of poor Gaspard."

"No one has told me so," said Defarge, shaking his head.

Having said it, he passed behind the little counter, and stood behind his wife's chair, looking over that barrier at the person to whom they were both opposed.

The spy drained his little glass of cognac, took a sip of fresh water, and asked for another glass of cognac. Madame Defarge poured it out for him, and took to her knitting again.

"You seem to know this quarter well; that is to say, better than I do?" observed Defarge.

"Not at all, but I hope to know it better. I am deeply interested in its miserable inhabitants."

"Hah!" muttered Defarge.

"The pleasure of conversing with you, Monsieur Defarge, recalls to me," pursued the spy, "that I have the honour of cherishing some interesting associations with your name. When Doctor Manette was released, you, his old domestic, had the charge of him, I know. He was delivered to you. You see I am informed of the circumstances?"

"Such is the fact, certainly," said Defarge.

"It was to you," said the spy, "that his daughter came; and it was from your care that his daughter took him, accompanied by a neat brown monsieur; how is he called? – Lorry – of the bank of Tellson and Company – over to England."

"Such is the fact," repeated Defarge.

"I have known Doctor Manette and his daughter, in England."

"Yes?" said Defarge.

"You don't hear much about them now?" said the spy.

"No," said Defarge.

"In effect," Madame struck in, looking up from her work and her little song, "we never hear about them. We received the news of their safe arrival, and perhaps another letter, or perhaps two; but, since then, they have gradually taken their road in life."

"Perfectly so, madame," replied the spy. "She is going to be married."

"Going?" echoed Madame. "She was pretty enough to have been married long ago. You English are cold, it seems to me."

"Oh! You know I am English."

"I perceive your tongue is," returned Madame; "and what the tongue is, I suppose the man is."

He did not take the identification as a compliment; but he made the best of it, and turned it off with a laugh. After sipping his cognac to the end, he added:

"Yes, Miss Manette is going to be married. But to one who, like herself, is French by birth. And speaking of Gaspard, it is a curious thing that she is going to marry the nephew of Monsieur the Marquis, in other words, the present Marquis. But he lives unknown in England. He is no Marquis there; he is Mr Charles Darnay. D'Aulnais is the name of his mother's family."

Madame Defarge knitted steadily, but the intelligence had a palpable effect upon her husband. Do what he would, behind the little counter, as to the striking of a light and the lighting of his pipe, he was troubled, and his hand was not trustworthy. The spy would have been no spy if he had failed to see it.

Having made, at least, this one hit, whatever it might prove to be worth, and no customers coming in to help him to any other, Mr Barsad paid for what he had drunk, and took his leave. For some minutes after he had left, the husband and wife remained exactly as he had left them, lest he should come back.

"Can it be true," said Defarge, in a low voice, looking down at his wife as he stood smoking: "what he has said of Ma'amselle Manette?"

"As he has said it," returned Madame, lifting her eyebrows a little, "it is probably false. But it may be true."

"If it is – " Defarge began, and stopped.

"If it is?" repeated his wife.

" – And if it does come, while we live to see it triumph – I hope, for her sake, Destiny will keep her husband out of France."

"Her husband's destiny," said Madame Defarge, with her usual composure, "will lead him to the end that is to end him. That is all I know."

"But it is strange," said Defarge, almost pleading with his wife to admit it. "After all our sympathy for Monsieur her father, and herself, her husband's name should be proscribed under your hand at this moment, alongside his who has just left us?"

"Stranger things than that will happen when it does come," answered Madame. "I have them both here, of a certainty; and they are both here for their merits; that is enough."

She rolled up her knitting when she had said those words, and presently took the rose out of the handkerchief that was wound about her head. Either Saint Antoine had an instinctive sense that the objectionable decoration was gone, or Saint Antoine was on the watch for its disappearance; howbeit, the wine shop soon recovered its habitual aspect.

In the evening, Madame Defarge was accustomed to pass from place to place and from group to group. There were many like her – such as the world will do well never to breed again. All the women knitted – worthless things; but, the mechanical work was a mechanical substitute for eating and drinking.

Her husband smoked at his door, looking after her with admiration. "A great woman," said he, "a grand woman, a frightfully grand woman!"

Darkness closed around, and then came the ringing of church bells and the distant beating of the military drums in the Palace Courtyard, as the women sat knitting, knitting. Another darkness was closing in, when the church bells, then ringing pleasantly in many an airy steeple over France, would be melted into thundering cannon. So much was closing in about the women who sat knitting, knitting, that they their very selves were closing in around a structure yet unbuilt, where they were to sit knitting, knitting, counting dropping heads.

CHAPTER 14

One Night

One memorable evening the Doctor and his daughter sat under the plane tree together. The moon rose and shone upon their faces through its leaves.

Lucie was to be married tomorrow. She had reserved this last evening for her father, and they sat alone under the tree.

"You are happy, my dear father?"

"Quite, my child."

They had said little, though they had been there a long time.

"And I am very happy tonight, dear father. I am deeply happy in the love that Heaven has so blessed – my love for Charles, and Charles's love for me. But if my marriage were so arranged that it would part us, even by the length of a few of these streets, I should be more unhappy and self-reproachful now than I can tell you. Even as it is – "

Even as it was, she could not command her voice.

In the sad moonlight, she clasped him by the neck, and laid her face upon his breast.

"Dearest dear! Can you tell me, this last time, that you feel quite, quite sure, no new affections of mine, and no new duties of mine, will ever interpose between us?"

Her father answered, with a cheerful firmness of conviction he could scarcely have assumed, "Quite sure, my darling! More than that," he added, as he tenderly kissed her: "my future is far brighter, Lucie, seen through your marriage, than it could have been without it."

"If I could hope *that*, my father!"

"Believe it, love! You, devoted and young, cannot fully appreciate the anxiety I have felt that your life should not be wasted – "

She moved her hand towards his lips, but he took it in his, and repeated the word.

" – wasted, my child – should not be wasted, struck aside from the natural order of things – for my sake. Just ask yourself, how could my happiness be perfect, while yours was incomplete?"

"If I had never seen Charles, my father, I should have been quite happy with you."

He smiled at her unconscious admission that she would have been unhappy without Charles, having seen him; and replied:

"My child, you did see him, and it is Charles. If it had not been Charles, it would have been another. Or, if it had been no other, I should have been the cause, and then the dark part of my life would have cast its shadow beyond myself, and would have fallen on you."

It was the first time, except at the trial, of her ever hearing him refer to the period of his suffering. It gave her a strange and new sensation while his words were in her ears; and she remembered it long afterwards.

"See!" said the Doctor of Beauvais, raising his hand towards the moon. "I have looked at her from my prison-window, when I could not bear her light."

The strange thrill with which she heard him go back to that time, deepened as he dwelt upon it; but there was nothing to shock her in the manner of his reference. He only seemed to contrast his present cheerfulness with the dire endurance that was over.

"I have looked at her, speculating thousands of times upon the unborn child from whom I had been rent. Whether it was alive. Whether it had been born alive, or the poor mother's shock had killed it. Whether it was a son who would some day avenge his father. Whether it would never know his father's story, and might even live to weigh the possibility of his father's having disappeared of his own will and act. Whether it was a daughter who would grow to be a woman."

She drew closer to him, and kissed his cheek and his hand.

"I have pictured my daughter, to myself, as perfectly forgetful of me – rather, ignorant of me, and unconscious of me. I have cast up the years of her age, year after year. I have seen her married to a man who knew nothing of my fate."

"My father! Even to hear that you had such thoughts of a daughter who never existed, strikes to my heart as if I had been that child."

"I know no more than that she was like her mother. In a more peaceful state, I have imagined her, in the moonlight, coming to me and taking me out to show me that the home of her married life was full of her loving remembrance of her lost father. My picture was in her room, and I was in her prayers. Her life was active, cheerful, useful; but my poor history pervaded it all."

"I was that child, my father, I was not half so good, but in my love that was I."

"And she showed me her children," said the Doctor of Beauvais, "and they had heard of me, and had been taught to pity me. I imagined that she always brought me back after showing me such things. But then, blessed with the relief of tears, I fell upon my knees, and blessed her."

"I am that child, I hope, my father. O my dear, will you bless me as fervently tomorrow?"

"Lucie, I recall these old troubles, loving you better than words can tell, and thanking God for my great happiness. My thoughts, when they were wildest, never rose near the happiness that I have known with you, and that we have before us."

He embraced her, solemnly commended her to Heaven, and humbly thanked Heaven for having bestowed her on him. By-and-by, they went into the house.

Only Mr Lorry was to be at the wedding. There was to be no bridesmaid but the gaunt Miss Pross. The marriage would make no change to their place of residence; they had been able to take the upper rooms in the house and they desired nothing more.

Doctor Manette was very cheerful at the little supper. They were only three at table, and Miss Pross made the third.

So, the time came for him to bid Lucie good night, and they separated. But, in the stillness of the third hour of the morning, Lucie came downstairs again, and stole into his room.

All was quiet; and he lay asleep, his white hair picturesque on the untroubled pillow, and his hands lying quiet on the coverlet. She put her needless candle in the shadow at a distance, crept up to his bed, and put her lips to his.

Into his handsome face, the bitter waters of captivity had worn; but he covered up their tracks with a determination so strong, that he held the mastery of them even in his sleep.

She put up a prayer that she might ever be as true to him as her love aspired to be, and as his sorrows deserved. Then, she kissed his lips once more, and went away. So, the sunrise came, and the shadows of the leaves of the plane-tree moved upon his face, as softly as her lips had moved in praying for him.

CHAPTER 15

Nine Days

The marriage day was shining brightly, and they were ready outside the closed door of the Doctor's room, where he was speaking with Charles Darnay. They were ready to go to church; the beautiful bride, Mr Lorry, and Miss Pross.

"And so," said Mr Lorry, who had been moving round the bride to take in every point of her quiet, pretty dress. "And so it was for this, my sweet Lucie, that I brought you across the Channel. How little I thought what I was doing! How lightly I valued the obligation I was conferring on my friend Mr Charles! Don't cry, Miss Pross," added the gentle Mr Lorry.

"I am not crying," said Miss Pross; "*You* are."

"I, my Pross?" (By this time, Mr Lorry dared to be pleasant with her, on occasion.)

"You were, just now; I saw you do it."

"Dear me! This is an occasion that makes a man speculate on all he has lost. Dear, dear! You think there never might have been a Mrs Lorry?" asked the gentleman of that name.

"Pooh!" rejoined Miss Pross. "You were a bachelor in your cradle."

"Well!" observed Mr Lorry, beamingly adjusting his little wig, "that seems probable, too."

"And you were cut out for a bachelor," pursued Miss Pross, "before you were put in your cradle."

"Then, I think," said Mr Lorry, "that I was very unhandsomely dealt with. Enough! Now, my dear Lucie," drawing his arm soothingly round her waist, "I hear them moving in the next room, and Miss Pross and I are anxious not to lose the final opportunity of saying something to you that you wish to hear. You leave your good father, my dear, in hands as earnest and as loving as your own; he shall be taken every conceivable care of; during the next fortnight, while you are in Warwickshire and thereabouts, even Tellson's shall go to the wall (comparatively speaking) before him. And when, at the fortnight's end, he comes to join you and your beloved husband, on your other fortnight's trip in Wales, you shall say that we have sent him to you in the best health and in the happiest frame. Now, I hear Somebody's step coming to the door. Let me kiss my dear girl with an old-fashioned bachelor blessing, before Somebody comes to claim his own."

For a moment, he held the fair face from him to look at the well-remembered expression on the forehead, and then laid the bright golden hair against his little brown wig, with a genuine tenderness and delicacy which, if such things be old-fashioned, were as old as Adam.

The door of the Doctor's room opened, and he came out with Charles Darnay. He was so deadly pale that no vestige of colour was to be seen in his face. But, in the composure of his manner he was unaltered, except that to the shrewd glance of Mr Lorry it seemed as though some air of dread had lately passed over him.

He gave his arm to his daughter, and took her downstairs to the chariot that Mr Lorry had hired. The rest followed in another carriage, and soon, in a neighbouring church, where no strange eyes looked on, Charles Darnay and Lucie Manette were happily married.

They returned home to breakfast, and all went well, and in due course the golden hair that had mingled with the poor shoemaker's white locks in the Paris garret, were mingled with them again in the morning sunlight, on the threshold of the door at parting.

It was a hard parting, though it was not for long. But her father cheered her, and said at last, gently disengaging himself from her enfolding arms, "Take her, Charles! She is yours!"

And her agitated hand waved to them from a chaise window, and she was gone.

The Doctor, Mr Lorry, and Miss Pross, were left quite alone. It was when they turned into the welcome shade of the cool old hall, that Mr Lorry observed a great change to have come over the Doctor. It was the old scared lost look that troubled Mr Lorry; and through his absent manner of clasping his head and drearily wandering away into his own room when they got upstairs, Mr Lorry was reminded of Defarge the wine shop keeper, and the starlight ride.

"I think," he whispered to Miss Pross, after anxious consideration, "I think we had best not speak to him just now, or at all disturb him. I must look in at Tellson's; so I will go there at once and come back presently. Then, we will take him a ride into the country, and dine there, and all will be well."

When he returned two hours later, he ascended the old staircase alone, having asked no question of the servant; going thus into the Doctor's rooms, he was stopped by a low sound of knocking.

"Good God!" he said, with a start. "What's that?"

Miss Pross, with a terrified face, was at his ear. "He doesn't know me, and is making shoes!"

Mr Lorry said what he could to calm her, and went himself into the Doctor's room. The bench was turned towards the light, and his head was bent down, and he was very busy.

"Doctor Manette. My dear friend, Doctor Manette!"

The Doctor looked at him for a moment and bent over his work again. He had laid aside his coat and waistcoat; his shirt was open at the throat, as it used to be. Even the old haggard, faded face had come back to him. He worked hard as if he had been interrupted.

Mr Lorry glanced at the work in his hand, and observed that it was a shoe of the old size and shape. He took up another that was lying by him, and asked what it was.

"A young lady's walking shoe," he muttered, without looking up. "It ought to have been finished long ago. Let it be."

"But, Doctor Manette. Look at me!"

He obeyed, in the old mechanically submissive manner, without pausing in his work.

"You know me, my dear friend? Think again. This is not your proper occupation. Think, dear friend!"

Nothing would induce him to speak more. He looked up, for an instant at a time, when he was requested to do so; but no persuasion would extract a word from him. He worked and worked in silence. The only ray of hope that Mr Lorry had, was that he sometimes furtively looked up without being asked. He looked as though he were trying to reconcile some doubts in his mind.

Two things at once impressed themselves on Mr Lorry, as important above all others; the first, that this must be kept secret from Lucie; the second, that it must be kept secret from all who knew him. In conjunction with Miss Pross, he took immediate steps towards the latter precaution, by giving out that the Doctor was not well, and required a few days of complete rest.

These measures Mr Lorry took in the hope of his coming to himself. He therefore made arrangements to absent himself from Tellson's for the first time in his life, and took his post by the window in the same room.

He was not long in discovering that it was worse than useless to speak to him, since, on being pressed, he became worried. He resolved merely to keep himself always before him, as a silent protest against the delusion into which he had fallen, or was falling. He remained, therefore, in his seat near the window, reading and writing, and expressing in as many pleasant and natural ways as he could think of, that it was a free place.

Doctor Manette took what was given him to eat and drink, and worked on, that first day, until it was too dark to see. When he put his tools aside as useless, until morning, Mr Lorry rose and said to him:

"Will you go out?"

He looked down at the floor on either side of him in the old manner, looked up and repeated in the old low voice:

"Out?"

"Yes; for a walk with me. Why not?"

He made no effort to say why not, and said not a word more. But, Mr Lorry thought he saw, as he leaned forward on his bench in the dusk, with his elbows on his knees and his head in his hands, that he was in some misty way asking himself, "Why not?"

Miss Pross and he divided the night into two watches, and observed him at intervals from the adjoining room. He paced up and down for a long time before he lay down; but, when he did finally lay himself down, he fell asleep. In the morning, he went straight to his bench and to work.

On this second day, Mr Lorry saluted him cheerfully by his name, and

114

spoke to him on topics that had been of late familiar to them. He returned no reply, but it was evident that he heard what was said, and that he thought about it, however confusedly. This encouraged Mr Lorry to have Miss Pross in with her work, several times during the day; at those times, they quietly spoke of Lucie, and of her father then present, precisely in the usual manner, and as if there were nothing amiss.

When it fell dark again, Mr Lorry asked him as before:

"Dear Doctor, will you go out?"

As before, he repeated, "Out?"

"Yes; for a walk with me. Why not?"

This time, Mr Lorry feigned to go out when he could extract no answer from him, and, after remaining absent for an hour, returned. In the meanwhile, the Doctor sat at the window, looking down at the plane-tree; but, on Mr Lorry's return, he slipped away to his bench.

The time went very slowly on, and Mr Lorry's hope darkened, and his heart grew heavier again, and grew yet heavier every day. The third day came and went, the fourth, the fifth. Six, seven, eight days, nine days passed.

With a hope ever darkening, Mr Lorry passed through this anxious time. The secret was well kept, and Lucie was unaware and happy. But he could not fail to observe that the shoemaker, whose hand had been a little out at first, was growing dreadfully skilful and his hands had never been so nimble and expert, as in the dusk of the ninth evening.

CHAPTER 16

An Opinion

Worn out by anxious watching, Mr Lorry fell asleep at his post. On the tenth morning he was startled by the shining of the sun into the room where a heavy slumber had overtaken him in the dark of the night.

He rubbed his eyes and roused himself; but he doubted, when he had done so, whether he was not still asleep. For, going to the door of the Doctor's room and looking in, he perceived that the shoemaker's bench and tools were put aside again, and that the Doctor himself sat reading at the window. He was in his usual morning dress, and his face (which Mr

Lorry could distinctly see), though still very pale, was calmly studious and attentive.

Even when he had satisfied himself that he was awake, Mr Lorry felt giddily uncertain for some few moments whether the late shoemaking might not be a disturbed dream of his own. For, his friend stood before him in his accustomed clothing, and employed as usual.

The answer was obvious. If the events had not happened how came he, Jarvis Lorry, there? How could he have fallen asleep, in his clothes, on the sofa in Doctor Manette's consulting-room?

Within a few minutes, Miss Pross was at his side. If he had had any particle of doubt left, her talk would of necessity have resolved it. He advised that they should meet the Doctor as if nothing unusual had occurred. If he appeared to be in his customary state of mind, Mr Lorry would then cautiously proceed to seek direction and guidance from the opinion he had been, in his anxiety, so anxious to obtain.

Mr Lorry presented himself at the breakfast-hour in his usual white linen, and with his usual neat leg. The Doctor was summoned in the usual way, and came to breakfast.

At first he supposed that his daughter's marriage had taken place yesterday. An incidental allusion, purposely thrown out, to the day of the week, and the day of the month, set him thinking and counting, and evidently made him uneasy. In all other respects, however, he was composed. Mr Lorry determined to have the aid he sought. And that aid was his own.

Therefore, when the breakfast was done and cleared away, and he and the Doctor were left together, Mr Lorry said, feelingly: "My dear Manette, I am anxious to have your opinion, in confidence."

Glancing at his hands, which were discoloured by his late work, the Doctor looked troubled, and listened attentively.

"Doctor Manette," said Mr Lorry, touching him affectionately on the arm, "it is the case of a very dear friend of mine. Pray advise me well for his sake – and above all, for his daughter's – his daughter's, my dear Manette."

"Do I understand," said the Doctor, softly, "some mental shock – ?"
"Yes!"
"Be explicit," said the Doctor. "Spare no detail."
Mr Lorry saw that they understood one another, and proceeded.

"My dear Manette, it is the case of an old and a prolonged shock. It is the case of a shock under which the sufferer was borne down, one cannot say for how long, because I believe he cannot calculate the time himself. It is the case of a shock from which he has recovered, so completely, as to be a highly intelligent man, capable of close application of mind, and great exertion of body. But, unfortunately, there has been," he paused and took a deep breath – "a slight relapse."

The Doctor, in a low voice, asked, "Of how long duration?"

"Nine days and nights."

"How did it show itself? I infer," glancing at his hands again, "in the resumption of some old pursuit connected with the shock?"

"That is the fact."

"Now, did you ever see him," asked the Doctor, distinctly, though in the same low voice, "engaged in that pursuit before?"

"Once."

"And when the relapse came, was he mostly as he was then?"

"I think in all respects."

"You spoke of his daughter. Does she know of the relapse?"

"It has been kept from her, and I hope will always be kept from her. It is known only to myself, and to one other who may be trusted."

The Doctor grasped his hand, and murmured, "That was very kind. That was very thoughtful!" Mr Lorry grasped his hand in return, and neither of the two spoke for a little while.

"Now, my dear Manette," said Mr Lorry, at length, in his most considerate and most affectionate way, "I am a mere man of business, and unfit to cope with such intricate and difficult matters. Tell me, how does this relapse come about? Is there danger of another? Could a repetition of it be prevented? How should a repetition of it be treated? How does it come about at all? What can I do for my friend? No man ever can have been more desirous in his heart to serve a friend, than I am to serve mine, if I knew how. Pray discuss it with me to enable me to see it a little more clearly, and teach me how to be a little more useful."

Doctor Manette sat meditating after these earnest words were spoken, and Mr Lorry did not press him.

"I think it probable," said the Doctor, breaking silence with an effort, "that the relapse you have described, my dear friend, was not quite unforeseen by its subject."

"Was it dreaded by him?" Mr Lorry ventured to ask.

"Very much," he said with an involuntary shudder. "You have no idea how such an apprehension weighs on the sufferer's mind, and how difficult – how almost impossible – it is, for him to utter a word upon the topic that oppresses him."

"Would he," asked Mr Lorry, "be sensibly relieved if he could but impart that secret brooding to any one, when it is on him?"

"I think so, but I believe it would be impossible for him."

"Now," said Mr Lorry, gently putting his hand on the Doctor's arm again, after a short silence, "to what would you refer this attack?"

"I believe," returned Doctor Manette, "that some intense associations of a most distressing nature were vividly recalled."

"Would he remember what took place in the relapse?" asked Mr Lorry, with natural hesitation.

The Doctor looked desolately round the room, shook his head, and answered, in a low voice, "Not at all."

"Now, as to the future," hinted Mr Lorry.

"As to the future," said the Doctor, recovering firmness, "I should have great hope. As it pleased Heaven to restore him so soon, I should have great hope. He, yielding under the pressure of a complicated something, long dreaded and vaguely foreseen and contended against, and recovering after the cloud had burst and passed, I should hope that the worst was over."

"Well, well! That's good comfort. I am thankful!" said Mr Lorry.

"I am thankful!" repeated the Doctor, bending his head with reverence.

"Assuming for a moment, that my friend was overworked; would it show itself in some renewal of this disorder?"

"I do not think so. I do not think," said Doctor Manette with the firmness of self-conviction, "that anything but the one train of association would renew it. I think that, henceforth, nothing but some extraordinary jarring of that chord could renew it."

He spoke with the diffidence of a man who knew how slight a thing would overset the delicate organisation of the mind, and yet with the confidence of a man who had slowly won his assurance out of personal endurance and distress. It was not for his friend to abate that confidence. He approached his second and last point. He felt it to be the most difficult of all.

"The occupation resumed under the influence of this passing affliction so happily recovered from," said Mr Lorry, clearing his throat, "we will call – Blacksmith's work. We will say that he was unexpectedly found at his forge again. Is it not a pity that he should keep it by him?"

The Doctor shaded his forehead with his hand, and beat his foot nervously on the ground.

"He has always kept it by him," said Mr Lorry, with an anxious look at his friend. "Now, would it not be better to let it go?"

Still, the Doctor, with shaded forehead, beat his foot nervously on the ground.

"You do not find it easy to advise me?" said Mr Lorry. "I quite understand it to be a nice question. And yet I think – " And there he shook his head, and stopped.

"You see," said Doctor Manette, turning to him after an uneasy pause, "it is very hard to explain, consistently, the innermost workings of this poor man's mind. He once yearned so frightfully for that occupation, the idea that he might need that old employment, and not find it, gives him a sudden sense of terror, like that which one may fancy strikes to the heart of a lost child."

He looked like his illustration, as he raised his eyes to Mr Lorry's face. "You see, too, it is such an old companion."

"I would not keep it," said Mr Lorry, shaking his head; for he gained in firmness as he saw the Doctor disquieted. "I would recommend him to sacrifice it. I only want your authority. Give me your authority, like a dear good man. For his daughter's sake, my dear Manette!"

Very strange to see what a struggle there was within him!

"In her name, then, let it be done; I sanction it. But, I would not take it away while he was present. Let it be removed when he is not there; let him miss his old companion after an absence."

Mr Lorry readily engaged for that, and the conference was ended. They passed the day in the country, and the Doctor was quite restored. On the three following days he remained perfectly well, and on the fourteenth day he went away to join Lucie and her husband.

On the night of the day on which he left the house, Mr Lorry went into his room with a chopper, saw, chisel, and hammer, attended by Miss Pross carrying a light, and hacked the shoemaker's bench to pieces. The burning was commenced without delay in the kitchen fire; and the tools, shoes, and leather, were buried in the garden. So wicked do destruction and secrecy appear to honest minds, that Mr Lorry and Miss Pross, while engaged in the deed, almost felt, and almost looked, like accomplices in a horrible crime.

CHAPTER 17

A Plea

When the newly married pair came home, the first person who appeared, to offer his congratulations, was Sydney Carton. They had not been at home many hours, when he presented himself. He was not improved in habits, or in looks, or in manner; but there was a certain rugged air of fidelity about him, which was new to the observation of Charles Darnay.

He watched his opportunity of taking Darnay aside into a window, and of speaking to him when no one overheard.

"Mr Darnay," said Carton, "I wish we might be friends."

"We are already friends, I hope."

"You are good enough to say so, as a fashion of speech; but, I don't mean any fashion of speech. Indeed, when I say I wish we might be friends, I scarcely mean quite that, either."

"What do you mean?"

"Mr Darnay, trust me! Now, you know me; you know I am incapable of all the higher and better flights of men. If you doubt it, ask Stryver, and he'll tell you so."

"I prefer to form my own opinion, without the aid of his."

"Well! At any rate you know me as a dissolute dog, who has never done any good, and never will."

"I don't know that you 'never will.' "

"But I do, and you must take my word for it. Well! If you could endure to have such a worthless fellow of such indifferent reputation, coming and going at odd times, I should ask that I might be permitted to come and go as a privileged person here. Look on me as a useless (and I would add, if it were not for the resemblance I detected between you and me, an unornamental) piece of furniture, tolerated for its old service, and taken no notice of. I doubt if I should abuse the permission. It is a hundred to one if I should avail myself of it four times in a year. It would satisfy me, I dare say, to know that I had it."

"Will you try?"

"That is another way of saying that I am placed on the footing I have indicated. I thank you, Darnay. I may use that freedom with your name?"

"I think so, Carton, by this time."

They shook hands upon it, and Sydney turned away. Within a minute afterwards, he was, to all outward appearance, as unsubstantial as ever.

When he was gone, Charles Darnay made some mention of this conversation in general terms, and spoke of Sydney Carton as a problem of carelessness and recklessness. He spoke of him, in short, not bitterly or meaning to bear hard upon him, but as anybody might who saw him as he showed himself.

He had no idea that this could dwell in the thoughts of his fair young wife; but, when he afterwards joined her in their own rooms, he found her waiting for him with the old pretty lifting of the forehead strongly marked.

"We are thoughtful tonight!" said Darnay, drawing his arm about her.

"Yes, dearest Charles," with her hands on his chest, "we are rather thoughtful tonight, for we have something on our mind."

"What is it, my Lucie?"

"Will you promise not to press one question on me, if I beg you not to ask it?"

"Will I promise? What will I not promise to my Love?"

"I think, Charles, poor Mr Carton deserves more consideration and respect than you expressed for him tonight."

"Indeed, my own? Why so?"

"That is what you are not to ask me. But I think – I know – he does."

"If you know it, it is enough. What would you have me do, my Life?"

"I would ask you, dearest, to be very generous with him always, and very lenient on his faults when he is not by. I would ask you to believe that he has a heart he very seldom reveals, and that there are deep wounds in it. My dear, I have seen it bleeding."

"It is a painful reflection to me," said Charles Darnay, quite astounded, "that I should have done him any wrong. I never thought this of him."

"My husband, it is so. I fear he is not to be reclaimed; there is scarcely a hope that anything in his character or fortunes is reparable now. But I am sure that he is capable of good things, gentle things, even magnanimous things."

She looked so beautiful in the purity of her faith in this lost man, that her husband could have looked at her as she was for hours.

"And, O my dearest Love!" she urged, clinging nearer to him, laying her head on him, and raising her eyes to his, "remember how strong we are in our happiness, and how weak he is in our misery!"

The supplication touched him home. "I will always remember it, dear Heart! I will remember it as long as I live."

He bent over the golden head, and put the rosy lips to his, and folded her in his arms. If one forlorn wanderer then pacing the dark streets, could have heard her innocent disclosure, and could have seen the drops of pity kissed away by her husband from the soft blue eyes so loving of that husband, he might have cried to the night. The words would not have parted from his lips for the first time – "God bless her for her sweet compassion!"

CHAPTER 18

Echoing Footsteps

Lucie sat in the still house in the tranquilly resounding corner, listening to the echoing footsteps of years.

There was something coming in the echoes. Fluttering hopes and doubts – hopes, of a love as yet unknown to her: doubts, of her remaining upon earth, to enjoy that new delight – divided her breast.

That time passed, and her little Lucie lay on her bosom. Then, among the advancing echoes, there was the tread of her tiny feet and the sound of her prattling words. Let greater echoes resound as they would, the young mother at the cradle side could always hear those coming. They came, and the shady house was sunny with a child's laugh.

Lucie heard in the echoes of years none but friendly and soothing sounds. Her husband's step was strong and prosperous among them; her father's firm and equal.

Even when there were sounds of sorrow among the rest, they were neither harsh nor cruel. Golden hair, like her own, lay in a halo round the worn face of a little boy, who said with a radiant smile, "Dear papa and mamma, I am very sorry to leave you both, and to leave my pretty sister; but I am called, and I must go!" They were not tears of agony that wetted his young mother's cheek, as the spirit departed from her embrace that had been entrusted to it.

Thus, the rustling of an Angel's wings got blended with the other echoes. Little Lucie, comically studious at the task of the morning, or dressing a doll at her mother's footstool, chattered in the tongues of the Two Cities that were blended in her life.

The Echoes rarely answered to the actual tread of Sydney Carton. Some half-dozen times a year, at most, he claimed his privilege of coming in uninvited, and would sit among them through the evening, as he had once done often. He never came there heated with wine. And one other thing regarding him was whispered in the echoes, which has been whispered by all true echoes for ages and ages.

No man ever really loved a woman, lost her, and knew her with a blameless though an unchanged mind, when she was a wife and a mother, but her children had a strange sympathy with him. Carton was the first stranger to whom little Lucie held out her chubby arms, and he kept his place with her as she grew. The little boy had spoken of him, almost at the last. "Poor Carton! Kiss him for me!"

These were among the echoes to which Lucie, sometimes pensive, sometimes amused and laughing, listened in the echoing corner, until her little daughter was six years old.

But, there were other echoes, from a distance, that rumbled menacingly in the corner all through this space of time. And it was now, about little Lucie's sixth birthday, that they began to have an awful sound, as of a great storm in France with a dreadful sea rising.

On a night in mid-July, 1789, Mr Lorry came in late, from Tellson's, and sat himself down by Lucie and her husband in the dark window. It was a hot, wild night.

"I began to think," said Mr Lorry, pushing his brown wig back, "that I should have to pass the night at Tellson's. We have been so full of business all day, that we have not known what to do first, or which way to turn. There is such an uneasiness in Paris and positively a mania among some of our customers there for sending their property to England."

"That has a bad look," said Darnay.

"A bad look, you say, my dear Darnay? Yes, but we don't know what reason there is in it. People are so unreasonable! Some of us at Tellson's are getting old, and we really can't be troubled out of the ordinary course without due occasion."

"Still," said Darnay, "you know how gloomy and threatening the sky is."

"I know that, to be sure," agreed Mr Lorry, trying to persuade himself that his sweet temper was soured, and that he grumbled, "but I am determined to be peevish after my long day's botheration. Where is Manette?"

"Here he is," said the Doctor, entering the dark room at the moment.

"The precious child is safe in bed?"

"And sleeping soundly."

"That's right; all safe and well! I don't know why anything should be otherwise than safe and well here, thank God; but I have been so put out all day, and I am not as young as I was!"

Saint Antoine had been, that morning, a vast dusky mass of scarecrows heaving to and fro, with frequent gleams of light above the billowy heads, where steel blades and bayonets shone in the sun. A tremendous roar arose from the throat of Saint Antoine, and a forest of naked arms struggled in the air like shrivelled branches. Fingers convulsively clutched at every weapon or semblance of a weapon that was thrown up from the depths below, no matter how far off.

Who gave them out, whence they last came, where they began, through what agency they crookedly quivered and jerked, scores at a time, over the heads of the crowd, like a kind of lightning, no eye in the throng could have told. But, muskets were being distributed – so were cartridges, powder, and ball, bars of iron and wood, knives, axes, pikes, every weapon that distracted ingenuity could discover or devise. People who could lay hold of nothing else, set themselves with bleeding hands to force stones and bricks out of their places in walls. Every pulse and heart in Saint Antoine was on high-fever strain and at high-fever heat. Every living creature there held life as of no account, and was demented with a passionate readiness to sacrifice it.

All this raging circled round Defarge's wine shop, and Defarge himself, already begrimed with gunpowder and sweat, issued orders, issued arms.

"Keep near to me, Jacques Three," cried Defarge; "and do you, Jacques One and Two, separate and put yourselves at the head of as many of these patriots as you can. Where is my wife?"

"Eh, well! Here you see me!" said Madame, composed as ever, but not knitting. Madame's right hand was occupied with an axe, and in her girdle were a pistol and a cruel knife.

"Where do you go, my wife?"

"I go," said Madame, "with you at present. You shall see me at the head of women, by-and-by."

"Come, then!" cried Defarge, in a resounding voice. "Patriots and friends, we are ready! The Bastille!"

With a roar that sounded as if all the breath in France had been shaped into the detested word, the living sea rose, wave on wave, depth on depth, and overflowed the city to that point. Alarm-bells ringing, drums beating, the sea raging and thundering on its new beach, the attack began.

Deep ditches, double drawbridge, massive stone walls, eight great towers, cannon, muskets, fire and smoke. Through the fire and through the smoke – in the fire and in the smoke, for the sea cast him up against a cannon, and on the instant he became a cannonier – Defarge of the wine shop worked like a manful soldier.

Deep ditch, single drawbridge, massive stone walls, eight great towers, cannon, muskets, fire and smoke. One drawbridge down!

"Work, comrades all, work! Work, Jacques One, Jacques Two, Jacques One Thousand, Jacques Two Thousand, Jacques Five-and-Twenty Thousand; in the name of all the Angels or the Devils – whichever you prefer – work!"

"To me, women!" cried Madame Defarge. "We can kill as well as the men when the place is taken!" And to her, with a thirsty cry, trooping women variously armed, but all armed in hunger and revenge.

A white flag from within the fortress, and a parley – suddenly the sea rose immeasurably wider and higher. Defarge of the wine shop was swept over the lowered drawbridge, past the massive stone outer walls, in among the eight great towers – surrendered!

The force of the ocean bearing him on, made drawing breath or turning his head virtually impossible, until he was landed in the outer courtyard of the Bastille. There, against an angle of a wall, he made a struggle to look about him. Jacques Three was nearly at his side; Madame Defarge, still heading some of her women, was visible in the inner distance, knife in hand. Everywhere was tumult, exultation, deafening and maniacal bewilderment and astounding noise.

"The Prisoners!"

"The Records!"

"The secret cells!"

"The instruments of torture!"

"The Prisoners!"

Of all these cries, "The Prisoners!" was the cry most taken up by the sea that rushed in. The foremost billows rolled past, bearing the prison officers with them, and threatening them all with instant death if any secret nook remained undisclosed. Defarge laid his strong hand on the breast of one of these men and separated him from the rest, and got him between himself and the wall.

"Show me the North Tower!" said Defarge. "Quick!"

"I will faithfully," replied the man. " But there is no one there."

"What is the meaning of One Hundred and Five, North Tower?" asked Defarge.

"Monsieur, it is a cell."

"Show it me!"

"Pass this way, then."

Jacques Three, disappointed by the dialogue taking a turn that did not seem to promise bloodshed, held by Defarge's arm as he held by the turnkey's. Through gloomy vaults where the light of day had never shone, past hideous doors of dark dens and cages, down cavernous flights of steps, and again up steep rugged ascents of stone and brick, more like dry waterfalls than staircases, Defarge, the turnkey, and Jacques Three, went with all speed. When they had done descending, and were winding and climbing up a tower, they were finally alone. Hemmed in here by the massive thickness of walls and arches, the storm within the fortress and without was only audible to them in a dull way.

The turnkey stopped at a low door, put a key in a clashing lock, swung the door slowly open, and said, as they all bent their heads and passed in: "One Hundred and Five, North Tower!"

There was a small, heavily grated, unglazed window high in the wall. There was a small chimney, heavily barred across, a few feet within. There was a stool, and table, and a straw bed. There were the four blackened walls, and a rusted iron ring in one of them.

"Pass that torch slowly along these walls, that I may see them," said Defarge to the turnkey.

The man obeyed, and Defarge followed the light closely.

"Stop! Look here, Jacques!"

"A. M.!" croaked Jacques Three, as he read greedily.

"Alexandre Manette," said Defarge in his ear, following the letters with his forefinger. "And here he wrote 'a poor physician.' What is that in your hand? A crowbar? Give it me!"

He crawled upon the hearth, and, peering up the chimney, struck and prised at its sides with the crowbar, and worked at the iron grating across it. In a few minutes, some mortar and dust came dropping down, which he averted his face to avoid. In a crevice in the chimney into which his weapon had slipped or wrought itself, he groped with a cautious touch.

"Collect everything together in the middle of the cell. So! Light them, you!"

The turnkey fired the little pile, which blazed high and hot. Stooping again to come out at the low-arched door, they left it burning, and retraced their way to the courtyard, seeming to recover their sense of hearing as they came down, until they were in the raging flood once more.

They found it surging in search of Defarge himself. Saint Antoine wanted its wine shop keeper foremost in the guard upon the governor who had defended the Bastille and shot the people. Otherwise, the governor would not be marched to the Hotel de Ville for judgement. Otherwise, the governor would escape, and the people's blood (suddenly of some value, after many years of worthlessness) would be unavenged.

There was but one quite steady figure, and that was a woman's. "See, there is my husband!" she cried, pointing him out. "See Defarge!" She stood immovable close to the grim old officer, and remained close to him. She remained close to him and he was almost at his destination, when the long gathering rain of stabs and blows fell heavy on him. He dropped dead under it, and she, suddenly animated, took her cruel knife and hewed off his head.

Now Saint Antoine was ready to execute his horrible idea of hoisting up men for lamps to show what he could be and do. "Lower the lamp yonder!" cried Saint Antoine, after glaring round for a new means of death; "here is one of his soldiers to be left on guard!" The swinging sentinel was posted, and the sea rushed on.

CHAPTER 19

Fire Rises

There was a change in the village where the fountain fell, and where the mender of roads went forth daily to hammer the stones on the highway. Far and wide lay a ruined country, yielding nothing but desolation. Every green leaf, every blade of grass and blade of grain, was as shrivelled and poor as the miserable people.

For scores of years gone by, Monseigneur had squeezed the countryside and wrung it, and had seldom graced it with his presence except for the pleasures of the chase.

As the mender of roads worked in the dust, he raised his eyes from his lonely labour, and saw a rough figure approaching on foot. It was a shaggy-haired man, of almost barbarian aspect, tall, in wooden shoes, rough, steeped in the mud and dust of many highways.

He came like a ghost at noon in the July weather, as he sat on his heap of stones under a bank, taking such shelter as he could get from a shower of hail.

The man looked at him, looked at the village in the hollow, at the mill, and at the prison on the crag.

"How goes it, Jacques?" he asked.

"All well, Jacques."

"Touch then!"

They joined hands, and the man sat down on the heap of stones.

"No dinner?"

"Nothing but supper now," said the mender of roads, with a hungry face.

"It is the fashion," growled the man. "I meet no dinner anywhere."

He took out a blackened pipe and lit it until it was a bright glow: he then dropped something into it from between his finger and thumb, that blazed and went out in a puff of smoke.

"Tonight?" said the mender of roads.

"Tonight," said the man, putting the pipe in his mouth.

"Where?"

"Here. When do you cease to work?"

"At sunset."

"Will you wake me, before departing? I have walked two nights without resting. Let me finish my pipe, and I shall sleep like a child. Will you wake me?"

"Surely."

The wayfarer slipped off his great wooden shoes, and lay down on his back on the heap of stones. He was fast asleep directly.

The road-mender seemed fascinated by the figure on the heap of stones. His eyes were so often turned towards it, that he used his tools mechanically. The traveller had travelled far; his great shoes, stuffed with leaves and grass, had been heavy to drag over the many long leagues, and his clothes were chafed into holes, as he himself was into sores. When he lifted his eyes from the man to the horizon, he saw in his small fancy similar figures, stopped by no obstacle, tending to centres all over France.

The man slept on until the sun was low in the west, and the sky was glowing. Then the mender of roads roused him.

"Good!" said the sleeper, rising on his elbow. "Two leagues beyond the summit of the hill?"

"About."

"About. Good!"

The mender of roads was soon at the fountain, squeezing himself in among the lean cattle brought there to drink. When the village had taken its poor supper, it did not creep to bed, as it usually did, but came out of doors again, and remained there looking in one direction only. Monsieur Gabelle, chief functionary of the place, became uneasy. He went out on his housetop alone, and looked in the same direction as the villagers. He glanced down from behind his chimneys at the darkening faces by the fountain below.

The night deepened. The trees surrounding the old château moved in a rising wind. Up the two terrace flights of steps the rain ran wildly, and beat at the great door, like a swift messenger rousing those within. East,

West, North, and South, through the woods, four heavy-treading, unkempt figures crushed the high grass and cracked the branches, striding on cautiously to come together in the courtyard. Four lights broke out there, and moved away in different directions, and all was black again.

But, not for long. Presently, the château began to make itself strangely visible by some light of its own, as though growing luminous. Then, a flickering streak played behind the architecture of the front, picking out transparent places, and showing where balustrades, arches, and windows were. Then it soared higher, and grew broader and brighter. Soon, from a score of the great windows, flames burst forth, and the stone faces awakened, stared out of fire.

Only a few people were left there – a horse was saddled and ridden away. It splashed through the darkness, finally stopping by the village fountain, and the foaming horse stood at Monsieur Gabelle's door. "Help, Gabelle! Help, every one!" A bell rang impatiently, but there was no other help. The mender of roads, and two hundred and fifty particular friends, stood with folded arms at the fountain, looking at the pillar of fire in the sky. "It must be forty feet high," said they, grimly; and never moved.

The rider clattered away through the village, to the prison on the crag. "Help, gentlemen-officers! The château is on fire; valuable objects may be saved from the flames! Help, help!" The officers at the gate looked towards the soldiers who looked at the fire; gave no orders and answered, "it must burn."

The château was left to itself. With the rising and falling of the blaze, the stone faces showed as if they were in torment. One face became obscured: anon struggled out of the smoke again, as if it were the face of the cruel Marquis, burning at the stake.

The château burned; the nearest trees scorched and shrivelled; trees at a distance, fired by the four fierce figures, begirt the blazing edifice with a new forest of smoke. Molten lead and iron boiled in the marble basin of the fountain; the water ran dry. Great rents and splits branched out in the solid walls; stupefied birds wheeled about and dropped into the furnace; four fierce figures trudged away, East, West, North, and South, guided by the beacon they had lighted, towards their next destination.

The village had surrounded Gabelle's house, summoning him forth for personal conference. He barred his door, and again withdrew to his housetop; this time resolved, if his door were broken in, to pitch himself head foremost over the parapet, and crush a man or two below.

He passed a long night up there, with the distant château for fire and candle, and the beating at his door for music. But, the friendly dawn appeared at last, and the people happily dispersed. Monsieur Gabelle came down.

Within a hundred miles, and in the light of other fires, there were other functionaries less fortunate, that night and other nights. The rising sun found them hanging across once-peaceful streets, where they had been born and bred. There were other villagers and townspeople less fortunate than the mender of roads and his fellows, upon whom the functionaries and soldiery turned with success, and whom they strung up in their turn. But the fierce figures were steadily wending East, West, North, and South.

CHAPTER 20

Drawn to the Loadstone Rock

Little Lucie had had three more birthdays while the angry ocean flowed, knowing no ebb.

The shining Bull's Eye of the Court was gone. The Court, from that exclusive inner circle to its outermost rotten ring of intrigue and corruption, was all gone together. Royalty was gone; had been besieged in its Palace and "suspended," when the last tidings came over.

The August of the year 1792 arrived, and Monseigneur was by this time scattered far and wide.

As was natural, the headquarters and great gathering place of Monseigneur, in London, was Tellson's Bank. It was the spot to which such French intelligence as was most to be relied upon, came quickest. Those nobles who had seen the coming storm in time, and anticipating plunder or confiscation, had made provident remittances to Tellson's, were always to be heard of there by their needy brethren. To which it must be added that every newcomer from France reported himself and his tidings at Tellson's, almost as a matter of course. Tellson's was therefore, to French intelligence, a kind of High Exchange. This was so well known that Tellson's sometimes wrote the latest news out in a line or so and posted it in the Bank windows, for all to read.

On a steaming, misty afternoon, Mr Lorry sat at his desk, and Charles Darnay stood leaning on it, talking with him.

"I understand that I am too old?" said Mr Lorry.

"A long journey, uncertain means of travelling, a disorganised country, a city that may not be even safe for you."

"My dear Charles," said Mr Lorry, with cheerful confidence, "you touch some of the reasons for my going. It is safe enough for me; nobody will care to interfere with an old fellow of nearly eighty when there are so many people there much better worth interfering with. And if it were not a disorganised city there would be no need to send somebody to our House there. As to the uncertain travelling and the long journey – if I were not prepared to submit myself to a few inconveniences for the sake of Tellson's, after all these years, who ought to be?"

"I wish I were going myself," said Charles Darnay, somewhat restlessly.

"Indeed! You are a pretty fellow to object and advise!" exclaimed Mr Lorry. "You wish you were going yourself? And you a Frenchman born? You are a wise counsellor."

"My dear Mr Lorry, it is because I am a Frenchman born, that the thought has passed through my mind often. One cannot help thinking, having had some sympathy for the miserable people, and having abandoned something to them," he spoke here in his former thoughtful manner, "that one might be listened to, and might have the power to persuade to some restraint."

"The truth is, my dear Charles," Mr Lorry lowered his voice, "you can have no conception of the difficulty with which our business is transacted, and of the peril in which our books and papers over yonder are involved. Shall I hang back, because I am a little stiff about the joints? Why, I am a boy, sir, to half a dozen old codgers here!"

"How I admire your youthful spirit, Mr Lorry."

"Nonsense, sir! And, my dear Charles," said Mr Lorry, "you are to remember, that getting things out of Paris at this present time, no matter what things, is next to an impossibility. At another time, our parcels would come and go, as easily as in business-like Old England; but now, everything is stopped."

"And do you really go tonight?"

"I really go tonight, for the case has become too pressing to admit of delay."

"And do you take no one with you?"

"I intend to take Jerry. Jerry has been my bodyguard on Sunday nights for a long time past and I am used to him. Nobody will suspect Jerry of being anything but an English bull-dog, or of having any design in his head but to fly at anybody who touches his master."

"I must say again that I heartily admire your gallantry and youthfulness."

"I must say again, nonsense, nonsense! When I have executed this little commission, I shall, perhaps, accept Tellson's proposal to retire and live at my ease. Time enough, then, to think about growing old."

This dialogue had taken place at Mr Lorry's usual desk, with Monseigneur swarming within a yard or two of it, boastful of what he would do to avenge himself on the rascal-people before long.

The House approached Mr Lorry, and laying a soiled and unopened letter before him, asked if he had yet discovered any traces of the person to whom it was addressed? The House laid the letter down so close to Darnay that he saw the direction – the more quickly because it was his own right name. The address, turned into English, ran:

"Very pressing. To Monsieur heretofore the Marquis St Evrémonde, of France. Confided to the cares of Messrs. Tellson and Co., Bankers, London, England."

On the marriage morning, Doctor Manette had made it his one urgent and express request to Charles Darnay, that the secret of this name should be – unless he, the Doctor, dissolved the obligation – kept just between them. Nobody else knew it to be his name; his own wife had no idea; Mr Lorry could have none.

"No," said Mr Lorry, in reply to the House. "I believe I have asked everybody now here, and no one can tell me where this gentleman is to be found."

It was near to closing time in the Bank and Mr Lorry held the letter out inquiringly. This Monseigneur looked at it, that Monseigneur looked at it. This, That, and The Other, all had something disparaging to say, in French or in English, concerning the Marquis who was not to be found.

"A nephew, I believe of the Marquis who was murdered," said one. "Happy to say, I never knew him."

"A coward who abandoned his post," said another (who had been got out of Paris, legs uppermost and half suffocated, in a load of hay), "some years ago."

"Set himself in opposition to the last Marquis, abandoned the estates when he inherited them, and left them to the ruffian herd. They will recompense him now, I hope, as he deserves."

Darnay, unable to restrain himself any longer said: "I know the fellow."

"Will you take charge of the letter?" said Mr Lorry. "You know where to deliver it?"

"I do."

"Will you undertake to explain, that we suppose it to have been addressed here, on the chance of our knowing where to forward it, and that it has been here some time?"

"I will do so. Do you start for Paris from here?"

"From here, at eight."

"I will come back, to see you off."

Very ill at ease, Darnay made the best of his way into the quiet of the Temple, opened the letter, and read it. These were its contents:

"Prison of the Abbaye, Paris. June 21, 1792.

Monsieur heretofore the Marquis.

I have been seized, and brought to Paris. My house has been destroyed.

The crime for which I am imprisoned is, they tell me, treason against the majesty of the people, in that I have acted against them for an emigrant. It is in vain I say that I have acted for them, and not against, according to your commands. And that I tell them that I had collected no rent. The only response is, that I have acted for an emigrant, and where is that emigrant?

Ah! Most gracious Monsieur heretofore the Marquis, where is that emigrant? I cry in my sleep where is he? I send my desolate cry across the sea, hoping it may perhaps reach your ears.

For the love of Heaven, I beg you, Monsieur, to help and release me. My fault is that I have been true to you. I pray you be you true to me!

From this prison of horror, whence I every hour tend nearer to destruction, I send you, Monsieur, the assurance of my dolorous and unhappy service.

Your afflicted Gabelle."

The peril of an old servant and a good one, whose only crime was fidelity to himself and his family, stared him in the face.

He knew very well, that in his horror of the deed that had given the old family name such a bad reputation, and in his resentful suspicions of his uncle, he had acted imperfectly. He knew very well, that in his love for Lucie, his renunciation of his social place, had been hurried and incomplete. He knew that he ought to have systematically worked it out and supervised it, and that he had meant to do it, and that it had never been done.

The happiness of his chosen English home, the necessity of being always actively employed, the swift changes and troubles of the time which had followed on one another so fast; he knew very well, that to the force of these circumstances he had yielded. That he had watched the times for a time of action, and that they had shifted and struggled until the time had gone by. The nobility were trooping from France by every highway and byway, and their property was in course of confiscation and destruction, and their very names were blotting out.

But he had oppressed no man, he had imprisoned no man. Monsieur Gabelle had held the impoverished estate on his own written instructions, to spare the people, to give them what little there was to give – such fuel as the heavy creditors would let them have in the winter. Such produce as could be saved from the same grip in the summer.

Charles Darnay would go to Paris.

The Loadstone Rock was drawing him to itself, and he must go. He was uneasy that bad aims were being worked out in his own unhappy land by bad instruments. And he who could not fail to know that he was better than they, was not there, trying to do something to stay bloodshed, and assert the claims of mercy and humanity. And now he had Gabelle's letter: the appeal of an innocent prisoner, in danger of death, to his justice, honour, and good name.

His resolution was made. He must go to Paris.

Yes. The Loadstone Rock was drawing him, and he must sail on, until he struck. He saw hardly any danger. His intentions with which he had done what he had done, even though he had left it incomplete, he felt would be gratefully acknowledged in France if he was there to justify them. Then, that glorious vision of doing good, arose before him, and he even saw himself in the illusion with some influence to guide this raging Revolution that was running so fearfully wild.

His resolution made, he considered that neither Lucie nor her father must know of it until he was gone. Lucie should be spared the pain of separation; and her father, always reluctant to turn his thoughts towards the dangerous ground of old, should come to the knowledge of the step, as a step taken.

He walked until it was time to return to Tellson's and take leave of Mr Lorry. As soon as he arrived in Paris he would present himself to this old friend, but say nothing of his intention now.

A carriage with post-horses was ready at the Bank door, and Jerry was booted and equipped.

"I have delivered that letter," said Charles Darnay to Mr Lorry. "I would not consent to your being charged with any written answer, but perhaps you will take a verbal one?"

"That I will, and readily," said Mr Lorry, "if it is not dangerous."

"Not at all. Though it is to a prisoner in the Abbaye."

"What is his name?" said Mr Lorry, with his open pocket-book in his hand.

"Gabelle."

"Gabelle. And what is the message?"

"Simply, 'that he has received the letter, and will come.' "

"Any time mentioned?"

"He will start upon his journey tomorrow night."

"Any person mentioned?"

"No."

He helped Mr Lorry to wrap himself in a number of coats and cloaks, and went out with him from the warm atmosphere of the old Bank, into the misty air of Fleet Street. "My love to Lucie, and to little Lucie," said Mr Lorry at parting, "and take precious care of them till I come back." Charles Darnay shook his head and doubtfully smiled, as the carriage rolled away.

That night, the fourteenth of August, he sat up late, and wrote two fervent letters; one to Lucie, explaining the strong obligation he was under to go to Paris. The other was to the Doctor, consigning Lucie and their dear child to his care. To both, he wrote that he would despatch letters in proof of his safety, immediately after his arrival.

It was hard, that day of being among them. An affectionate glance at his wife made him resolute not to tell her what impended (he had been half moved to do it, so strange it was to him to act in anything without her quiet aid), and the day passed quickly. Early in the evening he embraced her, and her scarcely less dear namesake, pretending that he would return by-and-by (an imaginary engagement took him out, and he had secreted a valise of clothes ready), and so he emerged into the heavy mist of the heavy streets, with a heavier heart.

The unseen force was drawing him fast to itself. He left his two letters with a trusty porter, to be delivered half an hour before midnight, and no sooner; took horse for Dover; and began his journey. "For the love of Heaven!" was the poor prisoner's cry with which he strengthened his sinking heart.

BOOK 3

THE TRACK OF A STORM

CHAPTER 1

In Secret

The traveller fared slowly towards Paris from England in the autumn of the year 1792. Bad roads, bad equipages, and bad horses, managed to delay him but the changed times were fraught with other obstacles. Every town-gate and village taxing-house had its band of citizen-patriots, with their national muskets in a most explosive state of readiness, who stopped all comers and goers. They questioned them, inspected their papers or looked for their names in lists of their own. They turned them back, or sent them on, or stopped them and held on to them as their capricious judgement or fancy deemed best for the dawning Republic One and Indivisible, of Liberty, Equality, Fraternity, or Death.

A very few French leagues of his journey were accomplished, when Charles Darnay began to realise that there was no hope of return until he was declared a good citizen at Paris. Whatever might befall now, he must on to his journey's end. Every common barrier that dropped across the road behind him, he knew to be another iron door in the series that was barred between him and England.

The universal watchfulness stopped him on the highway twenty times in a stage, slowing his progress twenty times in a day, by riding after him and taking him back, riding before him and stopping him by anticipation, riding with him and keeping him in charge. He had been days upon his journey, when he went to bed tired out, in a little town on the high road, still a long way from Paris.

Nothing but the production of Gabelle's letter from his prison would have got him so far. He was, therefore, not surprised to find himself awakened in the middle of the night by a functionary.

"Emigrant, I am going to send you on to Paris, under an escort."

"Citizen, I desire nothing more than to get to Paris, though I could dispense with the escort."

"Silence!" growled a red-cap, striking at the coverlet with the butt-end of his musket. "Peace, aristocrat!"

"It is as the good patriot says," observed the timid functionary – "You are an aristocrat, and must have an escort – and must pay for it."

"I have no choice," said Charles Darnay.

"Rise and dress yourself, emigrant."

Darnay complied, and was taken back to the guard-house. Here he paid a heavy price for his escort, and hence he started with it on the wet roads at three o'clock in the morning.

The escort were two mounted patriots in red caps and tri-coloured cockades, armed with national muskets and sabres, riding one on either side of him. A loose line was attached to his bridle, the end of which one of the patriots kept girded round his wrist. In this state they traversed all the leagues that lay between them and the capital.

They travelled in the night, halting an hour or two after daybreak, and lying by until the twilight fell. The escort were so wretchedly clothed, that they twisted straw round their bare legs, and thatched their ragged shoulders to keep the wet off. Charles Darnay did not allow the restraint that was laid upon him to awaken any serious fears in his breast.

But when they came to the town of Beauvais he could not ignore the fact that affairs were very alarming. An ominous crowd gathered to see him dismount and many voices called out loudly, "Down with the emigrant!"

He stayed in the saddle and said: "Emigrant, my friends! Do you not see me here, in France, of my own will?"

"You are a cursed emigrant," cried a farrier, making at him, hammer in hand, "and a cursed aristocrat!"

The postmaster interposed himself and soothingly said, "Let him be! He will be judged at Paris."

"Judged!" repeated the farrier, swinging his hammer. "Ay! And condemned as a traitor." At this the crowd roared approval.

As soon as he could make his voice heard Darnay said: "Friends, you deceive yourselves. I am no traitor."

"He lies!" cried the smith. "He is a traitor since the decree. His life is forfeit to the people. His cursed life is not his own!"

The postmaster instantly turned his horse into the yard and barred the crazy double gates. The farrier struck a blow upon them with his hammer, and the crowd groaned; but no more was done.

"What is this decree that the smith spoke of?" Darnay asked the postmaster, when he had thanked him.

"Truly, a decree for selling the property of emigrants."

"When passed?"

"The fourteenth."

"The day I left England!"

"Everybody says it is but one of several, and that there will be others – if there are not already – banishing all emigrants, and condemning all to death who return. That is what he meant when he said your life was not your own."

"But there are no such decrees yet?"

"What do I know!" said the postmaster, shrugging his shoulders; "there may be, or there will be. It is all the same."

They rode forward again when the town was asleep. They passed on, jingling through impoverished fields that had yielded no fruits that year.

Daylight at last found them before the wall of Paris. The barrier was closed and strongly guarded when they rode up to it.

"Where are the papers of this prisoner?" demanded a resolute-looking man in authority.

Naturally struck by the disagreeable word, Charles Darnay pointed out that he was a free traveller and French citizen, in charge of an escort which the disturbed state of the country had imposed upon him, and which he had paid for.

"Where," repeated the same personage, without taking notice, "are the papers of this prisoner?"

The patriot had them in his cap, and produced them. Casting his eyes over Gabelle's letter, the same personage in authority showed some disorder and surprise, and looked at Darnay with a close attention.

He left escort and escorted without saying a word, and went into the guard room. Meanwhile, they sat upon their horses outside the gate. Looking about him, Charles Darnay observed that the gate was guarded by both soldiers and patriots – the latter far outnumbering the former. And ingress into the city for peasants' carts bringing in supplies, and for similar traffic and traffickers, was easy enough, whereas egress, even for the homeliest people, was very difficult. Some knew their turn for examination to be so far off, that they loitered about. The red cap and tricolour cockade were universal, both among men and women.

When he had sat in his saddle some half-hour, taking note of these things, Darnay found himself confronted by the same man in authority, who directed the guard to open the barrier. Then he delivered to the escort a receipt for the escorted. Charles Darnay was told to dismount. The two patriots, leading his tired horse, turned and rode away without entering the city.

He accompanied his conductor into a guard-room, smelling of common wine and tobacco. Some registers were lying open on a desk, and an officer of a coarse, dark aspect, presided over these.

"Citizen Defarge," said he to Darnay's conductor, as he took a slip of paper to write on. "Is this the emigrant Evrémonde?"

"This is the man."

"Your age, Evrémonde?"

"Thirty-seven."

"Married, Evrémonde?"

"Yes."

"Where is your wife, Evrémonde?"

"In England."

"You are consigned, Evrémonde, to the prison of La Force."

"Just Heaven!" exclaimed Darnay. "Under what law, and for what offence?"

The officer looked up from his slip of paper for a moment.

"We have new laws, Evrémonde, and new offences, since you were here."

" I have come here voluntarily, in response to that written appeal of a fellow-countryman. I demand no more than the opportunity to help him without delay. Is not that my right?"

"Emigrants have no rights, Evrémonde," was the stolid reply. The officer wrote until he had finished, sanded it, and handed it to Defarge, with the words "In secret."

Defarge motioned with the paper to the prisoner that he must accompany him. The prisoner obeyed, and a guard of two armed patriots attended them.

"Did you," said Defarge, in a low voice, as they went down the guardhouse steps and turned into Paris, "marry the daughter of Doctor Manette, once a prisoner in the Bastille that is no more?"

"Yes," replied Darnay, looking at him with surprise.

"My name is Defarge, and I keep a wine shop in the Quarter Saint Antoine. Possibly you have heard of me."

"My wife came to your house to reclaim her father? Yes!"

The word "wife" seemed to serve as a gloomy reminder to Defarge, to say with sudden impatience, "In the name of La Guillotine, why did you come to France?"

"You heard me say why, a minute ago. Do you not believe it is the truth?"

"A bad truth for you," said Defarge, speaking with knitted brows, and looking straight before him.

"Indeed I am lost here. All here is so unprecedented, so changed, so sudden and unfair, that I am absolutely lost. Will you render me a little help?"

"None." Defarge spoke, always looking straight before him.

"Will you answer me a single question?"

"Perhaps. According to its nature. You can say what it is."

"In this prison that I am going to so unjustly, shall I have some free communication with the world outside? I am not to be buried there, prejudged, and without any means of presenting my case?"

"You will see. But other people have been similarly buried in worse prisons, before now."

"But never by me, Citizen Defarge."

Defarge glanced darkly at him, and walked on in silence. The deeper he sank into this silence, the fainter hope there was – or so Darnay thought – of his softening. He, therefore, quickly said, "It is of the utmost importance to me, that I communicate to Mr Lorry of Tellson's Bank, an English gentleman here in Paris, the simple fact, that I have been thrown into La Force. Can that be done?"

"My duty," Defarge doggedly rejoined, "is to my country and the People. I am the sworn servant of both. I will do nothing for you."

Charles Darnay felt it hopeless to entreat him further. As they walked on in silence, he realised the people were used to the spectacle of prisoners passing along the streets. A few passers turned their heads, and a few shook their fingers at him as an aristocrat. In one narrow, dark, and dirty street, an excited orator, mounted on a stool, was addressing an excited audience on the crimes against the people, of the king and the royal family. The few words he heard made it known to Charles Darnay that the king was in prison. On the road (except at Beauvais) he had heard absolutely nothing.

That he had fallen among far greater dangers than those which had developed themselves when he left England, he of course knew now. He had to admit that he might nòt have made this journey, if he could have foreseen the events of a few days. And yet, troubled as the future was, it was the unknown future, and in its obscurity there was ignorant hope. "La Guillotine," was hardly known to him, or to most people, by name. The frightful deeds that were soon to be done, were probably unimagined at that time in the brains of the doers. How could they have a place in the shadowy conceptions of a gentle mind?

Of unjust treatment in detention and hardship, and in cruel separation from his wife and child, he foresaw the likelihood but, beyond this, he dreaded nothing distinctly. He arrived at the prison of La Force.

A man with a bloated face opened the strong wicket, to whom Defarge presented "The Emigrant Evrémonde."

"What the Devil! How many more of them!" exclaimed the man.

The prison of La Force was gloomy, dark and filthy, with a horrible smell of foul sleep in it.

"In secret, too," grumbled the gaoler, looking at the written paper. "As if I was not already full to bursting!"

He stuck the paper on a file, and Charles Darnay awaited his further pleasure for half an hour.

"Come!" said the chief, at length taking up his keys, "come with me, emigrant."

Through the dismal prison twilight, his new charge accompanied him by corridor and staircase, until they came into a large, low, vaulted chamber, crowded with prisoners of both sexes. The women were reading and writing, knitting and sewing; the men for the most part stood behind their chairs.

The crowning unreality of his long unreal ride, was, they all at once rose to receive him. So strangely clouded were these refinements by the prison manners and gloom, so spectral did they become in the inappropriate squalor and misery through which they were seen, that Charles Darnay seemed to stand in a company of the dead. Ghosts all! All turned on him eyes that were changed by the death they had died in coming there.

It struck him motionless. The gaoler at his side, and the other gaolers moving about, looked extravagantly coarse compared to the sorrowing mothers and blooming daughters who were there. Surely, ghosts all.

"In the name of the assembled companions in misfortune," said a gentleman, coming forward, "I have the honour of giving you welcome to La Force. It would be an impertinence elsewhere, but it is not so here, to ask your name and condition?"

Charles Darnay roused himself, and answered.

"But I hope," said the gentleman, following the chief gaoler with his eyes, who moved across the room, "that you are not in secret?"

"I do not understand the meaning of the term, but I have heard them say so."

"Ah, what a pity! But take courage; several members of our society have been in secret, at first, and it has lasted but a short time." Then he added, raising his voice, "I grieve to inform the society – in secret."

There was a murmur of commiseration as Charles Darnay crossed the room to a grated door where the gaoler awaited him, and many voices gave him good wishes and encouragement. He turned at the grated door, to render the thanks of his heart; it closed under the gaoler's hand; and the apparitions vanished from his sight forever.

The wicket opened on a stone staircase, leading upward. When they had ascended forty steps, the gaoler opened a low black door, and they passed into a solitary cell. It struck cold and damp, but was not dark.

"Yours," said the gaoler.

"Why am I confined alone?"

"How do I know!"

"I can buy pen, ink, and paper?"

"Such are not my orders. You will be visited, and can ask then. At present, you may buy your food, and nothing more."

There were in the cell, a chair, a table, and a straw mattress. When the gaoler was gone, he thought, "Now am I left, as if I were dead." The prisoner walked to and fro in his cell, counting its measurement, and the roar of the city arose like muffled drums. "He made shoes, he made shoes, he made shoes." The prisoner paced faster, to draw his mind with him from that latter repetition. "He made shoes, he made shoes, he made shoes. Five paces by four and a half." With such scraps the prisoner walked faster and faster, obstinately counting and counting.

CHAPTER 2

The Grindstone

Tellson's Bank, established in the Saint Germain Quarter of Paris, was in a wing of a large house, approached by a courtyard and shut off from the street by a high wall. The house belonged to a great nobleman who had lived in it until he made a flight from the troubles, in his own cook's dress, and got across the borders.

What money would be drawn out of Tellson's, and what would lie there, lost and forgotten; what plate and jewels would tarnish in Tellson's hiding-places, while the depositors rusted in prisons; how many accounts with Tellson's never to be balanced in this world, must be carried over into the next; no man could have said. Mr Jarvis Lorry sat by a newly lighted wood fire, and on his courageous face there was a shade of horror.

He occupied rooms in the Bank. On the opposite side of the courtyard, under a colonnade, was extensive standing for carriages. Against two of the pillars were fastened two great flaring flambeaux, and in the light of these, was a large grindstone.

From the streets beyond the high wall, there came the usual night hum of the city.

"Thank God," said Mr Lorry, clasping his hands, "that no one near and dear to me is in this dreadful town tonight. May He have mercy on all who are in danger!"

Soon afterwards, the bell at the great gate sounded, and he thought, "They have come back!" and sat listening. But, there was no loud irruption into the courtyard, as he had expected, and he heard the gate clash again, and all was quiet.

The Bank was well guarded, and he got up to go among the trusty people who were watching it, when his door suddenly opened, and two figures rushed in, at sight of which he fell back in amazement.

Lucie and her father! Lucie with her arms stretched out to him, and with that old look of earnestness stamped upon her face.

"What is this?" cried Mr Lorry, breathless and confused. "Lucie! Manette! What has happened? What has brought you here?"

She panted out in his arms, imploringly, "O my dear friend! My husband! Charles!"

"What of Charles?"

"Here."

"Here, in Paris?"

"Has been here some days. An errand of generosity brought him here unknown to us; he was stopped at the barrier, and sent to prison."

The old man uttered an irrepressible cry. Almost at the same moment, the bell of the great gate rang again, and a loud noise of feet and voices came pouring into the courtyard.

"What is that noise?" said the Doctor, turning towards the window.

"Don't look!" cried Mr Lorry. "Don't look out! Manette, for your life, don't touch the blind!"

The Doctor turned, with his hand upon the fastening of the window, and said, with a cool, bold smile: "My dear friend, I have a charmed life in this city. There is no patriot in Paris who, knowing me to have been a prisoner in the Bastille, would touch me, except to overwhelm me with embraces. My old pain has given me a power that has brought us through the barrier, and gained us news of Charles, and brought us here. I knew it would be so, that I could help Charles out of all danger; I told Lucie so – What is that noise?" His hand was again upon the window.

"Don't look!" cried Mr Lorry, absolutely desperate. "No, Lucie, my dear, nor you!" He got his arm round her, and held her. "I solemnly swear to you that I know of no harm having happened to Charles; that I had no suspicion even of his being in this fatal place. What prison is he in?"

"La Force!"

"La Force! Lucie, my child, if ever you were brave in your life you will compose yourself now, to do exactly as I bid you. You must let me put you in a room at the back here. You must leave your father and me alone for two minutes."

"I will be submissive to you. I see in your face that you know I can do nothing else than this. I know you are true."

The old man kissed her, and hurried her into his room; then, hurried back to the Doctor. Together they looked out into the courtyard.

Looked out upon a throng of men and women. The people in possession of the house had let them in at the gate, and they had rushed in to work at the grindstone; it had evidently been set up there for their purpose, as in a convenient and retired spot.

But, such awful workers, and such awful work!

The grindstone had a double handle, and, turning at it madly were two men. Their hideous countenances were all bloody and sweaty. Shouldering one another to get next at the sharpening-stone, were men stripped to the waist. Hatchets, knives, bayonets, swords, all brought to be sharpened, all red with blood. As the frantic wielders of these weapons snatched them from the stream of sparks and tore away into the streets the same red hue was in their frenzied eyes.

All this was seen in a moment. The Doctor looked for explanation in his friend's ashy face.

"They are," Mr Lorry whispered the words, glancing fearfully round at the locked room, "murdering the prisoners. If you really have the power you think you have make yourself known to these devils, and get taken to La Force. It may be too late, I don't know!"

Doctor Manette pressed his hand, hastened bareheaded out of the room, and was in the courtyard when Mr Lorry regained the blind.

His streaming white hair, and the impetuous confidence of his manner, carried him in an instant to the stone. For a few moments there was a pause and then Mr Lorry saw him, surrounded by all, hurried out with cries of, "Help for the Bastille prisoner's kindred in La Force! Room for the Bastille prisoner in front there! Save the prisoner Evrémonde at La Force!"

He closed the window and the curtain, hastened to Lucie, and told her that her father was assisted by the people, and gone in search of her husband.

CHAPTER 3

The Shadow

At first, Mr Lorry's mind turned to Defarge, and he thought of finding out the wine shop again and taking counsel with its master regarding a safe dwelling-place for Lucie. But he lived in the most violent Quarter, and doubtless was influential there, and deep in its dangerous workings.

Noon came, but not the Doctor. Mr Lorry talked with Lucie. She said that her father had spoken of hiring lodgings for a short term, near the

Banking-house. Mr Lorry went out in search of such lodgings. He found a suitable one, high up in a removed by-street.

To this lodging he at once took Lucie and her child, and Miss Pross. He left Jerry with them, as a figure to fill a doorway, and returned to his own occupations.

The day wore itself out, and him with it, until the Bank closed. He was again alone in his room, considering what to do next, when he heard a foot upon the stair. In a few moments, a man stood in his presence, who addressed him by his name.

"Your servant," said Mr Lorry. "Do you know me?"

He was a strongly made man with dark curling hair, from forty-five to fifty years of age. For answer he repeated, without any change of emphasis, the words: "Do you know me?"

"I have seen you somewhere."

"Perhaps at my wine shop?"

Much interested and agitated, Mr Lorry said: "You come from Doctor Manette?"

Defarge gave into his anxious hand, an open scrap of paper. It bore the words in the Doctor's writing: "Charles is safe. The bearer has a short note from Charles to his wife. Let the bearer see his wife." It was dated from La Force, within an hour.

"Will you accompany me," said Mr Lorry, "to where his wife resides?"

"Yes," returned Defarge.

They went down into the courtyard and found two women – one, knitting.

"Madame Defarge, surely!" said Mr Lorry, who had left her in exactly the same attitude some seventeen years ago.

"It is she," observed her husband.

"Does Madame go with us?" inquired Mr Lorry, seeing that she moved as they moved.

"Yes. That she may be able to recognise the faces and know the persons. It is for their safety."

Beginning to be struck by Defarge's manner, Mr Lorry looked dubiously at him, and led the way. Both the women followed – the second woman being The Vengeance.

They found Lucie weeping, alone. She clasped the hand that delivered her husband's note – little thinking what it had been doing near him in the night.

"*Dearest,* take courage. I am well, and your father has influence here. You cannot answer this. Kiss our child for me."

That was all the writing. It was so much that she turned and kissed one of the hands that knitted. The hand made no response, dropping cold and heavy to its knitting again.

Lucie stopped in the act of putting the note in her bosom, and looked terrified at Madame Defarge. Madame Defarge met the look with a cold, impassive stare.

"My dear, Madame Defarge wishes to see those whom she has the power to protect, so that she may identify them. I believe," said Mr Lorry, rather halting, "I state the case, Citizen Defarge?"

Defarge looked gloomily at his wife, and gave no other answer than a gruff sound of acquiescence.

"You had better, Lucie," said Mr Lorry, "have the dear child here, and our good Pross. Our good Pross, Defarge, is an English lady, and knows no French."

The lady in question, who was convinced that she was more than a match for any foreigner, appeared with folded arms.

"Is that his child?" said Madame Defarge, stopping and pointing her knitting needle at little Lucie as if it were the finger of Fate.

"Yes, madame," answered Mr Lorry; "this is our poor prisoner's darling daughter, and only child."

"It is enough, my husband," said Madame Defarge. "We may go."

Lucie put her hand on Madame Defarge's arm. "You will be good to my poor husband and do him no harm."

"Your husband is not my business here," returned Madame Defarge, looking down at her. "It is the daughter of your father who is my business here."

"For my sake, then, be merciful to my husband. We are more afraid of you than of these others."

Madame Defarge received it as a compliment, and looked at her husband.

"As a wife and mother," cried Lucie, most earnestly, "I implore you to have pity on me and not to exercise any power that you possess, against my innocent husband, but to use it in his behalf!"

Madame Defarge looked, coldly as ever, at Lucie, and said, turning to her friend The Vengeance: "All our lives, we have seen our sister-women suffer – poverty, nakedness, hunger, thirst, sickness, misery, oppression and neglect of all kinds."

"We have seen nothing else," returned The Vengeance.

"We have borne this a long time," said Madame Defarge, turning her eyes again upon Lucie. "Is it likely that the trouble of one wife and mother would be much to us now?"

She resumed her knitting and went out. The Vengeance followed. Defarge went last, and closed the door.

"Courage, my dear Lucie," said Mr Lorry. "So far all goes well with us. Much better than it has of late gone with many poor souls. Cheer up, and have a thankful heart."

"I am not thankless, I hope, but that dreadful woman seems to throw a shadow on me and on all my hopes."

"Tut, tut!" said Mr Lorry; "A shadow indeed! No substance in it, Lucie."

But the shadow of these Defarges was dark upon himself, and in his secret mind it troubled him greatly.

CHAPTER 4

Calm in Storm

Doctor Manette did not return until the morning of the fourth day of his absence. So much of what had happened in that dreadful time was kept from Lucie until long afterwards. Eleven hundred defenceless prisoners of both sexes and all ages had been killed by the populace. All she knew was that there had been an attack upon the prisons, and that some had been dragged out by the crowd and murdered.

To Mr Lorry, the Doctor communicated that the crowd had taken him through a scene of carnage to the prison of La Force. He had found a self-appointed Tribunal sitting, before which the prisoners were brought singly, and by which they were rapidly ordered to be put forth to be massacred, released, or (in a few cases) to be sent back to their cells. He had announced himself by name and profession as having been for eighteen years a secret prisoner in the Bastille. One of the body sitting in judgement had risen and identified him – that man was Defarge.

He had ascertained, through the registers on the table, that his son-in-law was among the living prisoners, and had pleaded hard to the Tribunal for his life and liberty. Charles Darnay was then brought before the lawless Court, and examined. He seemed on the point of being released, when the tide in his favour met with some unexplained check (not intelligible to the Doctor). There were a few words of secret conference. The President had then informed Doctor Manette that the prisoner must remain in safe custody. The prisoner was removed to the interior of the prison again.

As Mr Lorry received these confidences, and as he watched the face of his friend now sixty-two years of age, a misgiving arose within. But, he had never seen his friend in his present aspect. For the first time the Doctor felt, now, that his suffering was strength and power. For the first time he felt that in that sharp fire, he had slowly forged the iron which could break the prison door of his daughter's husband, and deliver him. "As my beloved child was helpful in restoring me to myself, I will be helpful now in restoring the dearest part of herself to her."

The Doctor kept himself in his place, as a physician, and was soon the inspecting physician of three prisons, among them La Force. He could assure Lucie that her husband was mixed with the general body of prisoners. He saw her husband weekly, and brought sweet messages to her, straight from his lips.

This new life of the Doctor's was an anxious life; still, the sagacious Mr Lorry saw that there was a new pride in it. The Doctor knew that up to that time, his imprisonment had been associated in the minds of his daughter and his friend, with his personal affliction, deprivation, and weakness. Now he knew himself to be invested with forces to which they both looked for Charles's ultimate safety and deliverance, he took the lead and direction, and required them to trust to him.

"All curious to see," thought Mr Lorry, in his amiably shrewd way, "but all natural and right; so, take the lead, my dear friend, and keep it; it couldn't be in better hands."

But, though the Doctor tried hard, and never ceased trying, to get Charles Darnay set at liberty, or at least to get him brought to trial, the public current of the time set too strong and fast for him.

The new era began – the king was tried, doomed, and beheaded; as was his wife. The Republic of Liberty, Equality, Fraternity, or Death, declared for victory or death against the world in arms; the black flag waved night and day from the great towers of Notre Dame.

A revolutionary tribunal in the capital, and forty or fifty thousand revolutionary committees all over the land, struck away all security for liberty or life, and delivered over any good and innocent person to any bad and guilty one. Prisons were gorged with people who had committed no offence, and could obtain no hearing. Above all, one hideous figure grew as familiar as if it had been before the general gaze from the foundations of the world – the figure of the sharp female called La Guillotine.

It was the popular theme for jests – the best cure for headache, it prevented the hair from turning grey, it imparted a peculiar delicacy to the complexion. Models of it were worn on the breast.

It sheared off heads so many, that it, and the ground it most polluted, were a rotten red. It was taken to pieces, like a toy-puzzle for a young Devil, and was put together again when the occasion wanted it. It hushed the eloquent, struck down the powerful, abolished the beautiful and good.

Among these terrors, the Doctor walked with a steady head: confident in his power, cautiously persistent in his end, never doubting that he would save Lucie's husband at last. Yet the current of the time swept by, so that Charles had lain in prison one year and three months when the Doctor was thus steady and confident. So much more wicked and distracted had the Revolution grown in that December month, that the rivers of the South were encumbered with the bodies of the violently drowned by night. Still, the Doctor walked among the terrors with a steady head.

Silent, humane, indispensable in hospital and prison, using his art equally among assassins and victims, he was a man apart. In the exercise of his skill, the appearance and the story of the Bastille Captive removed him from all other men. He was not suspected or brought in question, any more than if he had indeed been recalled to life some eighteen years before.

152

CHAPTER 5

The Wood-sawyer

One year and three months. During all that time Lucie was never sure, from hour to hour, but that the Guillotine would strike off her husband's head next day. Every day, through the stony streets, the tumbrils now jolted heavily, filled with Condemned. Lovely girls; bright women; youths; stalwart men and old; gentle born and peasant born; all red wine for La Guillotine, all daily brought into light from the dark cellars of the loathsome prisons, and carried to her through the streets to slake her devouring thirst.

As soon as they were established in their new residence, and her father had entered on this routine, Lucie arranged the little household as exactly as if her husband had been there. Little Lucie she taught, as regularly, as if they were in their English home.

She did not greatly alter in appearance. The plain dark dresses, akin to mourning dresses, which she and her child wore, were as neat and as well attended to as the brighter clothes of happy days. She lost her colour, and the old, intent expression was a constant, not an occasional, thing; otherwise, she remained very pretty. Sometimes, at night on kissing her father, she would burst into the grief she had repressed all day, and would say that her sole reliance was on him. He always answered: "Nothing can happen to him without my knowledge. I know I can save him, Lucie."

On coming home one evening her father said to her, "My dear, there is a window, which Charles can sometimes reach at three in the afternoon. He might see you in the street, he thinks, if you stood in a certain place. But you will not be able to see him, my poor child. Even if you could, it would be unsafe for you to make a sign of recognition."

"O show me the place, my father, and I will go there every day."

From that time, in all weathers, as the clock struck two, she was there, and at four she turned away. When it was not too wet her child went too; at other times she was alone; but she never missed a single day.

It was the corner of a small winding street. The hovel of a woodcutter was the only house at that end; all else was wall. On the third day of her being there, he noticed her.

"Good day, citizeness."

153

"Good day, citizen."

This mode of address was now prescribed by decree.

"Walking here again, citizeness?"

"You see me, citizen!"

The wood-sawyer cast a glance at the prison, pointed and putting his ten fingers before his face to represent bars, peeped through them.

"But it's not my business," said he. And went on sawing his wood.

While the wood-sawyer was at work, she was always in his sight. To secure his good will, she always spoke to him first, and often gave him drink-money, which he readily received.

In all weathers Lucie passed two hours of every day at this place; and every day on leaving it, she kissed the prison wall. Her husband saw her (so she learned from her father) maybe once in five or six times. It was enough that he could and did see her when the chances served.

These occupations brought her round to the December month, wherein her father walked among the terrors with a steady head. On a lightly snowing afternoon she arrived at the usual corner. Her father joined her in her vigil.

A footstep in the snow – Madame Defarge.

"I salute you, citizeness," from the Doctor.

"I salute you, citizen." This in passing. Nothing more. Madame Defarge gone, like a shadow over the white road.

"Give me your arm, my love. Pass from here with an air of cheerfulness and courage, for his sake." They left the spot. "Charles is summoned for tomorrow."

"For tomorrow!"

"There is no time to lose. I am well prepared, but there are precautions to be taken. He has not received the notice yet, but I know that he will presently be summoned for tomorrow, and removed to the Conciergerie; I have timely information. You are not afraid?"

She could scarcely answer, "I trust in you."

"Do so, implicitly. Your suspense is nearly ended, my darling; he shall be restored to you within a few hours; I have encompassed him with every protection. I must see Lorry."

He stopped. There was a heavy lumbering of wheels within hearing. They both knew too well what it meant. One. Two. Three. Three tumbrils faring away with their dread loads over the snow.

"I must see Lorry," the Doctor repeated, turning her another way.

It was almost dark when they arrived at the Bank. The stately residence of Monseigneur was altogether blighted and deserted. Above a heap of dust and ashes in the court, ran the letters: National Property. Republic One and Indivisible. Liberty, Equality, Fraternity, or Death!

Who was with Mr Lorry – the owner of the riding-coat upon the chair – who must not be seen? From whom newly arrived, did he come out, agitated and surprised, to take his favourite in his arms? To whom did he appear to repeat her faltering words, when, turning his head towards the door from which he had issued, he said: "Removed to the Conciergerie. Summoned for tomorrow?"

CHAPTER 6

Triumph

The dread Tribunal of Judges, Public Prosecutor, and determined Jury, sat every day. Their lists went forth every evening, and were read out by the gaolers of the various prisons to their prisoners.

"Charles Evrémonde, called Darnay!"

Charles Evrémonde, called Darnay, stepped forward – he had seen hundreds pass away so.

His gaoler glanced over the list to assure himself that he had moved, and continued, pausing at each name. There were twenty-three names.

There were hurried words of farewell and kindness, but the parting was soon over. It was the incident of every day.

The passage to the Conciergerie was short and dark; the night in its vermin-haunted cells was long and cold. Next day, fifteen prisoners went to the bar before Charles Darnay's name was called. All the fifteen were condemned, in the space of an hour and a half.

"Charles Evrémonde, called Darnay," was at length arraigned.

His judges sat upon the Bench. Looking at the Jury and the turbulent audience, he might have thought that the usual order of things was reversed, and that felons were trying the honest men. Of the men, the greater part were armed; of the women, some wore knives, some daggers, some ate and drank, many knitted. Among these last, was one, with a spare piece of knitting under her arm. She was in a front row, by the side of a man whom he remembered as Defarge. He noticed that she once or twice whispered in his ear, and that she seemed to be his wife. What he most noticed was, that although they were as close to him as they could be, they never looked his way. They looked only at the Jury. Under the President sat Doctor Manette, in his usual quiet dress. As far as he could see, Doctor Manette and Mr Lorry were the only men unconnected with the Tribunal.

Charles Evrémonde, called Darnay, was accused by the Public Prosecutor as an emigrant, whose life was forfeit to the Republic, under the decree that banished all emigrants on pain of Death. It was nothing that the decree was dated since his return to France. Here he was, and there was the decree; he had been taken – his head was demanded.

"Take off his head!" cried the audience.

The President rang his bell for silence, and asked the prisoner whether it was not true that he had lived many years in England?

Undoubtedly it was.

Was he not an emigrant then? What did he call himself?

Not an emigrant, he hoped, within the sense and spirit of the law.

Why not? The President desired to know.

Because he had relinquished a title that was distasteful to him. He had left his country, he submitted, before the word emigrant in the present acceptation by the Tribunal was in use. To live by his own industry in England.

What proof had he of this?

He handed in the names of two witnesses; Théophile Gabelle, and Alexandre Manette.

But he had married in England? The President reminded him.

True, but not an English woman.

A citizeness of France?

Yes. By birth.

Her name and family?

"Lucie Manette, only daughter of Doctor Manette, the good physician who sits there."

Cries in exaltation of the good physician rent the hall.

On these few steps of his dangerous way, Charles Darnay had set his foot according to Doctor Manette's reiterated instructions. The same cautious counsel directed every step that lay before him, and had prepared every inch of his road.

The President asked, why had he not returned to France sooner?

Simply because he had no means of living in France, save those he had resigned. In England, he lived by giving instruction in the French language. He had returned when he did, on the pressing and written entreaty of a French citizen. He had come back, to save this citizen's life, and to bear his testimony, at whatever personal hazard, to the truth. Was that criminal in the eyes of the Republic?

The populace cried enthusiastically, "No!" and the President rang his bell to quiet them.

The President required the name of that citizen. The accused explained that the citizen was his first witness. He also referred with confidence to the citizen's letter, which had been taken from him at the Barrier, but which he did not doubt would be among the papers before the President.

The Doctor had taken care that it should be there and it was produced and read. Citizen Gabelle was called to confirm it. Doctor Manette was next questioned. His high personal popularity, and the clearness of his answers, made a great impression. He showed that the Accused was his first friend on his release from his long imprisonment and that the accused had remained in England, always faithful and devoted to his daughter and himself in their exile. Far from being in favour with the Aristocrat government there, he had actually been tried for his life by it, as the foe of England and friend of the United States. The Jury and the populace became one. When he appealed to Monsieur Lorry, an English gentleman then and there present, who could corroborate his account of the trial, the Jury declared that they had heard enough. They were ready with their votes.

All the voices were in the prisoner's favour, and the President declared him free.

Then, began one of those extraordinary scenes with which the populace sometimes gratified their fickleness. No sooner was the acquittal pronounced, than tears were shed as freely as blood at another time. Such fraternal embraces were bestowed upon the prisoner by as many of both sexes as could rush at him, that after his long and unwholesome confinement he was in danger of fainting from exhaustion. But the very

157

same people, carried by another current, could have rushed at him with the very same intensity, to rend him to pieces and strew him over the streets.

His removal, to make way for other accused persons who were to be tried, rescued him from these caresses. Five were to be tried together. So quick was the Tribunal to compensate itself and the nation for a chance lost, that these five were condemned to die within twenty-four hours.

When he and Doctor Manette emerged from the gate, there was a great crowd, in which was every face he had seen in Court – except two, for whom he looked in vain. On his coming out, the concourse made at him anew, weeping, embracing, and shouting.

They put him into a great chair they had among them. And in wild dreamlike procession, embracing whom they met and pointing him out, they carried him at length into the courtyard of the building where he lived. Her father had gone on before, to prepare Lucie, and when her husband stood upon his feet, she dropped insensible in his arms.

As he held her to his heart and turned her beautiful head between his face and the brawling crowd, so that his tears and her lips might come together unseen, a few of the people fell to dancing.

Instantly, all the rest fell to dancing. Then, they chose a young woman from the crowd to be carried as the Goddess of Liberty, and then swelling and overflowing out into the adjacent streets, they whirled away.

He grasped the Doctor's hand, and the hand of Mr Lorry, who came panting in breathless from his struggle against the crowd. He kissed little Lucie, who was lifted up to clasp her arms round his neck; and then he took his wife in his arms, and carried her up to their rooms.

"Lucie! My own! I am safe. Speak to your father, dearest. No other man in France could have done what he has done for me."

She laid her head upon her father's breast, as she had laid his poor head on her own breast, long ago. He was happy in the return he had made her, he was recompensed for his suffering, proud of his strength. "You must not be weak, my darling," he remonstrated; "don't tremble so. I have saved him."

CHAPTER 7

A Knock at the Door

"I have saved him." It was not a dream – he was really here. And yet his wife trembled, and a vague but heavy fear was upon her. The shadows of the wintry afternoon were beginning to fall, and the dreadful carts were rolling through the streets.

It was an ordinance of the Republic One and Indivisible of Liberty, Equality, Fraternity, or Death, that on the door or door post of every house, the name of every inmate must be legibly inscribed in letters of a certain size, at a certain convenient height from the ground. Mr Jerry Cruncher's name, therefore, duly embellished the door post down below; and, as the afternoon shadows deepened, he appeared, from overlooking a painter employed to add to the list the name of Charles Evrémonde, called Darnay.

For some months past, Miss Pross and Mr Cruncher had discharged the office of purveyors; the former carrying the money; the latter, the basket. Every afternoon at about the time when the public lamps were lighted, they fared forth on this duty, and made and brought home such purchases as were needful. They had just gone, leaving Lucie and her husband, her father, and the child, by a bright fire. Mr Lorry was expected back presently from the Banking House. Little Lucie sat by her grandfather with her hands clasped through his arm: and he, in a tone not rising much above a whisper, began to tell her a story. All was subdued and quiet, and Lucie was more at ease than she had been.

"What is that?" she cried, all at once.

"My dear!" said her father, stopping in his story, and laying his hand on hers, "The least thing startles you! You, your father's daughter!"

"I thought," said Lucie, excusing herself, with a pale face and in a faltering voice, "that I heard strange feet upon the stairs."

"My love, the staircase is as still as Death."

As he said the word, a blow was struck upon the door.

"Oh father. What can this be! Hide Charles. Save him!"

"My child," said the Doctor, rising, and laying his hand upon her shoulder, "I *have* saved him. What weakness is this, my dear! Let me go to the door."

159

He took the lamp in his hand, crossed the two intervening outer rooms, and opened it. A rude clattering of feet over the floor, and four rough men in red caps entered the room.

"The Citizen Evrémonde, called Darnay," said the first. "You are again the prisoner of the Republic."

The four surrounded him, where he stood with his wife and child clinging to him.

"Tell me how and why am I again a prisoner?"

"It is enough that you return straight to the Conciergerie, and will know tomorrow."

Doctor Manette, moved after these words were spoken, and confronting the speaker, and taking him, not ungently, by his red woollen shirt, said: "You know him, you have said. Do you know me?"

"Yes, I know you, Citizen Doctor."

"We all know you, Citizen Doctor," said the other three.

He looked from one to another, and said, in a lower voice, after a pause: "Answer his question to me then? How does this happen?"

"Citizen Doctor," said the first, reluctantly, "he has been denounced to the Section of Saint Antoine."

"Accused of what?" asked the Doctor.

"Citizen Doctor," said the first, with his former reluctance, "ask no more. If the Republic demands sacrifices from you, without doubt you as a good patriot will be happy to make them. The Republic goes before all. Evrémonde, we are pressed."

"One word," the Doctor entreated. "Will you tell me who denounced him?"

"It is against rule," answered the first; "but you can ask him of Saint Antoine here."

The Doctor turned his eyes upon that man.

"Well! Truly it is against rule. But he is denounced by the Citizen and Citizeness Defarge. And by one other."

"What other?"

"Do *you* ask, Citizen Doctor?"

"Yes."

"Then," said he of Saint Antoine, with a strange look, "you will be answered tomorrow. Now, I am dumb!"

CHAPTER 8

A Hand at Cards

Meanwhile Miss Pross threaded her way along the narrow streets, reckoning in her mind the number of purchases she had to make. Mr Cruncher, with the basket, walked at her side. They both looked right and left into most of the shops they passed.

Having purchased a few small articles of grocery, and a measure of oil for the lamp, Miss Pross bethought herself of the wine they wanted. She stopped at the sign of the Good Republican Brutus of Antiquity. As their wine was measuring out, a man parted from another man in a corner, and rose to depart. In going, he had to face Miss Pross. No sooner did he face her, than Miss Pross uttered a scream, and clapped her hands.

In a moment, the whole company were on their feet. Everybody looked to see a man and a woman standing staring at each other; the man with all the outward aspect of a Frenchman and a thorough Republican; the woman, evidently English.

It must be recorded, that not only was Miss Pross lost in amazement and agitation, but, Mr Cruncher was in a state of the greatest wonder.

"What is the matter?" said the man who had caused Miss Pross to scream; speaking in a vexed, abrupt voice and in English.

"Oh, Solomon, dear Solomon!" cried Miss Pross, clapping her hands again.

"Don't call me Solomon. Do you want to be the death of me?" asked the man, in a furtive way.

"Brother, brother!" cried Miss Pross, bursting into tears. "Have I ever been so hard that you ask me such a cruel question?"

"Then hold your meddlesome tongue," said Solomon, "pay for your wine. Who's this man?"

Miss Pross, shaking her loving and dejected head at her by no means affectionate brother, said through her tears, "Mr Cruncher."

"Let him come too," said Solomon. "Does he think me a ghost?"

Apparently, Mr Cruncher did, to judge from his looks.

"Now," said Solomon, stopping at the street corner, "what do you want?"

"How dreadfully unkind in a brother nothing has ever turned my love away from!" cried Miss Pross, "to give me such a greeting."

"There. Confound it! There," said Solomon, making a dab at Miss Pross's lips with his own. "Now are you content?"

Miss Pross only shook her head and wept in silence.

"If you expect me to be surprised," said her brother Solomon, "I am not surprised; I knew you were here; I know of most people who are here. So go your way as soon as possible, and let me go mine. I am busy. I am an official."

"My English brother Solomon," mourned Miss Pross, casting up her tear-fraught eyes, "an official among foreigners, and such foreigners!"

"I knew it. You want to be the death of me."

"The gracious and merciful Heavens forbid!" cried Miss Pross. "Far rather would I never see you again, dear Solomon. I have ever loved you truly, and ever shall. Say but one affectionate word to me, and I will detain you no longer."

He was saying the "affectionate" word, when Mr Cruncher unexpectedly interposed with the following singular question: "I say! Is your name John Solomon, or Solomon John?"

The official turned towards him with sudden distrust. He had not previously uttered a word.

"Come!" said Mr Cruncher. "Speak out. John Solomon, or Solomon John? She calls you Solomon, and she must know, being your sister. And I know you're John. Which of the two goes first? And that name of Pross warn't your name over the water."

"What do you mean?"

"Well, I can't call to mind what your name was, over the water, but I'll swear it was a name of two syllables."

"Indeed?"

"Yes. You was a spy – witness at the Bailey. What, in the name of the Father of Lies, was you called at that time?"

"Barsad," said another voice, striking in.

"That's the name for a thousand pound!" cried Jerry.

The speaker was Sydney Carton. He had his hands behind him, and he stood at Mr Cruncher's elbow. "Don't be alarmed, my dear Miss Pross. I arrived at Mr Lorry's, to his surprise, yesterday evening; we agreed that I would not present myself elsewhere until all was well, or unless I could be useful. I now beg a little talk with your brother. I wish for your sake Mr Barsad was not a Sheep of the Prisons."

Sheep was a cant word of the time for a spy, under the gaolers. The spy, who was pale, turned paler.

"I lighted on you, Mr Barsad," said Sidney Carton, "coming out of the prison of the Conciergerie while I was contemplating the walls, an hour or more ago. You have a face to be remembered. Made curious by seeing you and associating you with the misfortunes of a friend now very unfortunate, I walked in your direction. I walked into the wine shop here, and sat near you. I had no difficulty in deducing from your unreserved conversation, and the rumour openly going about among your admirers, the nature of your calling. And now I have a purpose."

"What purpose?" the spy asked.

"It might be dangerous, to explain in the street. Could you favour me, in confidence, with some minutes of your company – at the office of Tellson's Bank, for instance?"

"Why should I go there?"

"Really, Mr Barsad, I can't say, if you can't."

"Now, I told you," said the spy, casting a reproachful look at his sister, "if any trouble comes of this, it's your doing."

"Come, Mr Barsad!" exclaimed Sydney. "Do you go with me to the Bank?"

"I'll hear what you have got to say. Yes, I'll go with you."

"I propose that we first conduct your sister safely to the corner of her own street. As your escort knows Mr Barsad, I will invite him to Mr Lorry's with us. Are we ready? Come then!"

They left her at the corner of the street, and Carton led the way to Mr Lorry's, which was within a few minutes' walk. John Barsad, or Solomon Pross, walked at his side.

Mr Lorry had just finished his dinner, surprised to see a stranger.

"Miss Pross's brother, sir," said Sydney. "Mr Barsad."

"Barsad?" repeated the old gentleman, "Barsad? I remember the name – and the face."

"I said you had a remarkable face, Mr Barsad," observed Carton, coolly. "Pray sit down."

As he took a chair himself, he muttered, "Witness at that trial." Mr Lorry immediately remembered, and regarded his new visitor with an undisguised look of abhorrence.

"Mr Barsad has been recognised by Miss Pross as the affectionate

163

brother you have heard of," said Sydney. "I pass to worse news. Darnay has been arrested again."

Struck with consternation, the old gentleman exclaimed, "What do you mean! I left him safe and free within these two hours!"

"Arrested for all that. When was it done, Mr Barsad?"

"Just now, if at all."

"Mr Barsad is the best authority possible, sir," said Sydney, "and I have it from Mr Barsad's communication to a brother Sheep over a bottle of wine, that the arrest has taken place."

Mr Lorry was silently attentive.

"Now, I trust," said Sydney to him, "that the name and influence of Doctor Manette may stand him in as good stead tomorrow – you said he would be before the Tribunal again tomorrow, Mr Barsad?"

"Yes; I believe so."

"In as good stead tomorrow as today. But it may not be so. I admit, I am shaken, Mr Lorry, by Doctor Manette's not having had the power to prevent this arrest."

"In short," said Sydney. "This is a desperate time, when desperate games are played for desperate stakes. Let the Doctor play the winning game; I will play the losing one. No man's life here is worth purchase. Any one carried home by the people today may be condemned tomorrow. Now, the stake I have resolved to play for, in case of the worst, is a friend in the Conciergerie. And the friend I purpose to myself to win, is Mr Barsad."

"You need have good cards, sir," said the spy.

"I'll see what I hold. Mr Barsad," he went on, in the tone of one who really was looking over a hand at cards. "Sheep of the prisons, emissary of Republican committees, now turnkey, now prisoner, always spy and secret informer. Mr Barsad, now in the employ of the Republican French government, was formerly in the employ of the aristocratic English government, the enemy of France and freedom. That's an excellent card. Inference that Mr Barsad, still in the pay of the aristocratic English government, is the spy of Pitt, the treacherous foe of the Republic. That's a card not to be beaten. Have you followed my hand, Mr Barsad? I now play my Ace – Denunciation of Mr Barsad to the nearest Section Committee. Look over your hand, Mr Barsad, and see what you have. Don't hurry."

He drew a brandy bottle near, poured out a glassful, and drank it. He saw that the spy was fearful of his drinking himself into a fit state for the immediate denunciation of him. Seeing it, he poured and drank another glassful.

"Look over your hand carefully, Mr Barsad."

It was a poorer hand than he suspected. Mr Barsad saw losing cards in it that Sydney Carton knew nothing of. He had crossed the Channel, and accepted service in France: first, as a tempter and an eavesdropper among his own countrymen there: gradually, as a tempter and an eavesdropper among the natives. He knew that under the overthrown government he had been a spy upon Saint Antoine and Defarge's wine shop. He always remembered that that terrible woman had knitted when he talked with her. He had since seen her, in the Section of Saint Antoine, over and over again produce her knitted registers, and denounce people whose lives the guillotine then surely swallowed up. He knew, as every one employed as he was, that he was never safe. Once denounced, he foresaw that dreadful woman would produce that fatal register, and would quash his last chance of life.

"You scarcely seem to like your hand," said Sydney, with the greatest composure. "Do you play?"

"I admit that I am a spy, and that it is considered a discreditable station – though it must be filled by somebody."

"I play my Ace, Mr Barsad," said Carton, looking at his watch, "without any scruple, in a very few minutes."

"I should have hoped, gentlemen both," said the spy, always striving to hook Mr Lorry into the discussion, "that your respect for my sister – "

"I could not better testify my respect for your sister than by finally relieving her of her brother," said Sydney Carton.

"You think not, sir?"

"I have thoroughly made up my mind about it."

The smooth manner of the spy received such a check from the inscrutability of Carton – who was a mystery to wiser and more honest men than he – that it faltered here and failed him. While he was at a loss, Carton said, "And indeed, now I think again, I have another good card here, not yet enumerated. That friend and fellow Sheep, who spoke of himself as pasturing in the country prisons; who was he?"

"French. You don't know him," said the spy, quickly.

"French, eh?" repeated Carton, not appearing to notice him at all, though he echoed his word. "Well; he may be. Yet I know the face."

"I think not. It can't be," said the spy.

"It – can't – be," muttered Sydney Carton. "Can't – be. Spoke good French. Yet like a foreigner, I thought?" Carton struck his open hand on the table. "Cly! Disguised, but the same man. We had that man before us at the Old Bailey."

"Now, there you are hasty, sir," said Barsad. "Cly has been dead several years. He was buried in London, at the church of Saint Pancras-in-the-Fields. I helped to lay him in his coffin."

Here, Mr Lorry became aware, from where he sat, of a most remarkable shadow on the wall. It was the sudden extraordinary rising and stiffening of all the hair on Mr Cruncher's head.

"Let us be reasonable," said the spy. "I can show you a certificate of Cly's burial, which I happen to have in my pocket-book. Look at it! Take it in your hand; it's no forgery."

Mr Cruncher rose and stepped forward. Unseen by the spy, Mr Cruncher stood at his side, and touched him on the shoulder like a ghostly bailiff.

"That there Roger Cly, master," said Mr Cruncher. "So *you* put him in his coffin?"

"I did."

"Then who took him out of it?"

Barsad leaned back in his chair, and stammered, "What do you mean?"

"I mean," said Mr Cruncher, "that he warn't never in it. No! Not he! I'll have my head took off, if he was ever in it."

The spy looked round at the two gentlemen who looked in unspeakable astonishment at Jerry.

"I tell you," said Jerry, "that you buried paving-stones and earth in that there coffin. Don't go and tell me that you buried Cly."

"How do you know it?"

"What's that to you? Ecod!" growled Mr Cruncher.

Carton who, with Mr Lorry, had been lost in amazement at this turn of the business, now requested Mr Cruncher to explain himself.

"At another time, sir," he returned, "the present time is ill-conwenient. He knows well wot that there Cly was never in that there coffin."

"Humph! I see one thing," said Carton. "I hold another card, Mr Barsad. Here in raging Paris, with Suspicion filling the air, you will not outlive denunciation, when you are in communication with another aristocratic spy who, moreover, has feigned death and come to life again! A plot in the prisons – the foreigner against the Republic. A strong card – a certain Guillotine card! Do you play?"

"No!" returned the spy. "I confess that we were so unpopular that I only got away from England at the risk of being ducked to death, and that Cly never would have got away at all but for that sham. Though how this man knows it was a sham, is a wonder to me."

"Never you trouble your head about this man," retorted Mr Cruncher; "you have trouble enough giving your attention to that gentleman."

The Sheep of the prisons turned to Sydney Carton, and said, "It has come to a point. I go on duty soon, and can't overstay my time. You told me you had a proposal; what is it? Remember! I may denounce you if I think proper, and I can swear my way through stone walls, and so can others. Now, what do you want with me?"

"Not very much. You are a turnkey at the Conciergerie?"

"I tell you once for all, escape is not possible," said the spy.

"Why need you tell me what I have not asked? You are a turnkey at the Conciergerie?"

"I am sometimes."

"You can be when you choose?"

"I can pass in and out when I choose."

Sydney Carton said, rising: "So far, we have spoken before these two, because it was as well that the merits of the cards should not rest solely between you and me. Come into the dark room here, and let us have one final word alone."

CHAPTER 9

The Game Made

While Sydney Carton and Barsad were in the adjoining dark room, Mr Lorry looked at Jerry in considerable doubt and mistrust.

"Jerry," said Mr Lorry. "Come here."

Mr Cruncher came forward sideways, with one of his shoulders in advance of him.

"What have you been, besides a messenger?"

After some cogitation, accompanied with an intent look at his patron, Mr Cruncher conceived the idea of replying, "Agricultooral character."

"My mind misgives me much," said Mr Lorry, angrily shaking a forefinger at him, "that you have used the respectable and great house of Tellson's as a blind, and that you have had an unlawful occupation of an infamous description. If you have, don't expect me to keep your secret. Tellson's shall not be imposed upon. I am shocked at the sight of you."

"Now, what I would humbly offer to you, sir," pursued Mr Cruncher, "even if it wos so, which I don't say it is – wot I would humbly offer to you, sir, would be this. Upon that there stool, at that there Bar, sets that there boy of mine, brought up and growed up to be a man, wot will errand you, message you, general-light-job you, till your heels is where your head is, if such should be your wishes. If it wos so, which I still don't say it is, let that there boy keep his father's place, and take care of his mother. Let that father go into the line of the reg'lar diggin', and make amends for what he would have undug – if it wos so – by diggin' of 'em in with a will, and with conwictions respectin' the futur' keepin' of 'em safe. That, Mr Lorry," said Mr Cruncher, wiping his forehead with his arm, "is wot I would respectfully offer to you, sir."

"Say no more now," said Mr Lorry. "It may be that I shall yet stand your friend, if you deserve it, and repent in action – not in words. I want no more words."

Mr Cruncher knuckled his forehead, as Sydney Carton and the spy returned from the dark room. "Adieu, Mr Barsad," said the former; "our arrangement thus made, you have nothing to fear from me."

He sat down in a chair on the hearth. When they were alone, Mr Lorry asked him what he had done?

"Not much. If it should go ill with the prisoner, I have ensured access to him, once."

Mr Lorry's countenance fell.

"It is all I could do," said Carton. "To propose too much, would be to put this man's head under the axe, and, as he himself said, nothing worse could happen to him if he were denounced. It was obviously the weakness of the position. There is no help for it."

"But access to him," said Mr Lorry, "if it should go ill before the Tribunal, will not save him."

"I never said it would."

Mr Lorry's eyes gradually sought the fire; his sympathy with his darling, and the heavy disappointment of his second arrest, gradually weakened them; he was an old man now, and his tears fell.

"You are a good man and a true friend," said Carton, in an altered voice. "Forgive me if I notice that you are affected. I could not see my father weep, and sit by, careless. And I could not respect your sorrow more, if you were my father. You are free from that misfortune, however."

Though he said the last words, with a slip into his usual manner, there was a true feeling and respect both in his tone and in his touch, that Mr Lorry, who had never seen the better side of him, was wholly unprepared for. He gave him his hand. Carton gently pressed it.

"To return to poor Darnay," said Carton. "As I said to you when I first came, I had better not see her. I can put my hand out, to do what little helpful work that my hand can find to do, without that. You are going to her, I hope? She must be very desolate tonight."

"I am going now, directly."

"I am glad of that. She has such a strong attachment to you and reliance on you. How does she look?"

"Anxious and unhappy, but very beautiful."

"Ah!"

It was a long, grieving sound, like a sigh – almost like a sob. Mr Lorry looked at Carton's face, which was turned to the fire. A light, or a shade, passed from it swiftly and he lifted his foot to put back one of the little flaming logs, which was tumbling forward. He wore the white riding-coat and top-boots, then in vogue, and the light of the fire touching their light surfaces made him look very pale, with his long brown hair, all untrimmed, hanging loose about him.

Mr Lorry's eyes were again attracted to his face. Taking note of the wasted air about the naturally handsome features, and having the expression of prisoners' faces fresh in his mind, he was strongly reminded of that expression.

"And your duties here have drawn to an end, sir?" said Carton, turning to him.

"Yes. As I was telling you last night, I have at length done all that I can. I have my Leave to Pass. I was ready to go."

They were both silent.

"Yours is a long life to look back upon, sir?" said Carton, wistfully.

"I am in my seventy-eighth year."

"You have been useful all your life; steadily and constantly occupied; trusted, respected, and looked up to?"

"I have been a man of business, ever since I have been a man. Indeed, I may say that I was a man of business when a boy."

"See what a place you fill at seventy-eight. How many people will miss you when you leave it empty!"

"A solitary old bachelor," answered Mr Lorry, shaking his head. "There is nobody to weep for me."

"How can you say that? Wouldn't She weep for you? Wouldn't her child?"

"Yes, yes, thank God. I didn't quite mean what I said."

"It *is* a thing to thank God for; is it not?"

"Surely, surely."

"If you could say, with truth tonight, 'I have the love and attachment, the gratitude or respect, of no human creature. I have done nothing good or serviceable to be remembered by.' Your seventy-eight years would be seventy-eight heavy curses; would they not?"

"You say truly, Mr Carton; I think they would be."

Sydney turned his eyes again upon the fire, and, after a few moments, said: "Does your childhood seem far off? Do the days when you sat at your mother's knee, seem days of very long ago?"

Responding to his softened manner, Mr Lorry answered: "Twenty years back, yes; at this time of my life, no. For, as I draw closer to the end, I travel in the circle, nearer and nearer to the beginning. My heart is touched now, by many remembrances of my pretty young mother."

"I understand the feeling!" exclaimed Carton, with a bright flush.

Carton terminated the conversation here, by rising to help him on with his outer coat; "But you," said Mr Lorry, reverting to the theme, "you are young."

"Yes," said Carton. "I am not old, but my young way was never the way to age. Enough of me."

"And of me, I am sure," said Mr Lorry. "Are you going out?"

"I'll walk with you to her gate. You know my vagabond and restless habits. I shall reappear in the morning. You go to the Court tomorrow?"

"Yes, unhappily."

"I shall be there, but only as one of the crowd. My Spy will find a place for me. Take my arm, sir."

Mr Lorry did so, and they went downstairs and out in the streets. Carton lingered at a little distance, and turned back to the gate again when it was shut, and touched it. He had heard of her going to the prison every day. "She came out here," he said, looking about him, "let me follow in her steps."

It was ten o'clock at night when he stood before the prison of La Force, where she had stood hundreds of times. A little wood-sawyer was smoking his pipe at his shop-door.

"Good night, citizen," said Sydney Carton, pausing in going by; for the man eyed him inquisitively.

"Good night, citizen."

"How goes the Republic?"

"You mean the Guillotine. Sixty-three today. We shall mount to a hundred soon. Such a Barber!"

"Do you often go to see him – "

"Shave? Every day. What a barber! You have seen him at work?"

"Never."

"Go and see him when he has a good batch. He shaved sixty-three today, in less than two pipes! Word of honour!"

As the little man held out the pipe he was smoking, to explain how he timed the executioner, Carton felt the urge to strike the life out of him, so he turned away.

Sydney had not gone far out of sight, when he stopped and wrote on a scrap of paper. Then, he stopped at a chemist's shop, which the owner was closing.

Giving this citizen, too, good night, as he confronted him at his counter, he laid the scrap of paper before him. "Whew!" the chemist whistled softly, as he read it.

Sydney Carton took no heed, and the chemist said: "For you, citizen?"

"For me."

"You will be careful to keep them apart, citizen? You know the consequences of mixing them?"

"Perfectly."

Certain small packets were made and given to him. He put them, one by one, in the breast of his inner coat, counted out the money for them, and left the shop. "There is nothing more to do," said he, glancing upward at the moon, "until tomorrow. I can't sleep."

It was not a reckless manner in which he said these words aloud. It was the settled manner of a tired man, who had wandered and struggled and got lost, but who at length struck into his road and saw its end.

Long ago, he had followed his father to the grave. His mother had died, years before. These solemn words, which had been read at his father's grave, arose in his mind as he went down the dark streets. "I am the resurrection and the life, saith the Lord: he that believeth in me, though he were dead, yet shall he live: and whosoever liveth and believeth in me, shall never die."

Now, that the streets were quiet, and the night wore on, the words were in the echoes of his feet, and in the air. Perfectly calm and steady, he sometimes repeated them to himself as he walked; but, he heard them always.

Morning arrived and he stood upon the bridge listening to the water as it splashed the river-walls of the Island of Paris. The glorious sun, rising, seemed to strike those words, that burden of the night, straight and warm to his heart in its long bright rays.

He walked by the stream, far from the houses, and in the light and warmth of the sun fell asleep on the bank. When he awoke he lingered there yet a little longer, watching a trading-boat, that glided into his view and floated by him.

Mr Lorry was already out when he got back, and it was easy to surmise where the good old man was gone. Sydney Carton drank nothing but a little coffee, ate some bread, and, having washed and changed to refresh himself, went out to the place of trial.

The court was astir and a-buzz, and he stood in an obscure corner.

Mr Lorry and Doctor Manette were there. She was there, sitting beside her father.

When her husband was brought in, she turned a look upon him, so encouraging, so full of love and tenderness, yet so courageous for his sake, that it called the healthy blood into his face, brightened his glance, and animated his heart. If any had seen the affect of that look on Sydney Carton, it would have been seen to be the same result.

Every eye turned to the jury. Eager and prominent among them, was Jacques Three of St Antoine. A jury of dogs to try the deer.

Every eye then turned to the five Judges and the Public Prosecutor. No favourable leaning in that quarter today. Every eye then sought some other eye in the crowd, and gleamed approvingly; heads nodded at one another.

Charles Evrémonde, called Darnay. Released yesterday. Reaccused and retaken yesterday. Indictment delivered to him last night. Suspected and Denounced enemy of the Republic, Aristocrat, one of a family of tyrants, one of a race proscribed, for that they had used their abolished privileges to the infamous oppression of the people. Charles Evrémonde, called Darnay, absolutely Dead in Law.

The President asked, was the Accused openly denounced or secretly?

"Openly, President."

"By whom?"

"Three voices. Ernest Defarge, wine-vendor of St Antoine, Thérèse Defarge, his wife, and Alexandre Manette, physician."

A great uproar took place in the court, and in the midst of it, Doctor Manette stood, pale and trembling.

"President, I protest. You know the accused to be the husband of my daughter. Who is the false conspirator who says that I denounce the husband of my child!"

"Citizen Manette, be calm. To fail in submission to the authority of the Tribunal would be to put yourself out of Law. If the Republic demands of you the sacrifice of your child herself, you would have no duty but to sacrifice her. Listen to what is to follow. In the meanwhile, be silent!"

Doctor Manette sat down, with his eyes looking around, and his lips trembling; his daughter drew closer to him.

Defarge was produced and rapidly told the story of the Doctor's imprisonment, of the release, and of the state of the prisoner when released and delivered to him.

"Inform the Tribunal of what you did within the Bastille, citizen."

"I knew," said Defarge, looking down at his wife. "I knew that this prisoner, of whom I speak, had been confined in a cell known as One Hundred and Five, North Tower. He knew himself by no other name than One Hundred and Five, North Tower. I resolved, when the place should fall, to examine that cell. It fell. I went to the cell, with a fellow-citizen who is one of the Jury, directed by a gaoler. I examined it, very closely. In a hole in the chimney, where a stone had been worked out and replaced, I found a written paper. It is the writing of Doctor Manette. I give this paper to the hands of the President."

"Let it be read."

In a dead silence and stillness the prisoner looked at his wife; his wife only looked from him to look with solicitude at her father. Doctor Manette stared at the reader, Madame Defarge never took hers from the prisoner, Defarge never took his from his feasting wife, and all the other eyes there intent upon the Doctor, who saw none of them. The paper was read, as follows.

CHAPTER 10

The Substance of the Shadow

"I, Alexandre Manette, unfortunate physician, native of Beauvais, and afterwards resident in Paris, write this melancholy paper in the Bastille, during the last month of the year 1767. I write at stolen intervals. I will hide it in the wall of the chimney, where I have slowly made a hiding place. Some pitying hand may find it there, when I and my sorrows are dust.

I write with difficulty in scrapings of charcoal from the chimney, mixed with blood, in the last month of the tenth year of my captivity. Hope has quite left me. I realise that my reason will not long remain unimpaired. But I am at this time of sound mind – my memory is exact – I write the truth.

One night, in the third week of December 1757, I was walking by the Seine, an hour from my home when a carriage came along behind me. I stood aside to let it pass. The driver was told to stop.

The carriage stopped and the same voice called me by name. I answered. Two gentlemen were waiting when I came up with it.

They were both wrapped in cloaks, to conceal themselves, but they both seemed about my own age, and were greatly alike.

'You are Doctor Manette?' said one.

'I am.'

'Doctor Manette, formerly of Beauvais,' said the other.

'Gentlemen,' I returned. 'I am that Doctor Manette.'

'We were told that you were walking this way, so we followed, hoping to overtake you. Will you please enter the carriage?'

They had both moved, at these words, to place me between themselves and the carriage door. They were armed. I was not.

'Gentlemen,' said I, 'pardon me; but who seeks my assistance, and what is the nature of the case to which I am summoned.'

'Doctor, your clients are people of condition. Our confidence in your skill assures us that you will learn for yourself better than we can describe it. Will you please enter the carriage?'

I could do nothing but comply, and I entered in silence. They both entered after me. The carriage turned about, and drove on.

I repeat this conversation word for word.

The carriage left the streets behind, passed the North Barrier, and emerged upon the country road. At two-thirds of a league it left the main avenue, and presently stopped at a solitary house. We all three alighted, and walked to the door of the house. It was not opened immediately, in answer to the bell, and one of my two conductors struck the man who opened it across the face.

There was nothing extraordinary about this action, for I had seen common people struck more commonly than dogs. But when the other of the two, also struck the man, the look of the brothers was so alike, that I realised they were twin brothers.

Arriving at the house I heard cries coming from an upper chamber. I was immediately taken there and found a patient in a high brain fever lying on a bed.

The patient was a woman of great beauty not much past twenty. Her hair was torn and ragged, and her arms were bound to her sides with sashes and handkerchiefs, parts of a gentleman's dress. One piece was a fringed scarf bearing the letter E.

I turned her gently over, and looked into her face. Her eyes were wild, and she constantly repeated the words, 'My husband, my father, and my brother!' and then counted to twelve, and said, 'Hush!' Then she paused to listen, and then she cried the same words again.

'How long,' I asked, 'has this lasted?'

'Since about this hour last night.'

'She has a husband, a father, and a brother?'

'A brother.'

'I do not address her brother?'

He answered with great contempt, 'No.'

'She has some recent association with the number twelve?'

'With twelve o'clock.'

'Gentlemen, if I had known what I was coming to see, I could have come provided. Much time has been lost.'

One brother looked at the other, who said haughtily, 'There is a case of medicines here;' and brought it from a closet, and put it on the table.

I opened some of the bottles, and after many efforts gave the woman the dose that I desired to give. As I intended to repeat it and as it was necessary to watch its influence, I sat beside the bed. The cries continued, 'My husband, my father, and my brother!' the counting up to twelve, and 'Hush!' The only spark of encouragement was that my hand upon the sufferer's breast had a soothing effect. But the words were still cried out regularly.

I had sat there for half an hour, with the two brothers looking on, when one said:

'There is another patient.'

I was startled, and asked, 'Is it urgent?'

'You had better see,' he carelessly answered; and took up a light.

The other patient lay in a back room over a stable. Most of the ceiling was open, to the ridge of the tiled roof. On some hay on the ground, with a cushion thrown under his head, lay a handsome peasant boy – not more than seventeen. He lay on his back, his right hand clenched on his breast, looking straight upward. I could not see where his wound was, but I could see that he was dying.

'I am a doctor, my poor fellow,' said I. 'Let me examine it.'

'I do not want it examined,' he answered.

It was under his hand, and I soothed him enough to let me move his hand away. The wound was a sword-thrust, received some twenty-four hours before. He was dying. As I turned my eyes to the brother, I saw him looking down at this handsome boy as if he were a wounded animal.

'How has this been done, monsieur?' said I.

'A crazed young serf! Forced my brother to draw upon him, and has fallen by my brother's sword – like a gentleman.'

There was no pity in this answer. He seemed to say that it would have been better if the boy had died in the usual obscure way of his kind. He had no compassion for the boy, or for his fate.

The boy's eyes had slowly moved to him as he had spoken, and they now slowly moved to me.

'Doctor, they are very proud, these Nobles; but we common dogs are proud too. They plunder us, kill us; but we have a little pride left, sometimes. Have you seen her, Doctor?'

The shrieks and the cries could just be heard. He referred to them, as if she were lying in our presence.

I said, 'I have seen her.'

'She is my sister, Doctor. These Nobles have had their shameful rights in the modesty and virtue of our sisters, many years. She was a good girl, betrothed to a good young man – a tenant of his. We were tenants of he and his brother – the worst of a bad race.'

The boy spoke with difficulty but his voice grew stronger. 'We are robbed by that man as if we are common dogs and they superior Beings. We are taxed without mercy, obliged to work for him without pay, obliged to feed his tame birds on our wretched crops, and forbidden to keep a single tame bird ourselves. Our father says we should pray that our women might be barren and our miserable race die out!'

I had never before seen the sense of being oppressed, bursting forth like a fire.

'Nevertheless, Doctor, my sister married. He was ailing and she married him, that she might tend him in our cottage. She had not been long married, when that man's brother saw and admired her, and asked that man to lend her to him – for what are husbands among us! He was willing, but my sister was virtuous, and hated his brother. What did they do then, to persuade her husband to make her willing?'

The boy's eyes slowly turned to the onlooker, and I saw in the two faces that all he said was true.

'You know, Doctor, that it is among the Rights of these Nobles to harness us common dogs to carts, and drive us. They so harnessed him and drove him for days. But he was not persuaded. No! Taken out of harness one day at noon, to feed – if he could find food – he sobbed twelve times and died on her bosom.'

Only his determination to tell all wrong kept him alive. He forced his right hand to remain clenched, and to cover his wound.

'Then, with that man's permission, his brother took her away for his pleasure and diversion, for a little while. I took my other young sister to a safe place where, at least, she will never be *his* vassal. Then, I tracked the brother here, and last night climbed in, sword in hand.'

The room was darkening to his sight. I glanced around, and saw that the hay and straw were trampled over the floor, as if there had been a struggle.

'He came in and tossed me some money; then struck at me with a whip. But I, though a common dog, so struck at him as to make him draw. He drew to defend himself – thrust at me with all his skill for his life.'

I had seen the fragments of a broken sword, lying among the hay. A gentleman's weapon. Nearby, an old sword, once a soldier's.

'Lift me up, Doctor; lift me up. Where is he?'

'He is not here,' I said, thinking he referred to the brother.

'He! Proud as they are, he is afraid to see me. Where is the man who was here? Turn my face to him.'

I did so.

'Marquis,' said the boy, turned to him, right hand raised. 'In the days when all these things are to be answered for, I summon you and yours, to the last of your bad race, to answer for them. I summon your brother, the worst of the bad race, to answer for them separately. I mark this cross of blood upon you, as a sign.'

Twice, he put his hand to the wound in his breast, and with his forefinger drew a cross in the air. He stood for an instant then dropped, and I laid him down dead.

When I returned to the young woman, I found her still raving. I knew it might last many hours, and that it would probably end in her death.

I repeated the medicines I had given her, and sat at the side of the bed. The piercing quality of her shrieks never stumbled. They were always

'My husband, my father, and my brother! One, two, three, four, five, six, seven, eight, nine, ten, eleven, twelve. Hush!'

This lasted twenty-six hours from the time when I first saw her. I had come and gone twice, and was again sitting by her, when she began to falter. I did what little I could to assist but by-and-by she sank into a lethargy, and lay like the dead.

It was as if the wind and rain had lulled at last, after a long and fearful storm. I untied her and then I realised her condition. She was to be a mother. Then I lost the little hope I had for her.

'Is she dead?' asked the Marquis.

'Not yet,' said I.

'What strength these common bodies have!' he said, looking down at her.

'There is prodigious strength,' I answered him, 'in despair.'

He laughed and then frowned at my words.

'Doctor, finding my brother in this difficulty, I recommended that your aid should be sought. Your reputation is high, and you still have your fortune to make. The things that you see here, are things not to be spoken of.'

I listened to the patient's breathing, and avoided answering.

'Do you honour me with your attention, Doctor?'

'The communications of patients are always received in confidence.' I was guarded in my answer. I was troubled with what I had heard and seen.

Her breathing was so difficult to trace. There was life, and no more. Looking round, I found both the brothers intent upon me.

I am so fearful of being detected and sent to an underground cell and total darkness, that I must abridge this narrative. There is no failure in my memory; I recall every word ever spoken by those brothers.

She lingered for a week. Towards the last, I could understand a few syllables that she said to me, by placing my ear close to her lips. The brothers seemed careless what communication I might hold with her; as if – the thought occurred to me – I were dying too.

I observed that their pride bitterly resented the younger brother's (as I call him) having crossed swords with a peasant boy. They only considered that this was highly degrading to the family. Whenever I caught the younger brother's eyes, I knew he disliked me deeply, for knowing what I knew from the boy.

179

My patient died, two hours before midnight. I was alone with her, when her forlorn young head drooped, and all her earthly wrongs ended.

The brothers were waiting downstairs, impatient to leave.

'At last she is dead?' said the elder, when I went in.

'She is dead,' said I.

'I congratulate you, my brother,' he said as he turned round.

He now gave me a rouleau of gold. I took it from his hand, but laid it on the table, resolved to accept nothing.

'Pray excuse me,' said I. 'Under the circumstances, no.'

They exchanged looks, but bent their heads to me as I bent mine to them, and we parted without another word.

Early in the morning, the gold was left at my door in a little box, with my name on the outside. I decided after much anxiety to write privately to the Minister, stating the nature of the two cases to which I had been summoned, and the place to which I had gone. I knew about Court influence, and the immunities of the Nobles, and I expected that the matter would never be heard of. But, I wished to relieve my own mind. I had kept the matter a profound secret, even from my wife. This I stated in my letter. I did not realise the danger I was in; but I was aware there might be danger for others if they were to know the events.

I could not complete my letter that night. I rose early the next morning to finish it. It was the last day of the year. The letter was lying before me just completed, when I was told that a lady wished to see me.

The lady was young, and not marked for long life. She was in great agitation. She was the wife of the Marquis St Evrémonde. I connected the title by which the boy had addressed the elder brother, with the initial embroidered on the scarf, and realised that I had seen that nobleman very lately.

She had in part suspected, and in part discovered, the main facts of the cruel story, of her husband's share in it, and my involvement. She did not know that the girl was dead. Her hope was to avert the wrath of Heaven from a House that had long been hateful to so many.

She believed that there was a younger sister and her greatest desire was, to help that sister. I could tell her nothing, as I knew nothing. She had come to me, hoping that I could tell her the name and place of abode. I am still ignorant of both.

She was a good, compassionate lady, unhappy in her marriage. The brother distrusted and disliked her. When I handed her down to the door, there was a boy, two to three years old, in her carriage.

'For his sake, Doctor,' she said, pointing to him in tears, 'I would do all I can to make what poor amends I can, or he will never prosper in his inheritance. I feel that if no other innocent atonement is made for this, it will one day be required of him. What I have left to call my own – a few jewels – I will make it the first charge of his life to bestow, with the compassion of his dead mother, on this injured family, if the sister can be discovered.'

She kissed the boy, and said, caressing him, 'It is for thine own dear sake. Thou wilt be faithful, little Charles?' The child answered her bravely, 'Yes!' I kissed her hand, and she took him in her arms, and left. I never saw her more.

As she had mentioned her husband's name in the faith that I knew it, I added no mention of it to my letter. I sealed it and delivered it myself that day.

That night, the last night of the year, towards nine o'clock, a man in a black dress rang at my gate, demanded to see me, and softly followed my servant, Ernest Defarge, a youth, upstairs. When my servant came into the room where I sat with my wife – beloved of my heart! – we saw the man, who should have been at the gate, standing behind him.

An urgent case in the Rue St Honoré, he said. It would not detain me. He had a coach in waiting.

It brought me here, to my grave. When I was clear of the house, a black muffler was drawn tightly over my mouth from behind, and my arms tied. The two brothers crossed the road from a dark corner, and identified me with a single gesture. The Marquis took from his pocket my letter, showed it me, burnt it in the light of a lantern that was held. Not a word was spoken. I was brought to my living grave.

"If it had pleased *God* for either of the brothers, in all these frightful years, to grant me any tidings of my dearest wife I might have thought that He had not quite abandoned them. But, now I believe that the mark of the red cross is fatal to them, and that they have no part in His mercies. And them and their descendants, to the last of their race, I, Alexandre Manette, do this last night of the year 1767, denounce to Heaven and to earth."

A terrible sound arose when the reading of this document was done.

The narrative called up the most revengeful passions of the time, and there was not a head in the nation but must have dropped before it.

Little need to show how the Defarges had not made the paper public but had kept it, biding their time. Little need to show that this detested family name had long been anathematised by Saint Antoine, and was wrought into the fatal register. The man never trod ground whose virtues and services would have sustained him in that place that day, against such denunciation.

And all the worse for the doomed man, the denouncer, the father of his wife. When the President said that the good physician had rooted out an obnoxious family of Aristocrats, and would doubtless feel a sacred glow and joy in making his daughter a widow and her child an orphan, there was wild excitement, patriotic fervour, not a touch of human sympathy.

"Much influence around him, has that Doctor?" murmured Madame Defarge, smiling to The Vengeance. "Save him now, my Doctor, save him!"

At every juryman's vote, there was a roar. Back to the Conciergerie, and Death within four-and-twenty hours!

CHAPTER 11

Dusk

Lucie stood stretching out her arms towards her husband, with nothing in her face but love and consolation.

"If I might embrace him once! O, good citizens, if you would have so much compassion for us!"

There was but a gaoler left, along with two of the four men who had taken him last night, and Barsad. The people had all poured out to the show in the streets. Barsad proposed to the rest, "Let her embrace him then; it is but a moment." They passed her over the seats in the hall to a raised place, where he, by leaning over the dock, could fold her in his arms.

"Farewell, dear darling of my soul. My parting blessing on my love. We shall meet again, where the weary are at rest!"

They were her husband's words, as he held her to his bosom.

"I send a parting blessing to our child by you. I kiss her by you. I say farewell to her by you."

182

"My husband. No! A moment!" He was tearing himself apart from her. "We shall not be separated long. I feel that this will break my heart by-and-by; but I will do my duty while I can, and when I leave her, God will raise up friends for her, as He did for me."

Her father had followed her, and would have fallen on his knees, but Darnay put out a hand, crying: "No, no! What have you done that you should kneel to us! We know now what you underwent when you suspected my descent, and then knew it. We know now, the natural antipathy you strove against, and conquered, for her dear sake. We thank you with all our hearts. Heaven be with you!"

Her father's only answer was to draw his hands through his white hair, and wring them with a shriek of anguish.

"It could not be otherwise," said the prisoner. "All things have worked together as they have fallen out. It was the always-vain endeavour to discharge my poor mother's trust that first brought my fatal presence near you. Good could never come of such evil. Be comforted, and forgive me. Heaven bless you!"

As he was drawn away, his wife released him, and stood looking after him with her hands touching one another. As he went out she turned, tried to speak to her father, and fell at his feet.

Then Sydney Carton came and took her up. Only her father and Mr Lorry were with her. His arm trembled as it raised her. Yet, there was an air about him that had a flush of pride in it.

"Shall I take her to a coach? I shall never feel her weight."

He carried her lightly to the door, and laid her tenderly down in a coach.

When they arrived at the gateway, he lifted and carried her up the staircase to their rooms. There, he laid her down on a couch, where her child and Miss Pross wept over her.

"Don't recall her to herself," he said, softly, to the latter, "she is better so. Don't revive her to consciousness, while she only faints."

"Oh, Carton, dear Carton!" cried little Lucie, throwing her arms passionately round him, in a burst of grief. "Now that you have come, I think you will do something to help mamma, something to save papa! O, look, dear Carton! Can you, of all the people who love her, bear to see her so?"

He bent over the child, and laid her blooming cheek against his face.

He put her gently from him, and looked at her unconscious mother.

"Before I go," he said, and paused. "I may kiss her?"

It was remembered afterwards that when he bent and touched her face with his lips, he murmured some words. The child, who was nearest to him, told afterwards, that she heard him say, "A life you love."

In the next room, he turned suddenly on Mr Lorry and her father, and said to the latter: "You had great influence but yesterday, Doctor Manette. Try again. The hours between this and tomorrow afternoon are few and short, but try."

"I intend to try. I will not rest a moment."

"That's well. I have known such energy as yours do great things before now – though never," he added, with a smile and a sigh together, "such great things as this. But try!"

"I will go," said Doctor Manette, "to the Prosecutor and the President straight, and I will go to others whom it is better not to name. But there is a Celebration in the streets, and no one will be accessible until dark."

"That's true. Well! It is a forlorn hope at the best. When are you likely to have seen these dread powers, Doctor Manette?"

"Immediately after dark, I should hope. Within an hour or two."

"I shall go to Mr Lorry's at nine, to hear what you have done, either from our friend or from yourself."

Mr Lorry followed Sydney to the outer door, and, touching him on the shoulder, caused him to turn.

"I have no hope," said Mr Lorry.

"Nor have I."

"If any one of these men were disposed to spare him I doubt if they would dare after the demonstration in the court."

"And so do I. I heard the fall of the axe in that sound."

Mr Lorry leaned his arm upon the door-post, bowing his face. "He will perish; there is no real hope."

"Yes. He will perish: there is no real hope," echoed Carton. And walked with a settled step, downstairs.

CHAPTER 12

Darkness

Sydney Carton paused in the street, undecided where to go. "At Tellson's banking-house at nine," he said, with a musing face. "Should I, in the mean time, show myself? I think so. It is best that these people know there is such a man as I here; it is a sound and may be necessary preparation. But care! Let me think it out!"

He took a turn or two in the already darkening street, and traced the thought in his mind to its possible consequences. "It is best," he said, finally resolved, "that these people should know there is such a man as I here." And he turned his face towards Saint Antoine.

Defarge had described himself, that day, as the keeper of a wine shop in the Saint Antoine suburb. Having ascertained its situation, Carton came out of those closer streets again, and dined and fell sound asleep after dinner. For the first time in many years, he had no strong drink.

It was as late as seven o'clock when he awoke. As he passed along towards Saint Antoine, he stopped at a shop-window where there was a mirror, and slightly loosened his cravat, collar, and his wild hair. This done, he went on direct to Defarge's, and went in.

There were no customers in the shop but Jacques Three, of the croaking voice. This man, whom he had seen upon the Jury, stood drinking at the little counter, in conversation with the Defarges, man and wife.

As Carton walked in, took his seat and asked (in very indifferent French) for a small measure of wine, Madame Defarge cast a careless glance at him. Then looking more keenly she went up to him and asked him what it was he had ordered.

He repeated what he had already said.

"English?" asked Madame Defarge, raising her dark eyebrows.

After looking at her, he answered, in his former strong foreign accent. "Yes, madame. I am English!"

Madame Defarge returned to her counter to get the wine, and he heard her say, "I swear to you, like Evrémonde!"

Defarge brought him the wine, and gave him Good Evening. Then he went back to the counter, and said, "Certainly, a little like."

Madame sternly retorted, "I tell you a good deal like."

Carton followed the lines and words of his paper, with a slow forefinger. They were all leaning their arms on the counter close together. After a few moments' silence, while they all looked towards him, they resumed their conversation.

"It is true what Madame says," observed Jacques Three. "Why stop?"

"Well," reasoned Defarge, "one must stop somewhere, but where?"

"At extermination," said Madame.

"Magnificent!" croaked Jacques Three.

"Extermination is good doctrine, my wife," said Defarge, rather troubled; "in general, I say nothing against it. But this Doctor has suffered much; you saw his face when the paper was read."

"I saw his face!" repeated Madame, angrily. "I saw his face to be not the face of a true friend of the Republic."

"And you saw, my wife," said Defarge, in a deprecatory manner, "the dreadful anguish of his daughter!"

"Yes," said Madame; "I saw his daughter, more than once. I saw her today, and I have seen her other days in the street by the prison. Let me but lift my finger –!" She seemed to raise it (the listener's eyes were always on his paper), then let it fall on the ledge before her, as if the axe had dropped.

"The citizeness is superb!" croaked the Juryman.

"If it depended on thee," pursued Madame, addressing her husband, "thou wouldst rescue this man even now."

"No!" protested Defarge. "But I would leave the matter there."

"See you then, Jacques," said Madame Defarge, wrathfully; "This race is doomed to extermination. In the beginning, when the Bastille falls, he finds this paper of today, and he brings it home, and in the middle of the night, we read it. Ask him, is that so."

"It is so," assented Defarge.

"That night, I tell him, when the paper is read through, that I have now a secret to communicate. I was brought up among fishermen, and that peasant family so injured by the two Evrémonde brothers, as that Bastille paper describes, is my family. That sister of the mortally wounded boy upon the ground was my sister. That brother was my brother, those dead are my dead, and that summons to answer for those things descends to me! Ask him, is that so."

"It is so," assented Defarge once more.

"Then tell Wind and Fire where to stop," returned Madame; "but don't tell me."

Defarge interposed a few words for the memory of the compassionate wife of the Marquis; but only elicited a repetition of her last reply. "Tell the Wind and the Fire where to stop; not me!"

Customers entered, and the group broke up. The English customer paid for what he had had, counted his change, and asked, as a stranger, to be directed towards the National Palace. Madame Defarge took him to the door, and put her arm on his, in pointing out the road. The English customer considered whether to seize that arm, lift it, and strike under it sharp and deep.

But, he went his way, and at the appointed hour, arrived in Mr Lorry's room again. Doctor Manette had not been seen and had been gone more than five hours.

Mr Lorry waited until ten; but, Doctor Manette not returning, and he being unwilling to leave Lucie any longer, went back to her. In the meanwhile, Carton would wait alone by the fire for the Doctor. He waited and waited, and the clock struck twelve; but Doctor Manette did not come back. Mr Lorry returned, and found no tidings of him, and brought none. Where could he be?

They were discussing this when they heard him on the stairs. The instant he entered the room, it was plain that all was lost.

As he stood staring at them, his face told them everything.

"I cannot find it," said he, "and I must have it. Where is my bench? I have been looking everywhere for my bench. What have they done with my work?"

They looked at one another, and their hearts died within them.

They each put a hand upon his shoulder, and soothed him to sit down before the fire. He sank into the chair, and brooded over the embers, and shed tears.

Carton was the first to speak: "The last chance is gone. He had better be taken to her. But, before you go, will you hear me? Don't ask me why I make the stipulations I am going to make, and exact the promise I am going to exact; I have a good reason."

"I do not doubt it," answered Mr Lorry. "Say on."

Carton stooped to pick up Dr Manette's coat, which lay at his feet. As he did so, a small case fell lightly on the floor. Carton took it up, and there was a folded paper in it. He opened it, and exclaimed, "Thank God!"

"What is it?" asked Mr Lorry, eagerly.

"Let me speak of it in its place. First," he put his hand in his coat, and took a paper from it, "that is the certificate that lets me pass out of this city. Look at it. You see – Sydney Carton, Englishman?"

Mr Lorry held it open in his hand, gazing in his earnest face.

"Keep it for me until tomorrow. I shall see him tomorrow, and I had better not take it into the prison."

"Why not?"

"I don't know; I prefer not to do so. Now, take this paper that Doctor Manette has. It is a similar certificate, enabling him and his daughter and her child, at any time, to pass the barrier and the frontier! You see?"

"Yes!"

"Put it carefully with mine and your own. Now, observe! I never doubted until a short time ago that he could have such a paper. It may be soon recalled, and, I have reason to think, it will be."

"They are not in danger?"

"They are in great danger. They are in danger of denunciation by Madame Defarge. I know it from her own lips. I have lost no time, I have seen the spy. He says that a wood-sawyer, living by the prison wall, under the control of the Defarges, will say that he has seen her making signs and signals to prisoners. The pretence will be the common one, a prison plot, and it will involve all their lives, for all have been seen with her there. Don't look so horrified. You will save them."

"Carton! But how?"

"It will depend on you, and it could depend on no better man. This new denunciation will take place after tomorrow; probably two or three days afterwards. You know it is a capital crime, to mourn for a victim of the Guillotine. She and her father would unquestionably be guilty of this crime, and this woman would wait to add that strength to her case. You can buy the means of travelling to the coast as quickly as possible. Your preparations are complete, to return to England. Early tomorrow arrange to have your horses ready to leave at two o'clock in the afternoon."

"It shall be done!"

"Did I say we could depend upon no better man? Tell her, tonight, what you know of her danger as involving her child and her father. Dwell upon that, for she would lay her own fair head beside her husband's

188

cheerfully." He faltered for an instant; then went on as before. "Press upon her the necessity of leaving Paris, with them and you, at that hour. Tell her that it was her husband's last arrangement. Her father, even in this sad state, will submit himself to her; will he not?"

"I am sure of it."

"I thought so. Have all these arrangements made in the courtyard here, even to the taking of your own seat in the carriage. The moment I come to you, take me in, and drive away."

"I wait for you under all circumstances?"

"You have my certificate in your hand, and will reserve my place. Only wait for my place to be occupied, and then for England!"

"It does not all depend on one old man," said Mr Lorry, grasping his eager but steady hand. "I shall have a young man at my side."

"By the help of Heaven you shall! Promise me now that nothing will make you change these plans."

"Nothing, Carton."

"Remember these words tomorrow: change or delay for any reason and no life can possibly be saved."

"I will remember. I hope to do my part faithfully."

"And I hope to do mine. Now, good bye!"

Though he said it with a grave smile, and though he even put the old man's hand to his lips, he did not leave. He helped him to arouse the rocking figure and to walk on the other side of it to the courtyard of the house where Lucie waited. He entered the courtyard and remained a few moments alone, looking up at the light in her window. Before he went away, he breathed a blessing towards it, and a Farewell.

CHAPTER 13

Fifty-two

In the black prison of the Conciergerie, the doomed of the day awaited their fate. Fifty-two were on the list. Before their cells were quit of them, new occupants were chosen.

From the farmer-general of seventy, whose riches could not buy his life, to the seamstress of twenty, whose poverty and obscurity could not save her.

In every line of the narrative he had heard, Charles Darnay had heard his condemnation.

Nevertheless, it was not easy, with the face of his beloved wife fresh before him, to compose his mind to what it must bear. His hold on life was strong.

Before long, the consideration that there was no disgrace in the fate he must meet, and that numbers went the same road wrongfully, and trod it firmly every day, sprang up to stimulate him.

Before it was dark on the night of his condemnation, he had travelled thus far on his last way. Being allowed to purchase the means of writing, and a light, he sat down to write.

He wrote a long letter to Lucie, to say he had known nothing of her father's imprisonment, until he had heard of it from herself, and that he had been as ignorant as she of his father's and uncle's responsibility for that misery, until the paper had been read. His concealment from herself of the name he had relinquished, was the one condition – understandable now – that her father had attached to their betrothal. He besought her to console her father, by impressing him with the truth that he had done nothing for which he could justly reproach himself. Next to her preservation of his own last grateful love and blessing, and her overcoming of her sorrow, to devote herself to their dear child, he adjured her, as they would meet in Heaven, to comfort her father.

To Mr Lorry, he commended them all, and explained his worldly affairs. He never thought of Carton. His mind was so full of the others that he never once thought of him.

He had time to finish these letters before the lights were put out.

Now that he was composed, and hoped that he could meet the end with quiet heroism, a new action began in his waking thoughts, which was very difficult to master.

He had never seen the instrument that was to terminate his life. How high it was from the ground, how many steps it had, where he would be stood. Which way would his face be turned, would he be first, or the last. He was conscious of no fear.

The hours passed as he walked to and fro, and the clocks struck the numbers he would never hear again. Nine gone forever, ten gone forever, eleven gone forever, twelve coming on to pass away. He walked up and down, softly repeating their names to himself.

Twelve gone forever.

He knew that the final hour was Three, and he knew he would be summoned some time earlier, as the tumbrils jolted heavily and slowly through the streets. Therefore, he resolved to keep Two before his mind, as the hour, so to strengthen himself that he might be able, after that time, to strengthen others.

Walking regularly up and down with his arms folded, he heard One struck away from him, without surprise. He thought, "There is but another now," and turned to walk again.

Footsteps in the stone passage outside the door. He stopped. The key turned in the lock. As the door opened, a man said in a low voice, in English: "He has never seen me here. Go in alone; I wait near. Lose no time!"

The door was quickly opened and closed, and there stood before him with the light of a smile on his features, Sydney Carton.

There was something so bright and remarkable in his look, that, for a moment, the prisoner thought he was imagining it. But, he spoke, and it was his voice, and he took the prisoner's hand.

"Of all people, you least expected to see me?" he said.

"I find it hard to believe it is you. You are not" – the apprehension came suddenly into his mind – "a prisoner?"

"No. I have – some power – over one of the keepers here, and therefore I stand before you. I come from your wife, dear Darnay."

The prisoner wrung his hand.

"I bring you a request from her."

"What is it?"

"A most earnest entreaty, addressed to you in the most pathetic tones of the voice so dear to you."

The prisoner turned his face.

"You have no time to ask me what it means. You must comply with it – take off those boots you wear, and draw on these of mine."

There was a chair against the wall behind the prisoner. Carton had already pressed him down into it, and stood, barefoot.

"Draw on these boots of mine. Quick!"

"Carton, there is no escaping from this place. You will only die with me. It is madness."

191

"It would be madness if I asked you to escape; but do I? When I ask you to pass out at that door, tell me it is madness and remain here. Change that cravat and coat for mine. Let me also take this ribbon from your hair, and shake out your hair like mine!"

With wonderful quickness, and with a strength of will, he forced all these changes upon the prisoner.

"Dear Carton! It is madness. It never can be done. It has been attempted, and has always failed. I implore you not to add your death to mine."

"Do I ask you, my dear Darnay, to pass the door? When I ask that, refuse. There are pen and ink and paper on this table. Write what I shall dictate. Quick, friend, quick!"

Pressing his hand to his bewildered head, Darnay sat down at the table. Carton, with his right hand in his breast, stood close.

"Write exactly as I speak. 'If you remember,'" said Carton, dictating, "'the words that passed between us, long ago, you will understand this when you see it. You do remember them, I know. It is not in your nature to forget them.'"

He was drawing his hand from his breast; the prisoner chancing to look up as he wrote, the hand stopped, closing upon something.

"Have you written 'forget them'?" Carton asked.

"I have. Is that a weapon in your hand?"

"No; I am not armed."

"What is it in your hand?"

"You shall know directly. Write on. 'I am thankful that the time has come, when I can prove them. That I do so is no subject for regret or grief.'" As he said these words, his hand slowly moved down close to the writer's face.

The pen dropped from Darnay's fingers, and he looked about him vacantly.

"What vapour is that?" he asked.

"I am conscious of nothing. Take up the pen. Hurry, hurry!"

The prisoner made an effort to rally his attention. As he looked at Carton with clouded eyes, Carton – his hand again in his breast – looked steadily at him. "Hurry, hurry!"

The prisoner bent over the paper, once more.

"'If it had been otherwise,'" Carton's hand was again softly stealing down; "'I never should have used the longer opportunity. If it had been otherwise;'" Carton looked at the pen and saw it was trailing off into unintelligible signs.

Carton's hand moved back to his breast no more. The prisoner sprang up, but Carton's hand was close and firm at his nostrils, and his left arm caught him round the waist. He faintly struggled with the man who had come to lay down his life for him; but, within a minute or so, he was stretched insensible on the ground.

Quickly, Carton dressed himself in the clothes the prisoner had laid aside, combed back his hair, and tied it with the ribbon the prisoner had worn. Then, he softly called, "Come in!" and the Spy presented himself.

"You see?" said Carton, looking up, as he kneeled beside the insensible figure, putting the paper in the breast: "is your hazard very great?"

"Mr Carton," the Spy answered, with a timid snap of his fingers, "my hazard is not *that* if you are true to the whole of your bargain."

"Don't fear me. I will be true to the death. I shall soon be out of the way of harming you, and the rest will soon be far from here, please God! Now, get assistance and take me to the coach."

"You?" said the Spy nervously.

"Him, man, with whom I have exchanged. You go out at the gate by which you brought me in?"

"Of course."

"I was weak and faint when you brought me in, and I am fainter now. The parting interview has overpowered me. Such a thing has happened here. Your life is in your own hands. Quick! Call assistance!"

"You swear not to betray me?" said the trembling Spy.

"Man, man!" returned Carton, stamping his foot. "Take him to the courtyard, place him in the carriage and show him to Mr Lorry. Tell him to give him no restorative but air, and to remember my words of last night, and his promise, and drive away!"

The Spy withdrew, and Carton seated himself at the table, resting his forehead on his hands. The Spy returned immediately, with two men.

They raised the unconscious figure, placed it on a litter they had brought to the door, and bent to carry it away.

"The time is short, Evrémonde," said the Spy, in a warning voice.

"I know it well," answered Carton. "Be careful of my friend, I entreat you, and leave me."

"Come, then, my children," said Barsad. "Lift him, and come away!"

The door closed, and Carton was left alone. Straining to listen for any sound that might denote alarm, there was none. No cry was raised, or hurry made. Breathing more freely in a little while he listened again until the clock struck Two.

Several doors were then opened in succession, and finally his own. A gaoler, with a list, looked in, merely saying, "Follow me, Evrémonde!" and he followed into a large dark room. He could but dimly discern the others who were brought there to have their arms bound. The great majority were silent and still, looking fixedly at the ground.

As he stood by the wall a young woman rose from her seat and came to speak to him.

"Citizen Evrémonde," she said, touching him with her cold hand. "I am a poor little seamstress, who was with you in La Force."

He murmured, "true. I forget what you were accused of?"

"Plots. Though Heaven knows that I am innocent of any. Who would think of plotting with a poor little weak creature like me?"

The forlorn smile with which she said it, so touched him, that tears started from his eyes.

"I am not afraid to die, Citizen Evrémonde, but I have done nothing. I am not unwilling to die, if the Republic will profit by my death; but how can that be, Citizen Evrémonde?"

As the last thing on earth that his heart was to warm and soften to, it warmed and softened to this pitiable girl.

"I heard you were released, Citizen Evrémonde. I hoped it was true."

"It was. But, I was again taken and condemned."

"If I may ride with you, Citizen Evrémonde, will you let me hold your hand? I am not afraid, but it will give me more courage."

As the patient eyes lifted to his face, he saw a doubt and then astonishment. He pressed the hunger-worn young fingers, and touched his lips.

"Are you dying for him?" she whispered.

"And his wife and child. Hush! Yes."

"O you will let me hold your brave hand, stranger!"

"Hush! Yes, my poor sister; to the last."

The same shadows that are falling on the prison, are falling on the Barrier with the crowd about it, when a coach going out of Paris drives up to be examined.

"Who goes here? Papers!"

The papers are handed out, and read.

"Alexandre Manette. Physician. French. Which is he?"

This is he; this helpless, inarticulately murmuring, wandering old man.

"Lucie. His daughter. French. Which is she?"

This is she.

"The wife of Evrémonde; is it not? He has an assignation elsewhere. Lucie, her child. English. This is she?"

She and no other.

"Kiss me, child of Evrémonde. Now, thou hast kissed a good Republican. Sydney Carton. Advocate. English. Which is he?"

He lies here, in this corner of the carriage.

"Apparently the English advocate is in a swoon?"

It is hoped he will recover in the fresher air. He is not in strong health, and has separated sadly from a friend who is under the displeasure of the Republic.

Jarvis Lorry. Banker. English. Which is he?"

"I am he. Necessarily, being the last."

It is Jarvis Lorry who has replied to all the previous questions. It is Jarvis Lorry who stands with his hand on the coach door. The officials walk round the carriage and leisurely mount the box to look at what little luggage it carries on the roof.

"Behold your papers, Jarvis Lorry, countersigned."

"One can depart, citizen?"

"One can depart. A good journey!"

"I salute you, citizens. – And the first danger passed!"

These are again the words of Jarvis Lorry. There is terror and weeping in the carriage, there is the heavy breathing of the insensible traveller.

"Can we not go faster?" asks Lucie, clinging to the old man.

"I must not urge them too much; it would rouse suspicion."

"Look back, and see if we are pursued!"

"The road is clear, my dearest. So far, we are not pursued."

Houses in twos and threes pass by us, and open country, avenues of leafless trees. The hard uneven pavement is under us, the soft deep mud either side. Sometimes, we stick in ruts and sloughs in the track. The agony of our impatience is then so great, that we are for getting out and running – hiding – doing anything but stopping.

Out of the open country, in again, cottages in twos and threes, avenues of leafless trees. Have these men deceived us, and taken us back by another road? Is not this the same place twice over? Thank Heaven, no.

Leisurely, our four horses are taken out. The coach stands in the little street, bereft of horses, and with no likelihood of ever moving again. New horses one by one; leisurely, the new postilions follow, sucking and plaiting the lashes of their whips. All the time, our hearts beat at a terrifying rate.

We start our journey again. We are through the village, up the hill, and down the hill. The night comes on dark. He begins to revive, and to speak intelligibly; he thinks they are still together; he asks him what he has in his hand. Look out, and see if we are pursued.

The wind is rushing after us, but, so far, we are pursued by nothing else.

CHAPTER 14

The Knitting Done

While the Fifty-Two awaited their fate Madame Defarge held council in the shed of the wood-sawyer, erst a mender of roads.

"But our Defarge," said Jacques Three, "is undoubtedly a good Republican? Eh?"

"There is no better," The Vengeance protested, "in France."

"Peace, little Vengeance," said Madame Defarge, with a slight frown, "hear me speak. My husband, fellow-citizen, is a good Republican but he has his weaknesses, and he is so weak as to relent towards this Doctor."

"It is a great pity," croaked Jacques Three, dubiously shaking his head. "It is not quite like a good citizen; it is a thing to regret."

"See you," said Madame, "I care nothing for this Doctor. But, the Evrémonde people are to be exterminated, and the wife and child must follow the husband and father."

"She has a fine head for it," croaked Jacques Three. "I have seen blue eyes and golden hair there, and they looked charming when Samson held them up."

Madame Defarge cast down her eyes, and reflected a little.

"The child also," observed Jacques Three, "has golden hair and blue eyes. And we seldom have a child there. It is a pretty sight!"

"I cannot trust my husband in this matter," said Madame Defarge, coming out of her short abstraction. "I feel, since last night, that I dare not confide in him; also if I delay, he may warn them and then they might escape."

"That must never be," croaked Jacques Three. "No one must escape."

"In a word," Madame Defarge went on, "my husband has not my reason for pursuing this family to annihilation. I must act for myself, therefore. Come hither, little citizen."

The wood-sawyer advanced with his hand to his red cap.

"Concerning those signals, little citizen," said Madame Defarge, sternly, "that she made to the prisoners; you are ready to bear witness to them this very day?"

"Ay, ay, why not!" cried the sawyer. "Every day, in all weathers, from two to four, always signalling, sometimes with the little one. I know what I have seen with my eyes."

He made all manner of gestures while he spoke, in imitation of signals he had never seen.

"Clearly plots," said Jacques Three.

"There is no doubt of the Jury?" inquired Madame Defarge.

"Rely upon the patriotic Jury, dear citizeness. I answer for my fellow-Jurymen."

"Now, let me see," said Madame Defarge, pondering again. "Yet once more! Can I spare this Doctor to my husband? No, I cannot! You are engaged at three o'clock; you are going to see the batch of today executed. You?"

The question was addressed to the wood-sawyer, who hurriedly replied in the affirmative.

"I," said Madame, "am equally engaged at the same place. After, come you to me, in Saint Antoine, and we will give information against these people at my Section."

Madame Defarge beckoned the Juryman and The Vengeance a little nearer to the door. "She will be at home, awaiting the moment of his death. She will be mourning and grieving and in a state of mind to impeach the justice of the Republic. I will go to her."

"What an admirable woman!" exclaimed Jacques Three.

"Take my knitting," said Madame Defarge, placing it in her lieutenant's hands, "and have it ready for me in my usual seat."

"You will not be late?" said The Vengeance with alacrity.

"I shall be there before the commencement."

"Before the tumbrils arrive. Be sure you are there, my soul," said The Vengeance, calling after her.

Madame Defarge slightly waved her hand, to imply that she heard, and went round the corner of the prison wall.

There were many women at that time, upon whom the time laid a dreadfully disfiguring hand; but, none was more dreaded than this ruthless woman. Imbued from her childhood with a brooding sense of wrong, and an inveterate hatred of a class, opportunity had developed her into a tigress. She was absolutely without pity. Lying hidden in her bosom, was a loaded pistol, at her waist, was a sharpened dagger. Madame Defarge took her way along the streets.

When the journey of the coach, at that very moment awaiting its extra passenger, had been planned out last night, the difficulty of including Miss Pross had much engaged Mr Lorry's attention. Not only should the coach not be overloaded, but the time spent examining it and its passengers, should be reduced to the utmost. Their escape may well depend on the saving of a few seconds here and there. After anxious consideration, he proposed that Miss Pross and Jerry, who were free to leave the city, should leave at three o'clock in the quickest vehicle possible. Without luggage, they would soon overtake the coach, and, passing it, could order horses in advance, to ease its progress during the night, when delay was the most to be dreaded.

Seeing a way of rendering real service in the emergency, Miss Pross hailed it with joy. She and Jerry had seen the coach start, and knew who it was that Solomon had brought. Madame Defarge now drew nearer and nearer to the else-deserted lodging in which they now consulted.

"Now what do you think, Mr Cruncher," said Miss Pross, "of our not starting from this courtyard? A carriage has already left today, it might awaken suspicion."

"If you were to go before," said Miss Pross, "and stop the vehicle and wait somewhere for me; wouldn't that be best?"

Mr Cruncher thought it might be best.

"Where could you wait for me?" asked Miss Pross. "Would it be much out of the way, to take me in near the great cathedral door?"

"No, miss," answered Mr Cruncher.

"Then," said Miss Pross, "go to the posting-house, and make that change."

"I am doubtful," said Mr Cruncher, shaking his head, "about leaving you."

"Have no fear for me," returned Miss Pross, "Take me in at the cathedral, at Three o'clock, or as near it as you can. I am sure it will be better than our going from here."

With an encouraging nod or two, he immediately went out to alter the arrangements, and left her by herself to follow.

The necessity of composing her appearance so that it should attract no special notice in the streets, was a relief. She looked at her watch – twenty minutes past two. She had no time to lose.

Miss Pross got a basin of cold water and began laving her eyes, which were swollen and red. She constantly paused and looked round to see that there was no one watching her. In one of those pauses she cried out – a figure stood in the room.

Madame Defarge looked coldly at her, and said, "The wife of Evrémonde; where is she?"

It flashed upon Miss Pross's mind that all the doors were open, and would suggest the flight. Her first act was to shut them, all four. She then placed herself before the door of Lucie's chamber.

Madame Defarge's dark eyes followed her, resting on her when she was finished. Miss Pross, too, was a determined woman in her own way, and she measured Madame Defarge with her eyes.

"You might, from your appearance, be the wife of Lucifer," said Miss Pross. "But you shall not get the better of me. I am an Englishwoman."

Madame Defarge looked at her scornfully, but equally aware that the two were at bay. She saw a tight, hard, wiry woman before her. She knew that Miss Pross was the family's devoted friend; Miss Pross knew that Madame Defarge was the family's malevolent enemy.

"On my way there," said Madame Defarge, waving towards the fatal spot, "where my chair and knitting wait for me, I am come to make my compliments. I wish to see her."

"I know that your intentions are evil," said Miss Pross.

Each spoke her own language without understanding the other's words; both intent to deduce from look and manner, what the unintelligible words meant.

"It does no good to hide from me," saidMadame Defarge. "Tell her that I wish to see her. Do you hear?"

"No, you wicked foreign woman; I am your match."

Madame Defarge did not understand the words but realised she would get nowhere.

"Woman imbecile and pig-like!" exclaimed Madame Defarge, "I demand to see her. Either tell her, or stand out of the way and let me go to her!"

Neither of them for a single moment released the other's eyes. But Madame Defarge now advanced one step.

"I am a Briton," said Miss Pross, "I don't care an English Twopence for myself. I just know the longer I keep you here, the greater hope there is for my Ladybird."

So said Miss Pross, who had never struck a blow in her life. But her courage was of that emotional nature that it brought tears to her eyes. Madame Defarge mistook this for weakness. "Ha, ha!" she laughed, "you poor wretch! I address myself to that Doctor." Then she raised her voice and called out, "Citizen Doctor! Wife of Evrémonde! Any person but this miserable fool, answer the Citizeness Defarge!"

Perhaps the following silence whispered to Madame Defarge that they were gone. Three of the doors she opened swiftly, and looked in.

"There has been hurried packing – odds and ends upon the ground. There is no one in that room behind you! Let me look."

"Never!" said Miss Pross, who understood the request as perfectly as Madame Defarge understood the answer.

"If they are not in that room, they are gone, and can be pursued," said Madame Defarge to herself.

"As long as you don't know whether they are in that room or not, you are uncertain what to do," said Miss Pross to herself. "And if I can prevent your knowing it you shall not leave here while I can hold you."

"I will tear you to pieces, but I will have you from that door," said Madame Defarge.

"We are alone and not likely to be heard, and I pray for bodily strength to keep you here," said Miss Pross.

Madame Defarge made at the door. Miss Pross seized her round the waist in both her arms, and held her tight. Madame Defarge struggled in vain. Miss Pross, with the vigorous tenacity of love, always so much stronger than hate, clasped her tight, even lifting her from the floor in the struggle. Madame Defarge buffeted and tore her face; but, Miss Pross clung to her.

Soon, Madame Defarge's hands felt at her encircled waist. "It is under my arm," muttered Miss Pross, "you shall not draw it. I am stronger than you and will hold you till one of us faints or dies!"

Madame Defarge's hands were at her bosom. Miss Pross looked up and saw what it was, struck out – a flash and a crash, and stood alone – blinded with smoke.

As the smoke cleared, it passed out on the air, like the soul of the furious woman whose body lay lifeless on the ground.

In horror, Miss Pross passed the body and ran down the stairs to call for help. Happily, she checked herself and went back. Dreadful as it was to go in again, she went to get the bonnet and other things that she must wear. These she put on having first locked the door. She sat on the stairs a few moments to breathe and to cry, and then hurried away.

In crossing the bridge, she dropped the door key in the river. She arrived at the cathedral before her escort. Waiting there, she thought, what if the key were already found and identified, what if the door were opened and the remains discovered, what if she were stopped at the gate, and charged with murder! In the midst of these fluttering thoughts, the escort appeared.

"Is there any noise in the streets?" she asked him.

"The usual noises," Mr Cruncher replied; and looked surprised by the question.

"I don't hear you," said Miss Pross. "What do you say?"

It was in vain for Mr Cruncher to repeat what he said; Miss Pross could not hear him.

"I feel," said Miss Pross, "as if that crash was the last thing I should ever hear in this life."

"Blest if she ain't in a queer condition!" said Mr Cruncher, more and more disturbed. "Hark! There's the roll of them dreadful carts! You can hear that, miss?"

"I can hear," said Miss Pross, seeing that he spoke to her, "nothing.

There was first a great crash, and then stillness, that seems unchangeable, never to be broken as long as my life lasts."

"If she don't hear the roll of those dreadful carts," said Mr Cruncher, glancing over his shoulder, "it's my opinion that she never will hear anything else in this world."

And indeed she never did.

CHAPTER 15

The Footsteps Die Out For Ever

Along the Paris streets, the death-carts rumble. Six tumbrils carry the day's wine to La Guillotine.

So used are the regular inhabitants of the houses to the spectacle, that in many windows there are no people, and in some the occupation of the hands does not hesitate, while the eyes survey the faces in the tumbrils. Here and there, the inmate has visitors to see the sight.

Of the riders in the tumbrils, some observe these things with an impassive stare; others, with a lingering interest in the ways of life and men. Some, seated with drooping heads, are sunk in silent despair.

There is a guard of sundry horsemen riding with the tumbrils, and they are asked some question. The horsemen abreast of the third cart, frequently point out one man in it with their swords. He stands at the back of the tumbril with his head bent, to converse with a mere girl who sits on the side of the cart, and holds his hand. He has no curiosity for the scene about him, and always speaks to the girl. Here and there in the street of St Honoré, cries are raised against him. If they move him at all, it is only to a quiet smile, as he shakes his hair more loosely about his face. He cannot touch his face, his arms being bound.

On the steps of a church, awaiting the tumbrils, stands the Spy. He looks into the first: not there. He looks into the second: not there. He already asks himself, "Has he sacrificed me?" when his face clears, as he looks into the third.

"Which is Evrémonde?" says a man behind.

"At the back there."

202

"With his hand in the girl's?"

"Yes."

The man cries, "Down, Evrémonde! To the Guillotine all aristocrats!"

"Hush, hush!" the Spy begs, timidly.

"And why not, citizen?"

"He is going to pay the forfeit in five minutes more. Let him be at peace."

But the man continuing to exclaim, "Down, Evrémonde!" the face of Evrémonde is for a moment turned towards him. Evrémonde then sees the Spy, and looks at him, and goes his way.

The clocks are on the stroke of Three, and they come to the place of execution, and end. In front of La Guillotine, seated in chairs, are a number of women, busily knitting. On one of the foremost chairs, stands The Vengeance, looking about for her friend.

"Thérèse!" she cries. "Who has seen her? Thérèse Defarge!"

"She never missed before," says a knitting-woman of the sisterhood.

"No – nor will she miss now," cries The Vengeance, petulantly. "Thérèse."

She will scarcely hear thee, Vengeance. Send other women up and down to seek her, it is questionable whether they will find her!

The Vengeance stamped her foot in the chair. "Here are the tumbrils! And Evrémonde will be despatched in a wink. And she's not here! See her knitting in my hand, and her empty chair ready for her."

The tumbrils begin to discharge their loads. The ministers of Sainte Guillotine are robed and ready. Crash! A head is held up, and the knitting women count One.

The second tumbril empties and moves on; the third comes up. Crash! And the knitting women, never pausing in their work, count Two.

The supposed Evrémonde descends, and the seamstress is lifted out next after him. He still holds her hand as he promised. He gently places her with her back to the crashing engine and she looks into his face and thanks him. "But for you, dear stranger, I should not be so composed. I think you were sent to me by Heaven."

"Or you to me," says Sydney Carton. "Keep your eyes upon me, dear child, and mind no other object."

"I mind nothing while I hold your hand. I shall mind nothing when I let it go, if they are quick."

"They will be quick. Fear not!"

The two stand in the fast-thinning throng of victims, but they speak as if they were alone.

"Brave and generous friend, will you let me ask you one last question?"

"Tell me what it is."

"I have a cousin, an orphan, like myself, whom I love very dearly. She is five years younger than I, and lives in a farmer's house in the south. She knows nothing of my fate. How should I tell her! It is better as it is."

"Yes, yes: better as it is."

"What I have been thinking as we came along is this: If the Republic really does good to the poor, she may live a long time: she may even live to be old."

"What then, my gentle sister?"

"Do you think," the uncomplaining eyes fill with tears, and the lips part a little more and trembled, "that it will seem long to me, while I wait for her in the better land where I trust both you and I will be mercifully sheltered?"

"It cannot be, my child; there is no Time there, and no trouble there."

"You comfort me so much! Am I to kiss you now? Is the moment come?"

"Yes."

She kisses his lips; he kisses hers; they solemnly bless each other. Her hand does not tremble as he releases it. She goes next before him – is gone. The knitting women count Twenty-Two.

"I am the Resurrection and the Life, saith the Lord: he that believeth in me, though he were dead, yet shall he live: and whosoever liveth and believeth in me shall never die."

The murmuring of many voices, the upturning of many faces, all flashes away. Twenty-Three.

They said of him, that it was the most peaceful man's face ever beheld there, that he looked sublime and prophetic.

If he had been allowed to write down the thoughts that were inspiring him, they would have been these:

"I see Barsad, and Cly, Defarge, The Vengeance, the Juryman, the Judge, long ranks of the new oppressors who have risen on the destruction of the old. I see a beautiful city and a brilliant people rising from this abyss. I see the evil of this time and of the previous time gradually wearing out.

"I see the lives for which I lay down my life, peaceful, useful, prosperous and happy, in that England which I shall see no more. I see Her with a child upon her bosom, who bears my name. I see her father, aged and bent, but at peace. I see the good old man, so long their friend, enriching them with all he has, and passing tranquilly to his reward.

"I see that I hold a sanctuary in their hearts, and in the hearts of their descendants, generations hence. I see her weeping for me on the anniversary of this day. I see her and her husband lying side by side in their last earthly bed, and know that each was not more honoured in the other's soul, than I was in the souls of both.

"I see that child who bore my name, winning his way up in that path of life that once was mine. I see him winning it well. I see the blots I threw upon it, fade away. I see him – foremost of honoured men, bringing a boy of my name, with a forehead that I know and golden hair, to this place. It will then be fair to look upon, with not a trace of this day's disfigurement, and I hear him tell the child my story, with a tender and a faltering voice.

"It is a far, far better thing that I do, than I have ever done; it is a far, far better rest that I go to than I have ever known."